SILENT RAGE

Recent Titles by Julie Ellis from Severn House

THE HAMPTON SAGA

THE HAMPTON HERITAGE
THE HAMPTON WOMEN
THE HAMPTON PASSION

ANOTHER EDEN
BEST FRIENDS
DARK LEGACY
THE GENEVA RENDEZVOUS
THE HOUSE ON THE LAKE
ONE DAY AT A TIME
SECOND TIME AROUND
SINGLE MOTHER
SMALL TOWN DREAMS
A TURN IN THE ROAD
A TOWN NAMED PARADISE
VILLA FONTAINE
WHEN THE SUMMER PEOPLE HAVE GONE
WHEN TOMORROW COMES

SILENT RAGE

Julie Ellis

This first world edition published in Great Britain 2006 by
SEVERN HOUSE PUBLISHERS LTD of
9–15 High Street, Sutton, Surrey SM1 1DF.
This first world edition published in the USA 2006 by
SEVERN HOUSE PUBLISHERS INC of
595 Madison Avenue, New York, N.Y. 10022.

British Library Cataloguing in Publication Data

Ellis, Julie, 1933-
    Silent rage
    1.   Reporters and reporting - Fiction
    2.   Suspense fiction
    I.   Title
    813.5'4 [F]

    ISBN-10: 0-7278-6340-1

Typeset by Palimpsest Book Production Ltd.,
Polmont, Stirlingshire, Scotland.
Printed and bound in Great Britain by
MPG Books Ltd., Bodmin, Cornwall.

One

The staff of the *Westwood Sentinel*—located in upstate New York—were in a celebratory mood this mid-August Thursday morning of 2004. The word had spread with lightning speed: The new statistics on circulation reported a rise in the past six months to slightly over 15,000—very healthy for a town of 28,000. Very healthy for a publisher running for a seat on the Town Council.

'Wait till Adrienne gets the word,' Chuck Lansing—who *was* the Advertising Department—chortled as slender, dark-haired Sandy Taylor moved with her usual quick steps from the Composing Room and down the hall towards her own office. 'She's sure earned this!'

'It'll be great back-up for our ad rates.' Sandy managed a smile. She was struggling to mirror the expected delight in this new report, but her heart was pounding. In the Composing Room she had learned that in the past twenty-four hours American forces in Iraq had suffered more casualties. Almost a daily occurrence these past months.

Is Jamie all right? How can Adrienne be so convinced that both her sons will survive the carnage in Iraq? Jamie fighting with the marines—Andrew a foreign correspondent.

Each morning she was terrified—along with thousands of others across the nation—by the latest reports. She had nightmares about a pair of men in military uniform appearing at Adrienne's front door with terrible news.

'I knew our campaign against outsourcing would bring in new readers.' En route to his own office, Chuck trailed

1

her in high spirits. 'The lousy *Evening News* figures, "leave that to the big city newspapers." They're sure local folks are just interested in buying as cheap as they can at the malls—and to hell with lost jobs.'

'It's scary.' Sandy nodded. 'If we lose any more jobs in Westwood, we'll be labeled a depressed area.' Rumors were running wild about the likely closure of Westwood Manufacturing. The word was that Noel Ward, the founder and sole owner, was plotting to move all the jobs except for a small office staff to China. He complained about losing sales to competitors who'd already made this move.

'The *Evening News* says outsourcing is great. Adrienne was furious about last evening's editorial in their rag.'

'It's important that she win a seat on the Town Council in next month's election. Almost everybody says she can't lose.' Adrienne could be so eloquent, so charismatic. Like Andrew, his grandmother Claire often said. He was her favorite of the twins.

'Oh, by the way, congratulations.' Chuck hopped in his usual fashion to another topic. 'How does it feel to be promoted to Assistant Managing Editor?' An event that occurred less than twenty-four hours ago.

'I'm excited—and awed,' Sandy admitted. 'Of course, I'm just standing in for Jamie—until this insanity is over.' Adrienne cherished Jamie's devotion to the *Sentinel*. She laughed and said he was a clone of her.

'Nobody here works harder than you. Adrienne respects that. And when Jamie comes home, you'll be co-assistant managing editors.' *I see the glint in Chuck's eyes—he's sure that Jamie and I are serious about each other. And how confidently he says, 'when Jamie comes home.'*

'We all work hard—we love the paper.' Everybody on staff wore at least two hats, all proud of Adrienne's management. The *Sentinel* wasn't the usual small-town newspaper, devoted to local news, local people. Adrienne—Publisher since her husband died when Jamie and Andrew were eight—insisted on a section dealing with national and international news, despite the costs this required. *'We're part of the world—we don't exist in isolation.'* Everybody at the *Sentinel* called Adrienne by her given name, she thought tenderly. She insisted on that. To Adrienne every member of the staff was family. She agonized over any firing. Most had been with the paper for years. Sandy was the newcomer, on staff barely eighteen months.

'I'd better get cracking.' Chuck punctured Sandy's introspection. 'Spread the word about the increased circulation. Write up a "thank you" note for our readers. Maybe we'll be able to raise our rates. Everything else is going up in price. I keep warning Adrienne—we need to balance our budget.' He grimaced. 'Like the federal budget needs balancing.'

Sandy settled at her desk. Focus on work, she ordered herself. Stop living in a constant state of fear, waiting for the e-mails or a phone call that Jamie might manage to get through. His National Guard unit had been in Iraq for seven months—he'd expected to be home by now. Only a dozen days before he'd received word, she and Jamie had been debating about their wedding date. She was eager for a June wedding—he pressed for an earlier date. Nobody except Adrienne and Claire knew they planned to be married.

The sound of the phone was a jarring intrusion. She reached to reply.

'Sandy, someone just called in to report a hit-and-run accident at the corner of Cedar and Main.' Gloria, who doubled as receptionist and lifestyles editor, sounded shaken.

'Send Phil over to cover if he's available.'

'The woman who was hurt—' Gloria took a deep breath. 'The man who phoned in says it's Adrienne. He said it didn't look like an accident. Somebody was out to—to hurt her.'

Sandy's throat tightened in alarm. 'I'm on my way. You said the corner of Cedar and Main?'

'The southwest corner,' Gloria confirmed. 'Police and ambulance are there.'

Sandy sped from the building to the parking area at the rear. Too distraught to be aware of the sultry heat that greeted her. Normally she would walk the few blocks to the scene. Today every moment seemed precious. Praying Adrienne had suffered only minor injuries, she drove with a surge of impatience. Approaching the scene, she saw a crowd of onlookers, a pair of police cars, an ambulance. A large segment of Main Street was cordoned off. A woman was being carried to the ambulance. Adrienne! Unconscious.

Sandy parked haphazardly, dashed to the ambulance, identified herself. A pair of detectives strode towards her. She knew the older man—Cliff Bronson—from encounters on her reporting assignment.

'It was a definite attempt on her life,' Bronson told Sandy. He had a reputation for being tough, she remembered. 'A real bird dog,' Adrienne had said. 'We have two women witnesses who say the driver went out of his way to hit her, and this man and his son.' He indicated the pair beside him. The boy was about ten or eleven, Sandy estimated. 'He said he called your newspaper. The kid got the license number of the car. They both saw the car go through a red light, then swing about to hit her.'

'Yeah—I got the license number,' the little boy told Sandy. His face bright with excitement. 'That's what they always do on TV shows!'

'That was very good,' Sandy approved. Her eyes clung to the ambulance as a medic closed the door and rushed to the front. *Adrienne's unconscious. How badly is she hurt?*

'You're a reporter?' the boy's father asked and Sandy nodded, her mind in chaos. 'You'll mention my son's name in the paper?'

'Give me your name and his,' Sandy instructed. In this case she was the *Sentinel's* reporter. 'Thank you for calling us.'

Siren screeching, the ambulance raced off. Sandy rushed back to her car, followed. *Please God, let Adrienne be all right.*

At the bustling hospital emergency room Sandy waited along with Detective Bronson and the younger detective while Adrienne received swift treatment. Everybody in town knew Adrienne. Almost everyone liked and admired her. Almost everyone.

'You'll track down the car owner?' Sandy questioned the detectives. 'You have the license number—'

'If this is what we think—a murder attempt—there's a good chance the car was stolen,' Bronson cautioned her.

'Running a newspaper, she must have enemies,' the younger detective said. Bronson had introduced him as Detective Ryan. 'The *Sentinel* has been real strong in this outsourcing situation. Has she received nasty letters lately?'

'She always receives nasty letters.' Sandy strained for patience. *When will the doctors tell us about Adrienne's condition?* 'Not just on the outsourcing situation. She's always fighting for causes important to this town. We have a file—I'll see that it's turned over to you and—' She stopped short because a doctor—grim-faced, foreboding—was walking toward them.

The doctor gazed from the detectives to Sandy. 'Are you Sandy Taylor?'

'Yes . . .' Her eyes clung to him.

'She's asked to see you.' He paused. 'I'm sorry—she has very little time. There's nothing we can do to save her.' Shaken, Sandy listened while the doctor described Adrienne's condition.

'May I go to her?' she interrupted him. *This is unreal. I had breakfast with her three hours ago—and now she's dying?*

'Please do.' He beckoned to a nurse.

Lightheaded, her heart pounding, Sandy walked into the cubicle where Adrienne lay on a high hospital bed, propped up against a mound of pillows. Conscious now. Pale, fighting for each breath.

'Adrienne!' Sandy rushed to her side, took the outstretched hand in hers.

'The boys always warned me I talk too much,' Adrienne said with an effort at humor. 'The boys' were the twins—Jamie and Andrew. 'I sure pissed off somebody.'

'You're a fighter,' Sandy whispered. 'You'll beat this.' Knowing it was a lie.

'Tell my boys I love them . . .' Adrienne's voice was labored. Thready. 'I wanted so much to see you and Jamie married.' All at once her eyes clung to Sandy's. 'Be careful. Sandy, be careful.' Each word was an effort. 'Don't—'

'Why must I be careful?' Sandy was bewildered. 'Careful of what?'

But Adrienne was gone. Even before she summoned the nurse, Sandy knew Adrienne was gone.

At their request, Sandy had followed Detectives Bronson and Ryan to the police station. Now she sat with them in a small office and struggled to supply the information they needed.

'Take your time in answering,' Bronson said gently. 'We realize this has been a terrible shock for you.'

'I've told you about the three firings over the past couple of years.' Three bullies hated by their fellow workers—yet Adrienne had given them endless chances to mend their ways. 'They wrote threatening letters—she ignored them.'

'We'll need them,' Ryan told her.

'I'll have the files sent over to you later today.' She searched her mind. What other leads could she give them? 'It seems inconceivable that . . .' *Will they think I'm off the wall in suspecting somebody at Westwood Manufacturing?* 'I mean—' *No, they'll be sure I'm reaching for a suspect.*

'In a murder case nothing is inconceivable,' Bronson picked up. 'We'll follow any lead.'

'Adrienne—Mrs Moss—was running a fierce campaign against Westwood Manufacturing's rumored plans to outsource. It would mean a loss of almost a thousand jobs in Westwood.'

The two detectives exchanged a swift glance. 'We'll check it out,' Bronson assured her. 'Anything else?'

'Again, I'm reaching—' she warned.

'Reach,' Ryan ordered.

'There have been sharp words between the *Sentinel* and the *Evening News*.' They were the two daily newspapers in town. The *Evening News* was ultra-conservative. 'The *News* was fighting her run for a seat on the Town Council, misquoting her, circulating untrue, ugly stories. Everybody was sure she'd be elected. Except her opponent. He was running a dirty campaign.'

'We'll follow that up,' Bronson promised. 'Any other activity that might have caused friction?'

'That's all I can think of at the moment.'

'We'll follow every lead.' Bronson was brisk. 'And if you think of anything else, call immediately.' He reached in his jacket for a card, gave it to Sandy. 'Call on my cellphone number. That's always on.'

'Is there anyone else on the *Sentinel* who was close to Mrs Moss?' Ryan asked. 'Someone who might be aware of another motive for her murder?'

'Chuck Lansing, our Advertising Manager, has been with the paper for over twenty-four years. They were close. You might want to talk with him.'

Sandy sat behind the wheel in the steamy heat of her car and tried to accept Adrienne's death, feeling a towering sense of loss. Adrienne had been her godmother—always there for her. *When Mom died in that weird accident, Adrienne came to me immediately, took charge. I would have been lost without her.*

Why did Adrienne tell me to be careful? Careful of what?

Why must someone so fine, so important to the community die this way? Mom's best friend since she and Adrienne were little kids.

When Jamie went off to Iraq, Adrienne insisted she move into the house with her and Claire. *'You're working so hard. Why should you have to bother with keeping up an apartment? We have six bedrooms, and Martha to coddle us.'*

Now other words from Adrienne rebounded in her mind. *'Always remember, Sandy. Millions of women in small towns like Westwood are a power in making their communities a better place in which to live. We can do it here.'*

I must stand in for Adrienne, Sandy told herself with towering determination. Fight to stop Westwood Manufacturing from outsourcing. That was urgent. Adrienne's most fervent wish. How to do this—beyond the editorials in the *Sentinel?* It was a daunting task. How would have Adrienne proceeded?

Why did tragedy stalk her family and Adrienne's? Adrienne's husband and her father both dead in their early thirties. She'd been five, the twins eight. Her mother killed two years ago in a freakish accident. Now Adrienne. *Why?*

But no time for this, she scolded herself. Concentrate on what must be done. Adrienne's mother—Claire, to the staff of the *Sentinel*—must be told. Claire was elderly, opinionated, and fragile. But how could the blow be softened?

Sandy reached for the cell phone in the glove compartment, punched in Chuck's private number. He answered instantly.

'Yes.' He'd been waiting for this call.

'She—she didn't make it—' Sandy's voice broke. 'She was so brave—but she couldn't make it.'

'Oh, God!'

'And it wasn't an accident.' Sandy fought for composure. 'It was deliberate. Adrienne was murdered.'

For an instant Chuck seemed frozen in shock. His voice was harsh when he spoke. 'The killer will be caught,' he swore. 'The paper will fight for that—no matter how long it takes!'

'I'm going to the house now to tell Claire. Then I'll head back to the paper. And Chuck, can we bring Jamie and Andrew home for the funeral?'

'I'll make calls to Washington right now. I've got some contacts. They'll come home,' Chuck promised, took a deep anguished breath. 'This is unreal—'

'I should be back at the paper in an hour,' Sandy surmised. 'Call a meeting of the entire staff. Bring everybody into the conference room.' She hesitated a moment. 'Adrienne wouldn't want us to close down the paper even for a day. Tomorrow's edition must be a memorial to her.'

'It'll be out on schedule. The *Sentinel* has never taken a day off since Adrienne has been Publisher.'

'Two detectives, Bronson and Ryan, will be coming in to talk with you. They're chasing down any possible motives.'

'You told them about the three thugs that were fired, about Westwood Manufacturing and our battles with the *Evening News?* And the election scene?'

'Right.'

Chuck sighed. 'I don't know what else I can tell them.'

'This wasn't a random killing,' Sandy reminded him with fresh rage. 'Adrienne was the target.'

She was no longer Assistant Managing Editor, Sandy reminded herself when she was off the phone. She was Managing Editor until Jamie was released from military service. It was an awesome responsibility—but she must deal. The *Sentinel* must publish on schedule.

Chuck would fight with her. Adrienne used to say there was nothing Chuck didn't know about the business. Technically he ran the Advertising Department, but he was active in every area of the paper, ruled over the Composing Room.

With Chuck's help I can handle the paper until Jamie comes home. But when will that be? The news reports from Iraq are scary.

Chuck was calling Washington. Jamie would come home for Adrienne's funeral. Chuck would contact the magazine that Andrew was representing in Iraq. Andrew would be flown home. For a little while at least, Jamie would be home.

In this last year Andrew had become a celebrity for his reporting on the war in Afghanistan and Iraq. He'd left a job as a stringer for a major New York newspaper to become a foreign correspondent for the new *American Weekly* at the outbreak of fighting in Afghanistan, then moved into Iraq.

Adrienne had posted his articles on a corkboard in her office, but she refrained from being what she called 'a boastful mother.' Sometimes, Sandy mused, it seemed as though Adrienne made a point of soft-pedaling Andrew's success. Because it thrust Jamie into the shadows?

But Adrienne had been proud of Jamie, who had worked beside her since the day he graduated from Columbia's School of Journalism. Always, Sandy thought tenderly, Jamie remained in the shadows. Andrew was the adventurer, always reaching for new challenges. But Jamie loved working on the *Sentinel*. He threw himself with such enthusiasm into fighting Adrienne's causes.

Chuck and I must hold things together—Adrienne would expect that of us. How long before this insane war is over and Jamie comes home to take over?

Later in the day Detectives Bronson and Ryan would come to the office to talk with Chuck about possible suspects. Adrienne's killer must be caught. The *Sentinel* must do everything in its power to help the police.

Adrienne was always there for her. Now she felt a fierce

drive to avenge Adrienne's murder. Her life would be on hold until Adrienne's killer was convicted and behind bars— for life, without parole.

Two

Sandy pulled into the driveway of the imposing white columned colonial that Adrienne's father had built shortly before she was born. Adrienne had loved this house. In her mind Sandy heard Adrienne's voice that evening seven months ago when she'd moved into the house and felt herself already a part of the family:

'My father came back from fighting in World War II to take over the Sentinel. *He and Mother built this house just before I was born. We've had some rough times through the years. When Dad was determined to expand the paper from a weekly to a daily, he borrowed on the house. We came close to losing it. It's home, Sandy—for three generations. And now, I hope, for a fourth.'*

Gearing herself for what must be told, Sandy left the car and walked up the steps and across the porch to the front door—always left open during the daylight hours. *Will people still leave their doors unlocked when they learn that Adrienne was murdered?* She heard Martha—the family housekeeper for thirty-one years, since before the twins were born, and almost a member of the family now—singing as she moved about an upstairs room. The soft classical music coming from the sun-drenched library told her that Claire was there, listening to her beloved classical music and, perhaps, reading one of the myriad suspense novels of which she was so fond.

Sandy walked into the library—remembering how Adrienne had always teased the family for giving the room

such a formal name. But through the years two generations—and now a third—had collected a formidable number
of books. Stacked, for the most part, in neat rows. She
smiled, remembering Adrienne's definition of books—'our
best friends, always there for us.'

Claire glanced up with a welcoming smile that an instant
later turned to alarm. Sandy never arrived at the house at
this hour of the day. And her face was etched with pain.

'Something's happened,' Claire whispered, tightening
both hands into fists as though to prepare herself. Her face
drained of color. 'Something awful . . .'

No way to spare this fragile old lady, Sandy thought in
anguish. She launched into a report of what happened barely
an hour ago.

'Adrienne was on her way to an appointment with the
Mayor. She'd hoped that if the Town Council could come
up with some concessions, Westwood Manufacturing might
consider remaining in town.'

'It's wrong,' Claire whispered, anger mixing with grief.
'A mother should not survive her child. Who did this terrible thing?'

'The police are checking every possible lead.' Sandy sat
on a corner of the sofa. 'As soon as they have any news at
all, they'll tell us.'

'Ask Martha to bring me a cup of tea. And I'd like to be
alone for a while.'

Feeling a usurper, Sandy sat at the head of the table in the
Sentinel's spacious wood-paneled conference room while
the other staff members—summoned from wherever they
had been, their faces reflecting their shock and grief—filed
in somber silence to take their places at the table. Several
sat in folding chairs brought in to accommodate them.

This room was the locale for volatile discussions on the
Sentinel's destination, the causes it espoused, the problems
that erupted from year to year. Sitting at the head of the

table, Adrienne had always urged frankness from her staff. She listened to what each had to contribute. But no one had anticipated this meeting. The atmosphere was heavy with disbelief and pain.

Two hours after Adrienne Moss took her last breath, the staff listened, first to Sandy, then Chuck as the two outlined what must be done to bring out a special edition of the newspaper.

'The days of the "extra" are long gone,' Chuck reminded them. 'TV, radio, the Internet have replaced it. Already the whole town knows what has happened. Tomorrow morning's edition must be a tribute to Adrienne. Each of us will write of our feelings on this horrific day. Adrienne would not want us to close down for the day out of respect for her death—she'd expect us to carry on. I know it'll be rough, but tomorrow morning's edition of the *Sentinel* must come off the press as on any other morning.'

'Frank, you'll do a front-page article on Adrienne's murder as a news item.' Sandy struggled for poise. *I must do this—I can't fall apart.* 'The police are convinced this was not a routine hit-and-run accident. Contact the witnesses, interview the boy who memorized the license plate on the car involved. Jim—' she turned to the young photographer who had joined the staff nine years ago as a paperboy—'we'll need photos. The accident scene, the two women witnesses, the little boy and his father.'

'What about the driver?' asked Frank, their senior reporter. 'Did anybody get a good look at him? Will the police artist be able to make a sketch of him? It was a man?'

'It was a man,' Sandy confirmed. 'But nobody was able to recall anything about him. They'd been galvanized by the way the car—' Her voice broke. 'The deliberate way he mowed Adrienne down. It happened so fast . . .'

She listened while other staff members discussed areas to be covered, striving, despite their grief, to consider this as a strong newsworthy story. Adrienne's death was a tragedy that would be felt by the whole town. Not only because of the loss of a prominent, much-loved and admired citizen, but also because of the horror of a murder in the town of Westwood—where murder was a rare occurrence.

In a corner of her mind Sandy was haunted by the poignant moment when she'd told Claire that Adrienne had been murdered. There'd been no way to soften the blow. It had seemed as though Claire had aged, grown more fragile before her eyes.

'A mother should not outlive her child.'

For a long time these words would haunt her. Thank God for Martha. Adrienne used to call her Claire's guardian angel.

'All right,' Chuck wound up with closing instructions. 'We've got a special edition to get out. Everybody stands by until tomorrow morning's paper is put to bed.'

Sandy headed back to her office—Chuck at her side.

'I didn't have a chance to tell you,' he said. 'I'm in touch with the military authorities. I was assured Jamie will be flown home as soon as possible. Probably in a government plane. And Andrew's editor is trying to get through to him. They figure he's somewhere in Baghdad. He'll be flown home as soon as possible.'

'I called Mr Hollis—he's terribly upset.' He was Adrienne's longtime attorney and friend. 'He said he would handle all of the legal angles.'

'I suspect you'll wait for the twins to arrive before scheduling the funeral,' Chuck said. He smiled gently. 'At the moment you represent the family. Claire's in no condition to deal with it.'

'Jamie will know what to do.' Such a little while ago, Sandy thought, she was arranging—with Adrienne's help—for her mother's funeral. 'Adrienne had talked about cremation—as though she sensed her life would be cut short. She said she wanted her ashes buried at her husband's gravesite. But I'm sure Jamie must know that . . .'

15

Turning in at her office, she was conscious of the constant ringing of the office phones. The town was aware that one of their most important voices had been silenced. Every member of the staff focused now on bringing out the edition that would be a memorial to Adrienne. The hours moved past unnoticed. Coffee containers, remains of ordered-in food were strewn about desks.

And while they worked, Sandy knew that everyone grieved deeply. One question haunted them. Who had murdered the woman who had fought with such determination and courage to make Westwood a better town in which to live?

Slowly—reluctantly—several staff members left for the night. Clinging to the knowledge that tomorrow morning's *Sentinel* would be distributed on schedule.

Past 2 A.M., Chuck ordered Sandy home. 'We've done all we can today,' he said gently. 'Jamie will be flown home in the next twenty-four hours. Andrew's magazine is tracking him down. We have a paper to keep running—go home and get a few hours' sleep.'

'Our whole world changed since 8 A.M. this morning!'

'We'll survive this. We'll have to fight to keep our readers—after a brief period of support. To everyone in town Adrienne was the heart and soul of the *Sentinel*. But we'll cope,' he insisted. 'Now go home and get a few hours' sleep.'

Exhausted, Sandy agreed. Twenty minutes later she arrived home. The night was steamy, uncomfortable. Emerging from the garage, she heard the hum of the central air-conditioning unit. She saw a muted light in Claire's bedroom window. The other bedrooms were dark.

Martha had left a light in the foyer and at the head of the stairs. Slowly Sandy climbed the staircase. She considered knocking at Claire's door, discarded the idea. It might be an intrusion.

She'd left home this morning with her usual hope that

16

there'd be a call or an e-mail from Jamie some time during the day—though these occasions were, of necessity, rare. She would welcome his arrival home—but at what a price!

The carpeting softened her footsteps as she walked towards her bedroom. Striving for quiet, she opened the door and went inside. She'd set her clock alarm, she decided while she prepared for the night, though instinct told her it wouldn't be necessary. She welcomed the comfort of her bed as she settled in for the night. Every muscle seemed to ache. A twitch in one eyelid revealed the strain of the day.

Her thoughts turned again to Jamie. He would grieve much for his mother. He had always said—with rueful humor—that he couldn't compete with Andrew for her attention. They were identical twins but had different personalities. Andrew was the rebel, outgoing, the charmer. Jamie warm, intense, yet reserved.

In those first years after her father died and she and her mother moved to a town ninety minutes north of Westwood she had seen much of Jamie and Andrew. They had traveled to Westwood for many weekends. But the twins were three years her senior, and they'd delighted in teasing her. How often she was confused, mistaking Jamie for Andrew and vice-versa. Even then, though, she'd felt something special for Jamie.

But once Mom was teaching, then moved up to assistant principal and in her last four years principal, the weekends became infrequent. Still Adrienne and Mom had spoken frequently on the phone. Adrienne had been there for her in those heartbreaking days after Mom's death.

Lying sleepless until the first streaks of dawn appeared in the sky, she relived those last moments with Adrienne in the hospital emergency. Adrienne's last words ricocheted in her mind: *'Tell my boys I love them. I wanted so much to see you and Jamie married. Be careful, Sandy. Be careful.'*

Staring into the darkness, Sandy struggled for answers.

17

What was Adrienne trying to tell me? Of what must I be careful?

After three hours' sleep Sandy rose and prepared for the day. Walking down the stairs with cat-soft steps, she was aware of the aroma of fresh coffee floating from the kitchen. Martha was always up by 6 A.M., always prepared for the strange hours Adrienne and she herself kept when the *Sentinel* made such demands.

Martha walked into the hall. 'You're not leaving the house without breakfast, young lady. You can eat and be out in fifteen minutes. I've got your poached eggs up, toast takes a minute, and coffee's ready.'

Sandy capitulated. Nobody won when Martha made stipulations. 'How's Claire?'

'I'm sleeping on the futon in her room. She says she's throwing me out in a couple of days.' Martha grunted. 'Only if I see her sleeping through the night. And I hope the phone don't ring every two minutes today, the way it did yesterday. Everybody was calling to say how terrible they feel. Miss Adrienne's three ladies called to talk to Miss Claire. They said we were to call them if they could do anything to help.'

'I should have phoned them,' Sandy rebuked herself. 'But there was so much to do.' Adrienne's 'three ladies' were the friends she saw for dinner every Friday evening for years—and with whom she played bridge after dinner. Beth McDonald and Sara Adams, widowed early like herself, and long-divorced Dottie Lieberman.

'They understood,' Martha soothed her.

The two women walked into the kitchen. Breakfast was always eaten there.

'You look like you could do with some sleep, too,' Martha said, bringing coffee to the table. 'I'm expecting you home for dinner. All right, a late dinner,' she compromised. 'Any chance the boys will be home today?' To Martha, too, Jamie and Andrew were still 'the boys.'

'That's pushing it. I expect they'll be here by sometime tomorrow.'

A dozen minutes later Sandy was in her car and en route to the paper. She suspected Chuck had limited himself last night to a doze on the sofa in his office. That happened in moments of crisis, and right now he was determined the paper would go out on schedule.

The town was in its early morning quiet. Only an occasional delivery truck was on the road. Arriving at the paper, she noted more cars than usual in the parking area. A show of support, she thought with gratitude. Walking into the building, she paused at Chuck's office. He sat at his desk — bleary-eyed, swigging black coffee.

'The delivery trucks are out,' he told her without preliminaries. 'The paperboys, and papergirl,' he added, 'are at this moment picking up what they need for their routes.'

'Any word yet from Jamie or Andrew?' She lowered herself into a chair as she fought against yawns.

'I don't think either one is taking out time to tell us they're coming home.' Chuck handed a copy of the morning's edition to Sandy. 'Relax—we have tomorrow morning's paper to pull together.' In addition to his role as head of advertising, Chuck was also Financial Editor.

They focused on what needed to be lined up for the Saturday edition. Within an hour the Metro Editor and the Features Editor had arrived. Sandy doubled as the National News Editor—Jamie's role before he left for Iraq.

At moments past 8 A.M., with Gloria arriving for duty, the phones began to ring. Townspeople were full of questions. What are the police reporting about their search for Adrienne's killer? When will Adrienne Moss be buried? What security measures are residents urged to take? Grief blended with fear because a killer remained on the loose.

Gloria was briefed on how to handle incoming calls so that the work of getting the Saturday edition out wouldn't be interrupted. Both Chuck's private line and Sandy's were off the hook. She appeared in the doorway. She was harried but determined to keep the decks clear for Chuck and Sandy.

'Chuck, Dottie Lieberman is on the phone. She insists she has to talk to you.'

'Okay, I'll talk to her.' Chuck sighed. 'Dottie has the determination of a pit-bull.'

Moments later Dottie's voice—faintly shrill from exasperation at being stalled—came over the line, loud enough for Sandy to hear.

'Chuck, I'm reading this morning's *Sentinel.* I was truly touched. But I spoke with Beth McDonald and Sara Adams, and we feel the three of us—Adrienne's closest friends for so many years—should also write about our feelings for her. We want our letters to appear in the Sunday *Sentinel.*'

'No sweat,' Chuck reassured her. 'Just get the letters over to me by 3 P.M. tomorrow.'

'I'll fax them in ten minutes,' Dottie said. 'We've written them.' Her voice broke for an instant. 'They're our goodbye to Adrienne.'

Oh yes, Sandy thought in a surge of grief. This whole town had loved Adrienne. Except for a handful of people. One of whom had murdered her.

Three

Lieutenant Jamie Moss stood at a window in the recreation section of one of the many wings of the LRMC—the sprawling Landstuhl Regional Medical Center, the largest U.S. military hospital in Europe. He gazed out into the night without seeing, encased in shock.

An inconceivable report had been relayed to him. His mother—warm, dynamic, in love with life—had been murdered yesterday morning. He struggled to accept this . . . Who had done this? . . . Why?

Three days ago, in pre-dawn rain, he'd boarded a C-141 along with others wounded in the fighting in Iraq for the eight-hour flight to Ramstein Air Base in Germany, close to the French border. From there they'd been bussed three miles to Landstuhl.

His left arm had been sewed up, bandaged, placed in a protective sling. He'd expected to rejoin his company in a few days, as on two previous occasions. Each time he'd been lucky. He'd avoided the catastrophic injuries so common in this war.

But a dozen hours ago he'd been assaulted with the nightmarish news about his mother. Now he was awaiting a flight to Andrews Air Force Base, where he anticipated a connecting flight home. To attend her funeral.

'Stand by for boarding your flight.' A nurse walked through the area to advise those waiting for word that their C-17 was preparing for take-off. 'Report in thirty minutes.'

'Sugar, I can't stand nowhere,' a nineteen-year-old PFC

21

called back from his wheelchair in an effort at humor. 'But I'm sure as hell glad to be goin' home.'

Jamie glanced at the clock on the wall. It was past 9 P.M. Back home it was six hours earlier. Mid-afternoon. How were they holding up at the *Sentinel?*

Minutes before their take-off Jamie was approached by a pair of superior officers. He was informed that he was to receive an honorable discharge. 'This is your third injury,' one of the pair reminded him. 'You've served your time. You're going home to stay, Lieutenant Moss.'

The official confirmation would arrive within forty-eight hours, Jamie was told. He was simultaneously relieved and guilty. His men—except for two badly wounded—would stay in Iraq. *Shouldn't I be there with them?*

Within an hour forty-eight wounded were settled in the huge C-17. Jamie and two marines were ambulatory. Most of the others were on stretchers or in wheelchairs and headed for additional medical care at either Walter Reed Army Medical Center in Washington or the National Naval Medical Center in Bethesda. The few less seriously wounded would transfer to a C-130 that would carry them to their home bases.

The plane was airborne only a few minutes when twenty-eight-year-old Joe Kelly—a National Guardsman from Jamie's unit—called to him.

'You'll go to see my wife?' he asked. 'You said you would.'

Jamie moved to his side. 'My first day home,' he promised.

'I hope she wants me back—when I'm like this.' He gestured anxiously towards the stumps that were all that remained of his legs.

'Joe, she's not in love with your legs. It's you—the person you are.'

'She's out there supporting herself and two small kids for all these months. How am I to support my family? That's what a man's supposed to do.'

'The government will come through. They're doing great things—getting amputees back on their feet. It'll be that way for you. And I promise you,' he said, his throat tightening, 'when you're ready to go back to work, you'll have a job on my mother's newspaper.'

'I always wanted to go to journalism school. I was lucky to make it through a community college.' Joe took a deep breath. 'Do folks back home know how many of us are coming home this way? It's not like in other wars. We've got our body armor—at least, some of us—and that protects against a lot of injuries. But body armor don't protect our legs or arms, our faces or groins. Every day some of us lose arms or legs or both. Do people know that?' he repeated with sudden intensity.

'Sure they do,' Jamie said. Certain it was a lie. So clear in his mind the encounter last month when he'd met that British photographer when both of them had been hit by a roadside bomb.

While they waited for emergency care in a combat support hospital in Baghdad, the photographer told him about the BBC documentary that was shown in the United Kingdom back in February of this year. It contained heart-wrenching shots of the wounded arriving back in the United States, shots of the amputee ward at Walter Reed. The photographer's words were etched on Jamie's brain: *The correspondent told the television audience— while the camera panned the line-up of wounded—that American audiences were not allowed to see this documentary. Why?*'

The hours aboard seemed endless. At intervals Jamie worried about the current whereabouts of Andrew. Now a foreign correspondent in Iraq for a fancy new magazine that was attracting a lot of attention. Had he been reached? Was he on his way home? Was he all right?

Their paths had crossed for about twenty-four hours— which had pleased Mom when she'd heard. But Andrew enraged Major Evans—who had mistaken Andrew for him. Andrew and his damned delight in confusing people. Andrew said the major had no sense of humor. Still, most people considered Andrew charismatic.

At intervals he worried about what another correspondent—who knew both Andrew and him—had said. *'Oh, that Andrew, that wacky brother of yours! He thinks he's so clever. He talked about how Hemingway covered the Spanish Civil War from the lobby of his hotel in Madrid. That was the sharp way, he said. Wow, the explosive reports he sends in—most of them pure fiction.'*

He'd been furious with the guy. At first. Andrew could be irresponsible if he thought it was to his advantage. Was he filing fictional reports? That would be unconscionable. But instantly he rebuked himself for believing the exaggerated remarks of a newspaper stringer with no impressive credentials. The guy was probably jealous. How many times had he encountered that in the past?

He hadn't written home about his two previous injuries, Jamie recalled now. Why upset Mom and Sandy? He hadn't written about this latest. For a few hours he'd feared he'd lose his arm—but the doctors had saved it. He'd been lucky. And now he was going home. But not with joy. Mom wouldn't be there to welcome him.

Their C-17 landed at Andrews Air Force base at 12:42 A.M., U.S. eastern time.

'This is the usual arrival time,' a medic onboard told Jamie with a cynical smile. 'Planned that way. No reporters, no photographers hanging around to witness the cost of this creepy war.'

Ambulances were waiting to take the seriously wounded to Walter Reed and the medical center at Bethesda. Those on stretchers and wheelchairs were removed first. The few ambulatory wounded would be next, to stay the rest of the night at a nearby 'contingency aeromedical staging facility'—once an indoor tennis club and a community center.

24

In the morning C-130 transports would fly in to take the remainder to their home bases.

Jamie knew he wouldn't sleep. He doubted that any of the others with him were sleeping. Early in the morning the C-130s would arrive. He was on the list for a lift to the base at Troy, New York. From there he could catch a bus to Westwood. A homecoming so unlike what he'd anticipated.

By sunrise those expecting to take off were on the field awaiting the arrival of the C-130s. They watched the huge orange ball that was the sun rise over the horizon. The birth of a new day.

A cry of approval greeted the arrival of the first of the planes. The second to touch down would take its passengers to the base at Troy. Jamie took his place aboard. Home seemed close. But it wouldn't be home, he taunted himself, when Mom was gone.

He and Sandy and Mom had talked with joyful anticipation about the wedding that would follow on his return from Iraq—though the time he'd expected to remain there as a member of the National Guard had expired. This was not the war they'd expected to fight.

Always in the back of his mind had lingered the traitorous question: *'Will I return?'* In their infrequent phone calls and e-mails he and Sandy had pretended to ignore this— because it was too painful to consider. There must be more for them.

The war would end soon, they kept telling themselves. He would come home. He and Sandy would be married. Mom and Grandma would be ecstatic. But instead of a wedding, there would be a funeral.

How could this have happened? I won't have a moment's peace until Mom's killer is behind bars—for life. No chance of parole. I'll stay on the backs of the police—demand action. Follow my own leads. Mom's killer mustn't walk the earth a free man—or woman.

Four

Sandy winced as her alarm clock shrieked its 6 A.M. wake-up call, reached over to silence it. She'd slept at brief intervals in the course of the night. Troubled sleep that left her exhausted. Now she lay back against the pillow and reviewed the problems that would confront her today.

Thank God, Claire was holding up well. They'd talked until well past midnight. She understood—Claire needed to talk. Claire, too, had begun her working life as a newspaper reporter—but once married, she was assigned the role of homemaker and mother.

'I made up my mind when Adrienne was born,' Claire said with pride. 'She'd be in the newspaper business—like her father. Her world would be different from mine. Ralph just didn't understand that women have a right to move outside the home. But that was the thinking in those days.'

Adrienne had been more than a newspaperwoman, Sandy thought tenderly. She'd been a powerhouse in this town— devoted to making life better for its people. She fought for the good causes. She was always fair. Who wanted her dead?

The police said that—as they'd expected—the car that killed her had been stolen only hours earlier. Before the owner even realized it was gone. They'd brought the witnesses together with the police artist—but came up with nothing. They were exploring what vague leads were available: The three disgruntled former employees who'd made nasty threats; Westwood Manufacturing's CEO and top executives, so determined to outsource all except a token office and in nasty confrontation with those opposed; even people at their ultra-conservative competition, the *Evening News,* had been questioned. But since Thursday morning—when Adrienne was run down in murderous fashion—the anger of many of the townspeople had turned to fear because they realized a murderer was on the loose in their quiet town.

Sandy ordered herself out of bed and into the shower. Standing under the stinging hot spray, she confronted what must be done. Claire had pointed out that she must hold up funeral arrangements until Jamie and Andrew were home—though she'd made preliminary arrangements that were feasible. Her main efforts, Claire insisted, were to keep the *Sentinel* rolling. But already, Chuck reported, advertising was taking a nosedive.

'Not just with us,' he conceded. 'My spies tell me the *Evening News* is hitting the same snag. Only one subject of interest in town right now. Adrienne's murder.'

You need to get to the office early, Sandy rebuked herself. So much to be done!

Get moving—we have a newspaper to run. Am I up to this? Chuck will handle the business end, sure—but can I convince our readers that it'll be the same as when Adrienne was running the show? Adrienne was the heart and soul of the Sentinel.

Dressing, she clung to the knowledge that both Jamie and Andrew had been contacted, were en route home. Take one day at a time, she ordered herself. Somehow, she must cope.

Jamie gave momentary thought to renting a car to drive home, discarded it. He didn't see himself as a one-handed driver—he was the cautious type. Andrew would rent the most ostentatious car available, drive into town with the swagger of a James Bond, he suspected.

He was able to hitch a ride to the Troy bus station. He bought a one-way ticket to Westwood, began to pace about the lightly populated waiting room. Too impatient to sit until his bus pulled in. His mind a whirling kaleidoscope. Mom had been murdered. Why? By whom?

Now grief was invaded by rage. Mom was always crusading for some urgent cause—and for that she had to die? He was coming home to stay—but Mom was gone. Did the police have a substantial lead? Were they going full steam on the case? *What can I do to help nail the killer?*

Was Andrew on the way home or was he already there?

Andrew the flamboyant—who always managed to make Mom laugh. Andrew who charmed everybody. Almost everybody, he corrected himself, and felt uncomfortable as he remembered a conversation with the foreign correspondent 'embedded' in his company for the past month. The guy was jealous—he was making up bad jokes about Andrew.

Everybody was amazed by the difficulty in telling Andrew and him apart. 'Identical twins who are really identical,' Martha used to say in a blend of amusement and irritation. Sometimes Andrew was even able to fool Mom.

How was Sandy managing? Beautiful, bright Sandy, whom he loved more than he'd thought was possible. She couldn't know yet that he was coming home to stay. She must be terrified at the prospect of running the *Sentinel* on her own. And Grandma? Oh God, what a blow this must be to her.

The bus to Westwood was announced. Jamie rushed to board it, settled in a seat to the rear. In less than two hours they'd be pulling into town, he thought with relief. He'd slept little in the past forty-eight hours. Maybe he'd doze on the bus.

The arrival of a teenager with a Walkman at too high a volume eliminated any prospect of his dozing. He picked up a discarded newspaper on an empty seat across the aisle, tried to focus on the lead story.

He flinched at the report of war-prisoner abuse in Iraq. He remembered as a small boy hearing his father, who'd served in Vietnam, talk about the horrors of My Lai in agonizing detail. *'In every war there are some who disgrace their flag. Most American fighting men and women are honorable—but there is that tiny segment that turns you sick when you see what they do.'* His grandmother used to talk about his grandfather, who'd fought in World War II, all the way from North Africa and Sicily into Italy. *'Your grandfather would get so upset when he talked about American soldiers who got drunk and broke into houses in the villages, raped any female from eight to eighty. And he grieved for all the children born of rape—and disowned by both sides.'*

He had looked forward to the day he'd return home—but not like this. He'd anticipated a precious reunion. Plans to be made for a wedding. That would have to wait now until life resumed an even keel.

How was Sandy managing at the paper, he asked himself yet again. Chuck must be a big help—but Chuck's field was advertising, building circulation. Sandy had to breathe life into the *Sentinel.* The major objective of a small-town newspaper was to deal with community affairs, but the *Sentinel* made a strong point of trying to involve readers in national and world affairs.

Two rows below, a toddler began to cry. A harried young mother, coping with an older sibling, hastily offered a pacifier. Now all was quiet. Jamie's mind hurtled across the miles to Iraq. Some Iraqis welcomed them as liberators. Others loathed them as occupiers.

His face softened in recall. The children were eager to be friends if a smile was offered.

'American soldier nice!' They'd learned a few words of English, were proud to display their knowledge.

Any tiny gift brought awed gratitude. A pencil, a pen, a candy bar, a cookie. Most American soldiers were good-will emissaries, compassionate, striving in small ways to make life a little easier for the children.

He remembered a soldier in Baghdad who'd written back home about the horrendous shortages in the schools—where a pencil might be shared by three small students—and the resultant shipments of necessary supplies by civilians. Again, he was assaulted by a surge of guilt that he had come home while his men remained behind.

He gazed out the bus window—remembering how many times, when the going got rough, he asked himself if he'd ever return home. But he hadn't joined the National Guard as a playtime thing. It was his duty as an American. Still, he was haunted by doubts about the war.

Iraq had not attacked us. We'd gone in too fast—so arrogant to those who should be our allies. Abandoning diplomacy—and with no exit strategy. How the hell do we get out now? I sound like Dad talking about Vietnam.

The air-conditioning—so welcome on this sultry August morning—brought a shudder as he recalled the unconscionable heat of an Iraq summer. Nobody back home could envision the discomfort of those days and nights.

His impatience grew as the bus drew closer to Westwood. Everything was on Sandy's shoulders. She'd been through hell. He couldn't wait to see her, to hold her in his arms again. Together they would survive the horror of losing Mom. Losing her in such a horrendous fashion.

By the time the bus was a few miles out of Westwood he was sitting on the edge of his seat. Now they were approaching town. He saw everything as though for the first time, he thought—as if he'd never truly seen any of it before.

They were driving through the outlying areas. His heart pounded as his eyes devoured passing landmarks. His high school, the baseball field where he and Andrew had played as teenagers, the old church that dated back to the eighteenth century and last year had at last been restored with public funds. His throat tightened as the bus swung onto Main Street en route to the bus terminal.

Moments before the bus pulled to a stop in the terminal, he was on his feet. He'd go to the paper first. Sandy would be there—fighting to keep the *Sentinel* rolling. A monumental task for her, though in a year and a half on the paper she'd learned so much.

Later he'd go home to Grandma. What a terrible blow this was to her. Her only child. Thank God for Martha— grieving, too, but she'd be there to comfort Grandma. The way she'd comforted him and Andrew when they were hurt or sick. Martha was family.

Striding out of the bus terminal, he flinched for an instant at the sultry heat that enveloped him, then glanced about Main Street.

I'm home. Sometimes—when the going got rough—I asked myself if I'd ever make it back.

He turned onto Main Street, heading for the newspaper's headquarters just off Main and Christopher. He smiled at a pair of small boys on skateboards, who paused to smile shyly at him. The uniform, he realized, and his arm in the sling.

'Hi,' he greeted them.

'Hi,' they chorused with an air of pleased awe.

A few feet down he stopped short to read a poster in the window of the diner where he used to go for lunch. Astonished and touched by the black-edged poster that spoke of grief at his mother's death.

Posters appeared in other windows along Main Street. Sometimes he forgot how much his mother had given to this town—and how she was loved. But someone in this town had hated her enough to kill her.

When will Mom's murderer be caught? I want to tear him apart, watch him feel the pain Mom must have felt

31

when that car ran her down! Are the police going after this monster the way they must? We'll use the pages of the Sentinel *to help!*

Five

Sandy sat at the edge of her chair, unconsciously drumming on her desk with the hand not gripping the phone.

'I want to know why "the boys" aren't home yet.' Claire was fretful at the other end of the line—unusual for her. 'Their mother was murdered on Thursday, and here it's Saturday already.'

'I'm sure they're on their way home,' Sandy soothed. 'It took a while to reach them in Iraq—considering the conditions over there.'

'Why didn't Andrew call? He always knows how to pull strings—he could get a call through. How do we know he's all right?'

'Chuck talked several times with people over at the *American Weekly.*' Andrew was always Claire's favorite. Martha adored Jamie. 'Andrew's editor said he was fine— they were working to arrange a flight home for him.'

'Oh, all right, Martha—Sandy, I have to go. Martha's making me eat lunch when I know it'll just make me sick. She can be such a tyrant sometimes.'

Sandy put down the phone, reached for the latest batch of letters, e-mails and faxes that had arrived expressing sorrow about Adrienne's death. She froze at the sound of excited voices in the reception area. Her heart began to pound. Jamie was home!

She rushed from her office down the hall to the reception area. Chuck and several other staff members were

33

clustered about him as she arrived, pelting him with questions. *He's been wounded. His arm in a sling!*

'Jamie!' Her voice was rich with welcome, her face luminous. 'Thank God you're home.'

'I dreamt so often about the day I'd come home. I didn't expect it to be like this.' He moved forward, pulled her close.

'Okay, everybody, back to work,' Chuck ordered. 'We've got a paper to get out.'

His uninjured arm about Sandy, Jamie prodded her back to her office. Inside, he closed the door and kissed her with a seven-month hunger.

'I came as fast I could,' he told her when his mouth released hers. 'I was in Germany—in our hospital there—expecting to go back to my company in a couple of days. And then—' his face tightened in fresh anguish, 'I was told about Mom.' He fought for control. 'I still can't believe this is real.' He closed his eyes for a moment. 'Mom was such a dynamo—I expected her to be around forever.'

'What happened to your arm?' Sandy's eyes searched his. 'You said nothing about being wounded.' She prodded him into a chair, sat beside him.

'I had a big hole in my arm—it's okay now. I'll see Dr Maxwell about the follow-up.' Maxwell was the longtime family doctor. 'I was scared at first. Afraid I'd lose the arm. Third time I was hit—' His smile was wry.

'You were wounded before?' Sandy was startled. Shaken. 'You never said a word!'

'Why worry you?' he countered. 'I've got some shrapnel in one leg and in the good arm. But I'm fine,' he insisted and flinched. 'I'd be fine if Mom was all right.'

'If you were wounded before, why weren't you sent home?' Sandy was indignant.

'For small wounds we were treated in Baghdad or flown to Germany. In three or four days we were back in action. Only the serious cases were flown home.' His eyes darkened in recall. 'A correspondent back in Iraq told me nobody at home realized the horrible injuries. Nobody is shown photos of the amputees that are brought back to Walter Reed in Washington and the National Naval Medical Center in Bethesda. This isn't like the Gulf War,' he said bitterly. 'Landstuhl Medical Center treated four thousand Americans then—but more than three times that have been treated already in this go-round. And more are flown in every day.'

'And you have to go back into that—'Sandy shivered.

'No,' he said, startling her. 'I'm home for good.'

Sandy took a deep breath of relief. 'Oh, Jamie. Thank God.'

'Did you see Mom—at the end?' He was fighting for composure. 'Was she—was she able to say anything?'

'She was conscious only for a few moments. She said, "Tell my boys I love them." '

'That we knew.' Tears filled his eyes. 'She was the best.' Now he fought to continue. 'The army brass tell me my honorable discharge will come through any day. I won't be going back,' he emphasized—as though to convince himself. 'What are the police doing to catch that fiend? All I was told was that she was deliberately run down by a man in a stolen car. That there were witnesses who testified to that.'

Her voice unsteady, Sandy gave him all the facts available. 'The police are working hard on the case. It has top priority. The town is in shock.'

'What leads are they following?' Jamie's voice was harsh with rage. 'When are they going to find this creep?'

'The detectives are following several leads—the three men who were fired and made ugly threats, your mother's opposition in the race for a Town Council seat, even the people at Westwood Manufacturing who're threatening to outsource,' she added as he raised his eyebrows in question. 'The police will find him,' she insisted. 'How long can he hide?' She couldn't bring herself to admit he might be a thousand miles away by now.

'Is Andrew here yet?'

'No. Chuck has been in touch with people at his maga-zine—they say he's flying home.'

'Unless he's all tied up on a hot story.' Cynicism crept into Jamie's voice. Now he cleared his throat, in the way, Sandy realized, that said he regretted such a statement. 'I'd better run home to see Grandma. How's she handling this?'

'It's rough on her. Martha is with her every minute. Even sleeping in her room. Go to her,' Sandy said gently. 'She's been asking about you and Andrew.'

'Have—have any arrangements been made?' Jamie asked, seeming to recoil from this even as he asked.

'I've made preliminary arrangements for the funeral. As soon as Andrew arrives, we'll finalize this,' she said unsteadily. *It's so unreal—to be talking this way about Adrienne's funeral.*

'I'll go home, spend a little time with Grandma,' Jamie said, 'then I have to visit Joe Kelly's wife.' He closed his eyes for an instant, as though dreading this encounter.

'A soldier's wife?' *Bringing bad news?*

'Joe was in my National Guard unit. He'll be coming home soon. He lost both legs in an explosion near Baghdad. He didn't tell his wife. I've been delegated to do that.'

'Oh, Jamie!'

'He'll be in the amputee ward at Walter Reed for months. I told him he'd have a job on the paper when he came home. He's worrying every minute about how he'll support his wife and two small kids when he gets home. We'll find a place for him on the *Sentinel.*'

'Of course,' Sandy said softly.

'I'll be back in three or four hours,' Jamie surmised, rising to his feet. 'Everybody must be working long shifts—you'll need all the help you can get. Mom would expect me to pitch right in.' All at once he was defensive.

'Sure.' Sandy managed a shaky smile. 'Thank God you're here.'

'I can walk to the house, but Joe's wife lives on the other side of town.' He paused in thought. 'The battery in my car is probably dead by now—'

'Your mother sold it a few weeks ago. She planned to buy you a new one as a homecoming present the day you returned. She was waiting for you to choose.'

'That's my mom.' Jamie hesitated a moment. 'I'd like to drive her car. It would help me feel close to her.'

'Should you be driving just yet?' Sandy was solicitous.

'In a pinch I can use the bad arm,' he reassured her. 'And the traffic around town isn't apt to be heavy.'

'I'm so glad you're home, Jamie. So glad.'

Fighting off a sense of unreality, Jamie left the only house in which he'd ever lived with a feeling of gratitude that he was here—and guilt that he wasn't with his men in Iraq. He slid behind the wheel of the car and headed for Joe Kelly's house on the other side of town. Dreading the grief he was about to bestow on Joe's wife.

Again he gazed at familiar streets as though seeing them for the first time. Well-maintained, attractive houses in this prosperous area. Lush greenery on every side. Colorful displays of summer flowers. But it would never be the same town with Mom gone.

Images of devastated streets in Iraq where they'd fought so desperately flashed across his mind. Modest houses reduced to shambles, to rubble. May that never happen here, he prayed. Winced as he recalled the horror of 9/11—when over 2,000 innocent Americans were killed as the Twin Towers at the World Trade Center were reduced to rubble.

Now the scenery was changing. The houses were smaller, modest. The cars in driveways were old, weather-beaten. Yet the tiny lawns showed loving care. Flowers blossomed in abundance, as though announcing to the world that here dwelt happy families.

These were homes that were cherished, he thought with

compassion. But if Westwood Manufacturing resorted to outsourcing, how many of these house would be foreclosed for non-payment of mortgages?

Jamie slowed down, watched for addresses. Here it was: 23 Maple Road. Joe and Pat Kelly's tiny house, painted a smoky blue with white trim. Coleus lined the short path to the house. From the backyard came a light feminine voice, the chatter of two very small children.

He parked before the house, sat motionless, gearing himself for the task ahead. Timmy was three, he remembered, Emily almost a year. Joe kept snapshots of them and Pat in a shirt pocket—close to his heart, he always said.

Bracing himself for what he was about to inflict, he left the car and circled around to the rear of the house. Emily sat happily on a blanket on the grass and clapping her tiny hands. Timmy chortled with delight as his mother pushed the swing to exhilarating heights. The pretty, petite young woman pushing the swing was Pat, he guessed.

'I hope I'm not disturbing you,' he began and saw her alarm at the sight of him in uniform. 'Joe sent me to say "hello" for him,' he said quickly. 'I just arrived home today—'

'You're Lieutenant Moss.' Her smile was dazzling. 'He managed to get a call through to me. He said you'd be coming to see me. Oh . . .' She paused, her face somber now. 'Everybody in town was so shocked to hear about your mother. They're grieving with you. She was a wonderful lady.'

'Thank you. She'll be missed.'

'How is Joe?' Her eyes searched his. 'He doesn't say when he expects to come home. But he keeps telling me he'll be fine—'

'In time, yes.' Jamie searched for words.

'He said the doctors and nurses there are great.' But her unease was obvious. *Does she sense that Joe has been secretive about his injuries? That there's more than he's told her?* 'Let's go in the house and have some iced tea. We're going into a hot spell again.'

Pat introduced her two little ones to Jamie. 'Lieutenant Moss just saw your daddy,' she told them. 'Say hello.'

'Hello,' they chorused simultaneously—shy yet eager to welcome him.

'Emily was only three months old when Joe left for Iraq—she never truly knew him.' Pat's smile was wry. 'But Timmy remembers his daddy. Don't you, Timmy?'

Timmy was bashful, clung to his mother's hand while she cradled Emily in her arms. Together they walked into the house, settled themselves in the eat-in kitchen while Pat chattered as though, Jamie thought, she was fearful of what he had to say. Instinct told her Joe had not been totally honest about his injuries. That should make his task easier— but still he felt tense, knowing what he was about to drop on her would be devastating.

'Timmy, play with your truck,' Pat coaxed and settled Emily in the playpen in one corner of the kitchen.

'They're just as Joe described them,' Jamie told her. 'He was so excited when you wrote him that Emily had taken her first steps.'

'It was fantastic—we'd waited hopefully for her to walk. Then I took the two kids to a shoe store to buy new sneakers for Timmy, and the clerk brought out a tiny pair of red sneakers in what he figured was Emily's size. She reached out to take them and held up a foot. In three minutes she was wearing the red sneakers and walking across the floor. The store clerk took the picture I sent to Joe.'

Pat brought a pitcher of iced tea and two glasses to the table, then switched on the ceiling fan. No air-conditioning in these modest houses, Jamie thought in sympathy—and remembered the unbelievable heat in Iraq without it.

'You sounded as though Joe won't be home for a while.' Her eyes anxious.

'He'll be at Walter Reed for further treatment for a while.'

How much does she know about his injuries? Joe didn't tell me. Just that she doesn't know about his legs. 'We flew in from Germany together and—'

'Joe's in this country?' She was astounded. 'He didn't tell me. Why?'

'We flew in on the same C-17.' He struggled to continue. 'Pat, there's no easy way to tell you. Joe loves you very much—he was afraid of how you'd react—'

'To what?' Pat demanded. Her faced drained of color.

'In time he'll be able to walk again—with artificial limbs. But both legs had to be amputated at the knee.'

'Oh, my God—' Her whisper was steeped in anguish.

'He couldn't bring himself to you. He didn't know how you'd feel about him in this condition. But the doctors are sure they'll have him walking again. He'll be able to work. He'll have a job on the *Sentinel.*'

'I've loved Joe since our senior year in high school. We waited to marry until he graduated from community college. He's my whole life. Joe and the kids. How could he think I might not want him?' Tears spilled over unheeded. 'We'll work things out. So it'll take a while longer. We're a family—we'll manage. My mom looks after the kids when I work the dinner shift at Dido's Restaurant. We'll manage,' she repeated with defiance. 'And soon as we can arrange for it, I'm going down to Washington to Walter Read to tell Joe myself!'

At Gloria's coaxing Sandy ate her late lunch, ordered from their usual take-out place. She read the memos that Chuck had left on her desk earlier. But all the while part of her mind dwelt on Jamie's cynical reaction when she said that Andrew was flying home: *'Unless he's all tied up on a hot story.'*

Jamie was sorry that he'd said that, she remembered. She'd always thought that Jamie and Andrew were so close. That's what Adrienne always said. *'It's as though one isn't complete without the other. They're two halves of one.'*

Now she remembered what Chuck had brought up late last night, when the two of them were alone except for the pair in the Composing Room. Both exhausted from the day's efforts. Chuck admitted to some concern about the future of the *Sentinel.*

'Who'll own the paper with Adrienne gone? It'll go to the twins, of course—but suppose Andrew wants to sell? He's never showed any interest in being part of the paper. He's all wrapped up in foreign assignments, wherever there's danger and a big story.'

She'd assumed that Jamie would take over—never considered other possibilities. But Andrew would be an heir, also. She frowned as she considered the situation.

She knew that Adrienne alone owned the *Sentinel.* Claire was paid an annual income by the paper. It was an arrangement made years ago. And that was an odd conversation she'd had yesterday with Mr Hollis, Adrienne's longtime attorney. He asked if she had a personal attorney. *Why would I need an attorney?*

Was Mr Hollis concerned that Andrew would want to sell the paper and split the sale price with Jamie? Was he afraid that she would try to sue the paper because he knew that Adrienne had her sign a five-year contract? Just to give her a sense of security, she thought tenderly.

If the paper was sold, the new owner might want to terminate the whole staff immediately. The possibility was shattering. The *Sentinel* had been owned and operated by three generations of the Moss family. Would Andrew allow it to go into the hands of strangers?

She ordered herself to concentrate on the work at hand, was about to buzz Chuck about a couple of conflicts when she became aware of excited voices in the reception area. Jamie's voice. All at once she was anxious. Jamie was back—but why all the clamor? What had he discovered?

She rose from behind the desk. Her mind racing. *Have*

the police called at the house? Have they picked up a suspect?

She hurried down the hall to the reception area, where Jamie was surrounded by staff members. *Why is Jamie out of uniform? Why is he wearing a backpack?*

She saw him reach with his left arm—his wounded arm, though not in a sling now—to slide the backpack to the floor. Then comprehension broke through. *That isn't Jamie— it's Andrew!* When was the last time she'd seen Andrew for more than a few minutes? A weekend she and Mom had come to Westwood to stay with Adrienne. She was eleven, the twins were fourteen. Andrew and Jamie were taking off for summer camp.

All at once she realized Andrew had become aware of her presence. He moved towards her with a dazzling smile.

'You're little Sandy. Hey, you grew up just right.' He reached to pull her close. Now he turned to the others. 'It's great to be home—but not like this—' He frowned for a moment, as though rejecting reality. 'But Mom would want the paper to keep rolling. So everybody—back to the grind!'

'Have you been home?' Sandy asked Andrew. *Of course he hasn't. He has his backpack with him.* 'Your grand-mother has been asking for you.'

'I'll go home in a bit,' he promised. 'Right now, can you sit me down before a computer? My laptop was stolen right out of my backpack when I was renting a car at the airport.'

'Sure.' Sandy was taken aback. 'In your mother's office.'

She led the way. Her heart pounding. *How could I have mistaken Andrew for Jamie?* They were identical twins, yes—but she'd forgotten it wasn't just a physical identity. Their voices, too, were identical. It was disconcerting.

'I have to finish a story I started on the flight to Washington,' Andrew explained while they walked down the hall to his mother's office. '*American Weekly* must have it by midnight. I lost the first half when that son-of-a-bitch stole my laptop—but I'll pick it up again, e-mail the whole deal to them.'

She felt a momentary reluctance to walk into Adrienne's office. She sensed that for Andrew, too, this was a traumatic moment.

'The computer's new,' Sandy told him. 'Adrienne loved it. The printer's fast—and there's sure to be paper in the tray. She always refilled it when the supply got low.' *How can I talk this way when this room is ghost-ridden now?*

'Okay.' Andrew dropped his backpack on the floor, sat down at the computer. 'Do you suppose somebody could order coffee up for me? Black, no sugar.'

'I'll ask Gloria to bring you a mug. She keeps the coffee-maker in constant action.' Even in a time of crisis Andrew could focus on a story. Adrienne would approve of that.

'Did Jamie get home yet?' Andrew asked.

'About three hours ago,' Sandy told him. 'He came here first, then went home to see your grandmother. From there he was going to see the wife of a member of his unit in Iraq.' Sandy flinched in recall. 'A soldier who's coming home a double amputee.'

'Good old reliable Big Brother,' Andrew drawled. 'He beat me into the world by three minutes.' Sandy felt a touch of amusement in his voice. 'Salt of the earth. Oh, I parked in the paper's area at the rear. I won't have some gang of weird kids writing graffiti on the car or smashing the windshield, will I? The rental agency won't appreciate my returning a messed-up Jag.'

Sandy managed a faint smile. 'You've been away a long time.' The years at college and the years of overseas assignments. Home for occasional brief visits. 'This is quiet little Westwood. We don't have wild gangs here.'

Andrew's face tightened. 'But we have a vicious murderer on the loose. I remember we never used to lock the doors at the house until we were all in bed for the night.'

'Nobody locked their doors until three nights ago,' Sandy

said. 'Nobody will feel safe until your mother's murderer is captured.' Even Jamie had applied for a gun permit.

'I'll knock out my story, pop in the house to see Grandma. Then I'm going over to talk to the detectives assigned to Mom's case.' His face tightened. 'They have to understand we expect action. What have they dug up so far?'

'Not much.' Sandy was taken aback. 'The car had been stolen just a couple of hours before—before it happened . . .' Her voice petered out.

'What else do they know?' he pushed.

'They've checked out the three men who were fired and wrote hate mail,' she told him. *It's only been forty-eight hours*. 'One has been in prison for seventeen months. Another at Riker's Island down in New York for the past three weeks. As far as they can learn, the third man moved away almost two years ago.'

'Let them be damn sure he moved away.' Andrew slammed the computer desk with a fist. 'Once I've got this story off my hands, I want to sit down with you and hear every detail of what's been happening. Jamie and I won't let this creep get away. He's going to pay for what he did to Mom.'

Six

Sandy sat at her desk—her mind in chaos. *How could I have mistaken Andrew for Jamie? They're such different people.*

She felt traitorous. She should be able to know which was Jamie. Her mind shot back to the conversation she'd had some weeks ago with Karen Mitchell, her college professor turned friend. Karen was in heavy research for a book under contract—a study on identical twins.

'It's fascinating, Sandy. Identical twins aren't just physical replicas of each other. Their voices are identical. Their DNA is the same. Only their fingerprints are different. And their personalities. One is the aggressor, the other more reserved.'

She'd been interested in Karen's study because of Jamie and Andrew. She'd seen little of them in the past dozen years, but they'd been part of the earlier years. She remembered even now how they'd loved to tease her.

But she could look into their eyes and know which was Jamie, she told herself. Hadn't someone said that the eyes were the mirror of the soul? She loved Jamie. Jamie and Andrew were two different people. But for a shocking moment she'd mistaken Andrew for Jamie.

Now she forced herself into action. There was much to be done. Call Mr Hollis, tell him that Jamie and Andrew were home. Make an appointment for Jamie and Andrew with the people at the funeral home.

The phone rang. Sandy picked up.

45

'This is Detective Ryan. Detective Bronson and I would like to sit down with you to discuss Mrs Moss's relationship with Westwood Manufacturing. Could we do that in about an hour?'

'Yes,' Sandy told him. 'I'll bring together all the stories we've run on the subject—and the irate letters we received from Ward in response.'

Had Adrienne been murdered because she was raising such a storm in town about Westwood Manufacturing's rumored plans to move operations to China? Did Adrienne die because she tried to save this town from becoming a 'depressed area?'

The day was racing past. Sandy spent forty minutes with the two detectives, with Chuck called in to join the discussion. Shortly past 4 P.M.—moments after Andrew had left—Jamie returned to the paper. He paused at the entrance to Sandy's office, a large plastic bag held in the corner of his working arm.

'I should have been back earlier,' he apologized, 'but it took longer than I thought with Joe Kelly's wife.' His face reflected the anguish of that meeting. 'And earlier Grandma needed to talk. She's fighting to hold herself together. She kept asking about Andrew.'

'He's here. He needed to use a computer—to finish a story for his magazine. He left for the house five minutes ago.'

'I'll see him later.' *Are Jamie and Andrew feuding? Why do I feel this aura of hostility between them? But they'll fight together to nail Adrienne's killer. Both are determined to see that happen.* 'You know Martha —' He extended the bag with an air of indulgence. 'When she's upset, she bakes. She sent over a bunch of apple tarts. They're still warm.'

'Then we'd better get them out of that plastic bag.' Sandy reached to take it from him, looked inside. 'She sent over enough for the whole staff.'

'Take out two,' Jamie said. 'I'll ask Gloria to spread the others around, and I'll bring back coffee for us.'

Over apple tarts and coffee, Jamie came to the conclusion that he and Andrew must go to the funeral home today. 'For Grandma's sake we should bury Mom quickly.'

'Tomorrow afternoon?' Sandy asked after a moment. There had been no question of the police releasing Adrienne's body. Arrangements had been made immediately with the mortician. 'I know that seems awfully fast—'

'If the funeral home is able to handle it, then tomorrow afternoon.' Jamie was resolute.

'We can announce it in tomorrow morning's edition. It'll be a rush for people to schedule attendance,' Sandy conceded, 'but they'll be there.'

'I'll talk to Andrew—we'll go over together to the funeral home.' He paused. 'Will you go with us? To say goodbye to Mom?'

'I want to remember her the way I saw her last,' Sandy whispered. *But what did she mean when she told me to be careful?*

'Grandma will go with us. And Martha,' he guessed. 'Are there any papers we'll need to take with us?'

'Call Mr Hollis. He'll tell you what's necessary.' It was difficult to believe they were talking about burying Adrienne's ashes.

Again, it was close to midnight when Sandy turned off her office lights for the day. The floor was night-dark. The only sounds came from the Composing Room. Where was Jamie? He'd come back to the paper after dealing with Adrienne's funeral arrangements. He'd been working with Chuck since then on an editorial for tomorrow morning's edition.

She paused at the door to Chuck's office. He was at his computer. Seeming exhausted, Jamie leaned back in a chair beside his desk.

Chuck glanced up with a smile. 'Hi. Take this character home, will you? He needs a night's sleep.'

'Unless you plan on walking, you'd better drive home with me,' she reminded Jamie.

'Right. I left Mom's car at Phil's—the air-conditioning conked out,' he told Chuck. 'You don't know how I appreciate it after a summer in Iraq.' He rose to his feet, stretched. 'You plan on sleeping here?'

'I'll be out in another hour. You two beat it.' Chuck managed a rueful grin. 'You know my wife—Bernice threatens to send over a few changes of clothes and a comforter if I don't put in an appearance at the house by 2 A.M. That's my deadline.'

Sandy and Jamie drove home through the deserted streets, the sky dark with clouds. Only a police car prowled in the late night quiet—punctured now by the sounds of two battling tomcats. Sandy parked in their driveway. Now she and Jamie walked to the house. The front door was locked, as at every house in town tonight.

A light was on in the foyer. In the living room to the left Andrew was watching the late evening news on TV.

'Checking up on what's doing in Iraq,' Andrew said, his face taut. 'Nothing's getting better—only worse.'

Sandy saw the glint of surprise in his eyes at her presence.

'I moved into the house when Jamie went off to Iraq with his National Guard unit,' she explained. 'I was working long hours—Adrienne thought it would be easier on me if I didn't have to keep up my apartment.' *He doesn't know about Jamie and me. It's hardly something to talk about at a time like this.*

'Martha told me Mom kept my room always ready for me—whenever I could pop into town,' Andrew said. His eyes roamed from Jamie to Sandy, back to Jamie. *He's sensing there's something special between us.* 'I didn't expect this damn war to take us both away at the same time.'

'I'm calling it a night.' Jamie was brusque. 'What about you, Sandy?'

'That goes for me, too—before I fall on my face. Goodnight, Andrew.'

But despite her tiredness Sandy found sleep elusive. She lay awake, gazing into the darkness until she fell asleep from exhaustion. Sleep punctured by fearful dreams. Of a murderer stalking their town. Of threats to the *Sentinel.*

Was the murderer a hired killer, paid off by Westwood Manufacturing—or the *Evening News?* Would there be more killings? Who would be next?

Early on the gray, dismal Sunday afternoon the family, including Sandy and Martha, walked into the flower-laden church, to the pew reserved for them. Directly behind them sat Chuck and his wife plus several staff members of the *Sentinel.* Now Adrienne's three close friends were taking their places. Dottie Lieberman, a popular lawyer in town, Beth McDonald, a high school teacher, and Sara Adams, who inherited a small fortune at her husband's early death and devoted herself to volunteer work.

Pale and drawn, Chuck leaned forward to talk to Jamie. 'We drew straws to see who from the paper would come,' he explained. 'The others are busy with tomorrow's edition—but their hearts are here with the family.'

Already the church was half-filled. Sandy knew that the mourners would extend out onto the street before the service began. A town was in mourning today.

She sat beside Claire, holding one hand in hers. Jamie on her other side. The sweetness of the flowers was almost oppressive.

Adrienne's three close friends since childhood sat just behind the staff members. Every Friday evening for years the four women had dinner together and afterwards played bridge. Sandy had met them all: Dottie Lieberman—the successful local lawyer divorced for a dozen years because

49

her husband resented her career; Beth McDonald—who'd taught Jamie and Andrew in junior high; and Sara Adams— a stay-at-home mom until she was widowed and who had then focused on volunteer work. It was Sara who sobbed softly through much of the service.

Sandy was dismayed that Mr Hollis insisted that the will be read that same evening—it seemed so callous to rush that way—and Adrienne's friends seemed shocked and surprised that he had asked them to attend the reading. Probably Adrienne left some bequest to each of her friends, Sandy thought tenderly. Though no one ever expected to be attending the reading of her will at so early a time.

'We'll meet at my office at 8 P.M. sharp,' Hollis reminded the family as they headed for the limousine after Adrienne's ashes had been lowered into her late husband's gravesite. 'The reading won't take long.'

At the house they gathered in the living room while Martha went to the kitchen to prepare a quick dinner.

'No need for me to go to Mr Hollis's office with the rest of you,' Claire announced, seeming drained of strength. 'I'll have my dinner—because if I don't,' she added with a burst of spirit, 'Martha won't let me be. Then I'll go to bed.'

'I'll run out to the kitchen.' Sandy rose to her feet. 'Persuade Martha to let me set the table.' *Let Grandma have some time alone with Jamie and Andrew.*

As expected, Martha grumbled at Sandy's insistence on setting the table. She complained, too, about Mr Hollis's insistence she be at his office for the reading of the will.

'I don't like leaving Miss Claire alone even for an hour. Suppose she feels like having a cup of tea? She'll have to make it herself. Why do they need me there?'

'She'll be fine for an hour. It's just a formality to have you there.'

'I know what Miss Adrienne wrote into her will about me . . .' Martha's usual calm eroded for the moment. 'She told me long ago—not that I expected to be around to receive it.' Martha struggled to keep her voice even. 'She was leaving me her pearls—which she let me wear to my grand-niece's wedding two years ago.'

A few minutes before 8 P.M. Sandy and Martha, along with Jamie and Andrew, were seated in Mr Hollis's office. He was at his desk, expressionless. It was almost as though he dreaded this meeting, Sandy thought. He had been the family lawyer for thirty-eight years, for business and personal matters. He, too, grieved for Adrienne Moss.

Sandy sat with shoulders hunched in the coldness of the room. She remembered Adrienne's complaint: '*Air-conditioning in public places is always too high—set for the comfort of men in wool suits.*'

Moments later Adrienne's three friends arrived. Seeming self-conscious at being there, they sat in the semicircle of folding chairs brought in for the occasion.

Mr Hollis cleared his throat, shuffled the papers before him. 'I thought this occasion would be many years hence,' he said stiffly, 'that it would be my son and law partner who would perform this task.'

Sandy sat tense in her chair, willing him to get on with the reading. Seated here between Jamie and Andrew, she felt strangely trapped. Only Jamie's uniform told her this was the twin she loved, the man she was to marry.

With part of her mind she heard Mr Hollis read the bequests to Adrienne's three friends, pieces of jewelry to remember her by, and to Martha her double strand of pearls. Specific stocks and shares were to go to three local charities. And now Mr Hollis paused. He seemed almost reluctant to continue.

'To my sons Jamie and Andrew I leave each $25,000. My mother has been provided for in other arrangements.' Mr Hollis paused, as though gearing himself to continue. 'The balance of my worldly possessions are bequeathed to my goddaughter, Sandra Taylor.'

For a moment an aura of shock permeated the atmosphere.

'There must be some mistake,' Sandy gasped and turned to Jamie as though in apology.

'No mistake.' Mr Hollis was brusque. 'The will was drawn up six months ago and duly witnessed. It decrees that if any heir fights it, he or she is disqualified and his or her share will go to a designated local charity.' Mr Hollis held a long, labored breath. 'Mrs Moss was confident that her mother would remain in the family home for her remaining years.'

'Mom meant for you to inherit,' Andrew told Sandy after another awkward pause. 'You were very important to her.'

'But it's wrong!' Sandy turned from Andrew to Jamie, bewildered.

I mustn't fight the will—I must respect Adrienne's wishes. If I inherit, then Jamie will share. Leaving Andrew out in the cold. Except for the $25,000 bequest. Had Adrienne concluded that Andrew—already on the road to success— would need nothing from her?

'It's what Mom wanted,' Andrew reiterated after a moment of leaden silence. Unexpectedly he smiled. 'That means I'm your houseguest, Sandy. But I'll be taking off soon on another assignment in Iraq.'

'Andrew, it'll always be the family home,' Sandy stammered and turned to Jamie. *Why is he looking so thunderous?*

'I take it for granted there will no effort to fight the will.' Mr Hollis sent a cursory glance about those gathered before him. 'Andrew, Jamie, the $25,000 bequest to each of you is in the form of a CD held in trust for you. You won't have to wait for probate to receive this. Sandy, we'll need to talk about technical details. Call me in a few days—we'll set up an appointment.'

'Yes, Mr Hollis,' Sandy agreed, her mind in chaos.

She rose to her feet. Mr Hollis was closing the meeting.

Didn't the others understand? They all sat in mute silence—encased in disbelief. Then all at once the others, too, rose from their chairs. Martha crossed to hug her. Only Martha didn't seem shocked.

'You were like her daughter,' Martha said, tears sliding down her cheeks. 'With the boys over in Iraq you were her rock of Gibraltar.'

Stunned—uncomfortable at being privy to this—Adrienne's three close friends were trying to ignore the terms of the will. They embraced Martha, expressed their sympathy to Jamie and Andrew about their mother's death, and took off as though fearful of some furious outbreak.

'Let's go home,' Martha said. 'It's been a long day.'

Seven

On the drive home the four in the car avoided any talk about the will. To fill the silence that imprisoned the others, Martha rambled on about Adrienne's three close friends.

'It'll never be the same for them. All these years, since soon after your father died,' she told Jamie and Andrew, 'Miss Adrienne met them every Friday night for dinner and to play bridge.' She struggled against tears. 'She was—what do folks call it? The linchpin that held them together when things went bad for one of them.'

Sandy was dazed, struggling to comprehend what had happened. Adrienne, who was always so logical, had created an illogical situation. It had been an unspoken assumption by everyone at the paper that one day in the distant future Jamie would be the Publisher of the *Sentinel,* and in some fashion Andrew would be co-heir to his mother's estate.

As the car approached the house, Sandy saw the light in Claire's window. She hadn't gone to sleep. Martha would take her a cup of decaffeinated tea and a sleeping pill, she thought compassionately. At Martha's intervention, Dr Maxwell had prescribed this.

Claire would learn about Adrienne's will. She would ask Martha—and Martha would have to tell her. How would she accept the terms? Andrew was his grandmother's favorite. Would she be furious? *Will she hate me for inheriting most of Adrienne's estate?*

Emerging from the car, Martha decreed that she would

serve tea and muffins. 'You all just pecked at dinner,' she scolded.

Sandy fought against soaring discomfort as she sat in the living room with Jamie and Andrew. *Both steering away from any discussion of the will.* They focused on the intensifying fight in Iraq—for a few minutes.

Inevitably, the conversation returned to Adrienne's murder. Jamie and Andrew were impatient that the police were coming up with no suspect. *But they must understand—the police need time.*

'Let the cops go their way,' Andrew said, fire in his eyes. 'We'll do our own investigating. Mom's killer has got to pay!'

'Let's offer a reward.' Jamie's voice was electric. 'That ought to bring some action. A $50,000 reward for information that brings about a conviction.' *The money left to Jamie and Andrew in Adrienne's will.* 'We'll put up the money, Andrew—' His eyes asked for confirmation.

'Run it on the front page of tomorrow morning's edition,' Andrew ordered. 'Or is it too late for tomorrow?'

'We can manage it,' Sandy said. 'Let me get on the phone with—' She paused in sudden realization. 'You're Managing Editor now, Jamie.'

'You're the Publisher,' he reminded her, his eyes opaque— unnerving her, 'as of just past 8 P.M. tonight.'

'Jamie,' she protested—*I don't want to think about the will. It mustn't come between Jamie and me—*'how do we handle this?' She knew, but it seemed politic to place responsibility in Jamie's hands. And in truth, she told herself, he knew far more about the paper's operation than she.

Jamie rose to his feet. 'We'll go back to the paper now, reset the front page. Move the original articles to inside pages. Cut back as necessary. The morning *Sentinel* must go out on schedule—but let's make sure our reward offer is headlined.'

'What can I do to help?' Andrew, too, was on his feet.

'The *Sentinel* is a small-town newspaper,' Jamie said with an enigmatic smile. 'Not a national magazine. We'll manage.'

'Explain to Martha,' Sandy told Andrew. 'She'll understand.'

While Sandy drove, Jamie made notes for the front-page article to be inserted under the new headline.

'You promised to see Dr Maxwell about your arm,' she reminded him. 'You said the stitches should be coming out about now.'

'I made an appointment for tomorrow—10 A.M.,' he told her.

'Good.' *Why do I feel a wall coming up between Jamie and me?*

'Thank God we're in the computer age,' Jamie said as Sandy swung the car into the paper's parking area. 'We can reset with little sweat.'

'Chuck's here—' Sandy pointed to Chuck's suburban, which on occasion doubled as delivery truck. He has to be told about the will, she reminded herself. He'd been anxious, fearful that the paper would go to 'the boys' and that Andrew might want to sell.

'He's not soliciting ads at this hour,' Jamie surmised. 'But then he was Mom's right hand in so many ways.'

'Chuck been wonderful these last few days. I needed help,' Sandy admitted. Chuck knew that the will was going to be read this evening. He couldn't know the terms—he'd be shocked. Everybody expected Jamie to take over the paper.

She parked. Unexpectedly Jamie reached to pull her close, held her for a few moments. Warm, reassuring moments. Some of her tension evaporated. This was the Jamie she knew and loved. Adrienne's will mustn't come between them.

'Mom looked forward so to our wedding,' he murmured. 'But she'll be with us in spirit—we know that.'

'Jamie, I don't understand about the will—'

'Don't try,' he said again. *But he's stunned—he's hurt. He feels rejected by his mother.* 'Mom wanted you to inherit.'

Questions assaulted Sandy. Was this Adrienne's way of cutting Andrew off? But why? She adored him. She was so proud of his success. Was she afraid that Jamie wasn't up to running the paper? But that was absurd—he was far more capable than she. *What did Adrienne mean when she told me, 'Be careful, Sandy. Be careful—'?*

Was Adrienne upset that Jamie had not made a big splash—like Andrew—in the field she loved? Did she blame herself for that? But Jamie was devoted to the *Sentinel*— he was happy here. He meant the paper to be his life. *Our life.* But why did Adrienne cut Jamie—and Andrew—off with just a $25,000 bequest? It was so unlike her.

'I'll call Detective Bronson,' Jamie told Sandy as they walked towards the entrance. 'You said you have his card— that we were to call at any time of day or night. He must be told about our offer of a reward.'

They saw the light turned off in Chuck's office as they approached. Chuck emerged.

'What the hell are you two doing here?' he demanded.

Omitting any discussion of the will yet, Jamie explained about the decision to offer a $50,000 reward.

'I figure we ought to notify the detectives on the case,' Jamie began.

'Bronson and Ryan,' Chuck recalled. 'You two set up the new front page. I'll check with them.'

'Chuck, there's something you should know—not that it means anything. You know Mr Hollis insisted on a read-ing of the will tonight.' She took a deep breath, forced herself to continue. 'Adrienne left the paper to me.'

She saw the startled, disbelieving reaction in his eyes. He turned from her to Jamie, back to her.

'So we go on as usual,' Chuck said. 'Okay, let's get crack-ing.'

Jamie—with Sandy at his side—immediately called the Composing Room staff together.

'This is not the first time the *Sentinel* has had to make a last-moment change on the front page,' he reminded them. 'Prepare for another late night.'

The Composing Room staff—who also served as camera/platemaker technicians—listened intently to his instructions.

'We must make the public aware of this reward as soon as possible. In tomorrow morning's edition,' Jamie summed up. 'Sandy and I will have the new layout ready in forty minutes.'

By 4 A.M. it was clear the *Sentinel* was on schedule. Sandy and Jamie sat with Chuck in his office—all with an air of relief.

'The reward just might jog some memories,' Chuck said, his face somber. 'The police are coming up with nothing.'

'Another important matter . . .' Sandy searched for words. 'Do we stay on Adrienne's course?'

'Meaning what?' Jamie was puzzled.

'Your mother was on a heavy campaign to dissuade Westwood from outsourcing. You know what that'll do to this town. One thousand jobs are at stake.'

Chuck gazed from Sandy to Jamie. 'At this point we don't know if they're involved in her murder.'

'Let the police investigate,' Jamie said after a moment. 'You're right, Sandy. Mom would expect us to follow her lead. She'd made a commitment to fight outsourcing. We'll carry on for her.' He managed a faint smile. 'Maybe not today—but we'll keep it in work.'

'Let's go home,' Sandy told Jamie a few moments later, feeling drained of all strength. 'Let's grab at least three hours' sleep before another business day begins.'

Adrienne's ashes had been laid to rest. The will read. Tomorrow would be the beginning of a new business week. Life must move on.

Sandy and Jamie drove through town, darkened in slumber, almost devoid of traffic, in a silence broken only by the sound of a dog invading a garbage pail. Both were too exhausted for talk—until Sandy turned into their street.

Jamie broke the silence. 'Sandy, I was upset by Mom's will. I felt rejected—as though Mom was scolding me for something I did. Or something I didn't do. But at moments I thought about it—and now I understand. Mom wasn't cutting me out. She knows we're going to be married.' He paused. 'Unless as a new heiress,' he joshed, 'you're looking for more interesting fields.'

For an instant Sandy's eyes left the road. 'Jamie, you know better,' she protested. 'But I suppose we should wait a while.' They'd always talked about a wedding right after his return from Iraq. 'I mean—out of respect.'

'I don't think Mom would care—but yes, it would shock the town if we married too quickly.'

'Then what you're saying . . .' She sought for words. 'You're saying Adrienne meant to cut Andrew off.' Her mind was in turmoil. 'Why, Jamie?' In a corner of her mind she remembered that Jamie always felt Andrew was his mother's favorite. 'Why?' She was bewildered. 'I feel guilty, somehow.'

'Don't be.' Jamie was brusque. 'Mom never did anything without a reason.' His eyes enigmatic. 'But let's concentrate on what's important. We must track down Mom's killer. He can't be allowed to walk free. Sandy, I won't have a moment's rest until whoever killed Mom is behind bars for the rest of his life.'

At 7:10 A.M. on Monday, Sandy and Jamie left the parking area and walked into the *Sentinel's* reception room. Only slightly rested after two hours' sleep. Functioning on will power, Sandy told herself. This morning Jamie had abandoned his uniform for a sports shirt, chinos and loafers—his working clothes. Iraq was behind him. Also this morning—at Sandy's insistence—he would take over his mother's office.

Gloria was at her desk already. She reached for a copy of the morning's *Sentinel* and handed it to Jamie with an air of triumph. In moments of crisis she kept unconventional working hours.

'You sleeping here now?' Jamie joshed while he and Sandy viewed the headline above the new front-page article: $50,000 REWARD FOR INFORMATION LEADING TO CONVICTION.

'I came in at a few minutes past six—to help get the paperboys—and our one papergirl—out on their routes,' Gloria said. It was Gloria, Sandy recalled, who had campaigned for the addition of a papergirl. 'I don't think Chuck went home last night. Bernice called about twenty minutes ago. She's sending over a change of clothes. It's nice we have a shower available.'

'I don't suppose you've had time to put up coffee?' Jamie was wistful. They'd sneaked out of the house without breakfast while Martha was taking a tray up to Claire's room.

'What does that look like to you?' Gloria pointed to the corner table where the coffeemaker was in action. 'I'll bring coffee in a couple of minutes.'

Sandy and Jamie settled themselves in her office to debate about the following day's editorial.

'People are running scared.' Jamie was somber. 'We need to reassure them—and yet point out that until Mom's killer is nailed, we all need to be cautious. Doors and windows locked. Not just at night,' he emphasized and winced. 'For those without air-conditioning that's going to be rough.'

'More cops on duty?' Sandy lifted an eyebrow in question.

'That may be tough on the town budget. If Ward does outsource, we'll lose more than jobs. We'll lose tax revenue.' He grimaced. 'How did Noel Ward become such a creep? Five years ago he had a solid reputation among his workers. Westwood Manufacturing offered paid holidays, health insurance. They had a small turnover of employees. What happened over there?'

'The union came in,' Sandy reminded him. 'Salaries went up. Everything seemed to be working all right. Then business dropped off. The company began layoffs. Where they used to work three shifts at special periods, they cut down to one. Then—about two months ago—rumors started about the probability of outsourcing most of the jobs. That was devastating. In the last couple of weeks employees were conscious of special meetings in the conference room with out-of-town strangers. They're unnerved.'

'I can understand that.' Jamie reached for his mug of coffee. 'Okay, for now let's focus on tomorrow morning's edition.'

Forty minutes after they arrived, Sandy's private line buzzed. 'Sandy Taylor.'

'I've been hanging around the police station hoping for some break in the case.' It was Frank's voice, shrill with excitement. 'All hell's breaking loose down here. Tell Jim to meet me at Dottie Lieberman's house—354 Sycamore Drive. We'll want photos—'

'Frank, what's happened at Dottie Lieberman's house?' Sandy's heart was pounding.

'It looks like we have a serial killer on the loose. Dottie Lieberman's daughter dropped by her house for an early breakfast meeting.' *They're both lawyers, share cases.* 'She found her mother dead in bed. Suffocated. A red lollipop beside her. Dottie Lieberman has been murdered!'

Eight

Jamie leapt to his feet. 'Make sure we keep plenty of space on tomorrow morning's front page open. Run with Frank's story for now and Jim's photos,' he told Sandy. 'I'm going over to Dottie Lieberman's house. Check in the files—see what we have on Lieberman's law cases, dating back five years.'

'The police will want that, too.' Sandy pushed back her chair. 'I'll see that they get it.'

Sliding behind the wheel of his mother's car, Jamie discarded the sling, moved his arm: Yes! He could use the hand now. Remember to keep the 10 A.M. appointment with Dr Maxwell, he reminded himself. The stitches would come out. He drove from the parking lot at a faster pace than normal. His mind chasing after answers. *Dottie Lieberman's murder—so soon after Mom's—is no coincidence. If the police solve her murder, then they'll have Mom's killer.*

Nothing mattered so much as nailing the creep who was killing innocent women in this town. This was a serial killer. Who was to be the next victim?

At this early hour—just after 8 A.M.—he was encountering little traffic. One school bus was beginning its rounds. A produce truck headed for the supermarket. A *Sentinel* paperboy—running late—was completing his route. Most folks in town hadn't heard the news yet, but any minute now local radio and TV would be invading homes with the horrific news. He was driving past rows of well-maintained private homes, their residents preparing for another day.

62

The sky was blue, devoid of clouds. The sun was brilliant. Yesterday's humidity gone. An autumnal chill in the air.

Approaching Dottie Lieberman's multi-windowed contemporary, just four blocks away from the Mosses' colonial, he saw the coroner's van and two police cars parked. What an agonizing experience for Nora—to walk into her mother's house and find her like that.

He and Nora had been at school together. Their mothers were close friends. As kids they'd attended the same birthday parties; one summer he and Andrew had gone to the same camp as she had. Nora and Craig, her husband of two years, belonged, as he did, to the local environmental group. Now he noted the media trucks, TV and radio, parked on the other side of the road. Frank and Jim stood beside the line-up of cars, along with reporters and photographers from the weekly *Evening News* and several newspapers from nearby towns.

'The detectives gave us a quick briefing—nothing more,' Frank reported with an air of frustration as Jamie approached. 'All we know is that Dottie Lieberman was suffocated with her own pillow. No fingerprints, no forced entry. They haven't a clue as to who killed her.'

'Go back to the paper and start on your article—I'll phone in whatever new pops up,' Jamie instructed. 'Jim, give Frank what you have so far. Hang around here with me—maybe we'll pick up something new.'

A pair of cops on duty out front prevented any intrusion into the house. Jamie gritted his teeth in frustration. He needed to talk with Nora. *Somewhere there's a link between Mom's killing and Dottie Lieberman's.*

His mind clicked into high gear. Use the cell phone, try to get through to Nora. He reached into a jacket pocket. Call the paper—Gloria would get him Dottie Lieberman's home phone number. Ten minutes later he managed to get Nora on the phone.

'Jamie, I can't believe this.' Her voice broke. 'First Adrienne, now Mom. Who killed our mothers?'

'Let's talk about it when you can get away from the police,' Jamie said. 'We're going to catch that fiend, Nora. That's all I can think about now.'

They talked a few moments longer. Jamie was to meet Nora at her house at 3 P.M.

'Craig doesn't even know,' Nora realized in shock. 'I have to talk with him!'

With phones ringing constantly in the background, Sandy sat with Jamie and Chuck in what had been Adrienne's office and which—with some reluctance—Jamie now accepted as his. The hum of a newscaster's voice filtered from a radio down the hall. News of Dottie Lieberman's murder was dominating local radio and television programming.

'I have to meet with Nora Lieberman at her house at 3 P.M.,' Jamie reminded the other two. 'She's badly shaken but determined to do whatever she can to help track down her mother's killer—and Mom's.'

'Don't take a photographer with you,' Chuck advised. 'We've got plenty in the files that we can use.'

'Right,' Jamie agreed, in somber thought. 'I remember going with Mom to Nora's wedding.' His face softened. 'And Mom agreed with Nora that she had the right to use her single name professionally—though some folks in town rejected it. Mom threw out her pet retort: "We're living in the twenty-first century—let's act like that." '

Earlier Jamie had kept his appointment with Dr Maxwell. The stitches had been removed from his injured arm and Dr Maxwell assured him he'd have no further problems with the wound.

They ate without tasting the grilled-chicken sandwiches that Gloria had ordered without asking and had brought to them. Mugs of coffee sat at strategic positions while they talked.

'Something that has never happened in Westwood is

64

happening now,' Chuck said flatly. 'No denying it—we have a serial killer on our hands.'

'Two murders, each carried out in a different way.' Sandy's mind was in high gear. 'For serial killers, isn't that unusual?'

'Who can predict what goes on in the mind of a serial killer?' Chuck challenged. 'All we can do—every person in this town—is to be careful.'

That's what Adrienne said to me—'Be careful, Sandy. Be careful.'

'The whole town radiates an atmosphere of terror, but what can we tell people to lessen their fears?' Chuck spread his hands in a gesture of futility.

'The cops are uptight,' Jamie admitted. 'We got very little out of them at the news briefing. We know the story—and there's nothing else to go on. "Nothing's missing. No fingerprints. No forced entry—" '

Chuck broke in impatiently. 'How do they know that? Nobody has fancy locks around here. Even a sharp amateur could pick a local lock. And Dottie was a lawyer—a bright divorce lawyer for the most part—and very outspoken. She could have been killed by a resentful husband or wife.'

'One point bothers me.' Sandy squinted in thought. 'We keep thinking a serial killer is responsible for what's happened. But what's the link between the two murders? My every instinct tells me these are not random killings, that it wasn't a coincidence that Dottie Lieberman was the second victim, but what's the link between them?'

Jamie nodded. 'I thought about that as I was driving over to the Lieberman house. Some creep killed Mom— and now he—or she—is going after Mom's circle of close friends!'

All at once Sandy was ice-cold. 'You mean Beth McDonald and Sara Adams could be next?'

'That's possible. Or it could be anyone close to Adrienne.'

Chuck revised. 'Meaning you, Jamie, Andrew. Adrienne's mother or Martha. We can't know where he or she will strike again.'

'Two close friends, living within a block of each other, murdered within days.' Sandy fought for calm. 'Let's be honest—one of us is at risk for being the next on the list. And that could include you, too, Chuck.'

Andrew appeared in the doorway. 'I just heard the news.' Sandy stiffened. *Why am I always unnerved at seeing Jamie and Andrew in the same room?* 'What the hell's going on in this town?'

'A psycho is on the loose,' Jamie shot back. 'There's been a second murder—one of Mom's closest friends. Dottie Lieberman.'

Andrew gaped in disbelief. 'What are the police saying? Do they have any leads?'

'So far, nothing,' Jamie told him. 'Neither on Mom's killer nor on Dottie Lieberman's.'

'I suppose it's early to expect action.' Andrew tried to make a show of being fair. 'The cops need time. But we can't just sit around and do nothing!' He pondered for a moment. 'Let's do some searching on our own! Like circularizing the news of the reward.'

'It's running on the front page of the *Sentinel,*' Jamie shot back.

'Not everybody reads the *Sentinel.* Let's get out circulars, deliver one to every house, post one on every lamppost in town.' He exuded grim determination.

'We can do that,' Chuck agreed. 'I'll put it into work right away.'

'Great.' Now Andrew switched topics. 'I'm looking for a friendly computer not in use. I just spoke with my magazine. My photographer in Iraq e-mailed photos to *American Weekly*—and my editor wants me to do an accompanying article.'

'How can you do that?' Jamie was astonished.

'Easy.' Andrew refused to be disturbed. 'I know the terrain. I know the people. The photos tell the story. So,' he wound up, 'is there a computer available for me?'

'Take over my old office while you're here,' Jamie told him.

Sandy picked up an odd inflection in his voice. 'It's right next door.'

'Thanks a bunch.' Andrew turned to leave.

She heard Andrew exchanging greetings in the hall with Bob, one of the men from the Composing Room. *It's incredible—if Jamie wasn't sitting here with me, I'd swear that it was he talking to Bob.*

Jamie glanced at his watch. 'I'll have to leave soon for my appointment with Nora.'

Gloria charged into the room. 'I've got a call on hold. Somebody from the District Attorney's office insists on talking to the "Publisher."' Gloria turned to Sandy. Uncomfortable now. 'I told him you're the Publisher, but he insists I'm wrong.' She shrugged. 'He probably thinks women shouldn't have the vote.'

'Put the call through to Jamie's line,' Sandy ordered. 'Jamie is Acting Publisher.'

'Right.' Gloria seemed relieved.

Moments later the phone on Jamie's desk rang. He picked up, reached to hit speakerphone. 'Jamie Moss.'

'This is District Attorney Potter's assistant,' a young male voice said. A newcomer in town, Sandy recalled—and ruffling feathers. 'We have a new development in the Adrienne Moss murder.' The excitement he'd tried to mask crept through now. 'A man is coming here within the next thirty minutes. He claims he can identify Mrs Moss's killer—'

Jamie was skeptical. 'Someone after the reward?'

'I don't believe so. It could be a crank call—but that's not the impression we're getting. He insists that the Publisher of the *Sentinel* be present.'

'I'm Acting Publisher at the moment,' Jamie told him. 'I'll be there within the next twenty minutes. Along with Publisher Sandra Taylor.'

Nine

'It may be some nutcase,' Chuck warned when Jamie was off the phone. 'That happens.'

'We'll find out fast enough.' Jamie turned to Sandy. 'Let's get over to Eric Potter's office.'

'Right.' Sandy was on her feet.

They rushed to the parking area, took off in Sandy's car. Jamie shot an anxious glance at his watch.

'The character in Potter's office said his informant would be there in thirty minutes,' Sandy reminded him. 'We have plenty of time.'

Please God, let this not be just a nutcase looking for publicity. If he killed Adrienne, did he also kill Dottie Lieberman? It seems likely.

They arrived at Potter's headquarters, were immediately ushered into his private office.

'Eric, this is Sandra Taylor. She's the Publisher of Record,' Jamie introduced her. 'I'm Acting Publisher. What's this all about?'

'It may be nothing, but we have to follow any lead. This man claims he can bring in your mother's killer.' He cleared his throat, his eyes traveling to the door. 'You won't believe it—the guy is Noel Ward.'

Jamie and Sandy were astonished. 'The head of Westwood Manufacturing?' Jamie asked.

'I can't figure it out.' Potter shook his head in bewilderment. 'We know, of course, that lately he and Adrienne Moss were bitter enemies—'

'Exactly what did he say?' Sandy asked, trembling with rage. *Noel Ward hired a hit man—and now he's trying to wiggle out.*

'He said he needed to talk to us. He could bring in the killer under certain circumstances. And he insisted that the Publisher of the *Sentinel* be present at our meeting.'

'Why?' Jamie was puzzled. 'Because my mother was Publisher until—'

Potter shrugged. 'I don't have a clue.'

'He's trying to build a sympathetic public reaction.' Sandy's voice was scathing. 'A sympathetic jury pool.' *But who can have sympathy for a murderer?*

Moments later—well ahead of the projected thirty minutes—there was a light knock at the door.

'Come in,' Potter ordered.

The door opened. 'Mr Ward is here,' Potter's administrative assistant said and stepped aside.

Noel Ward—pale and drawn—walked into the room. A man of commanding presence. Somewhere in his fifties, Sandy guessed. Accustomed to having his way in every situation. Westwood's major employer—on the point of wreaking havoc on this town. And involved in Adrienne's murder?

'Mr Ward, please have a seat.' Potter was brisk, gestured to the third chair in a semi-circle before his cluttered desk. 'Have you met Jamie Moss and Sandra Taylor of the *Sentinel?*'

'Not officially,' Ward said, his face tightening. 'We've crossed paths.' *He knows I've been interviewing employees fearful of losing their jobs. That we have a major article in work.* 'No need for chit-chat. Mr Potter, I have an eighteen-year-old son. Warm, loving, always eager to please. But Evan is—' He took a deep, agonized breath. 'Evan is severely retarded. He's been home-schooled, to the extent that it was possible, watched over with care. His two true pleasures in life are driving—and he's good at it and in

70

normal times cautious—and watching television. As you may have heard, I'm in the process of considering out-sourcing my business, except for a small office staff.'

'A devastating situation for almost a thousand workers,' Sandy said passionately. 'A devastating situation for this town!'

For an instant her eyes clashed with Ward's. He turned away, gazed into space.

'We've faced some ugly talk. I've been upset, spoke in haste in my son's presence.' He paused, gearing himself to continue. 'Evan heard me say—in a moment of frustration—that I was sick of this battle. That it was all the fault of the woman who ran the *Sentinel.*' He was struggling now to continue. His voice dropped to a harsh whisper. 'I said I wished Adrienne Moss was dead.'

'Oh, dear God!' Involuntarily Sandy reached out a hand to Jamie. *This is the man responsible for Adrienne's death!*

'Evan had no understanding of what he was doing. He wanted to please his father.' Now—sensing the tumultuous feelings he'd evoked in Jamie and Sandy—Ward focused on the District Attorney. 'But before I bring him in, I want your promise that he will be tried as a minor. His birth certificate states his age as eighteen, but in truth—as medical records will show—he's barely nine.'

'You're telling me,' Eric Potter said with quiet delibera-tion, 'that your son, Evan Potter, killed Adrienne Moss.'

'Yes.' Ward fought for composure. 'He only meant to please me,' he reiterated. 'He doesn't understand what he's done.'

'He murdered my mother!' A vein throbbed in Jamie's forehead.

Ward closed his eyes for an instant—as though to escape reality. 'I know the grief he's brought to Mrs Moss's family and friends. To this town. It was a tragic act. But before I bring Evan in, I must know that he won't be tried as an adult.'

'He'll be tried as a juvenile,' Eric Potter agreed after a fleeting glance at Jamie. 'Provided his medical history confirms what you've said.' He paused, seeming to weigh the situation. 'But, Mr Ward—considering his mental capacity—how did he know to steal a car, not to use one of your family cars to run down Mrs Moss?' There was an undertone of accusation in his voice now. *Does he suspect that Ward told his son to kill Adrienne—but now blames the murder on the boy?*

'Evan knew that from the television,' Ward said tiredly. 'I told my wife it was bad for him to watch all those crime shows, but he's hyperactive, they relax him.'

'Are you willing to take a lie-detector test?' Potter threw at Ward.

'Any time, any place,' Ward shot back. 'I'm guilty only of making a careless remark in anger.'

'With tragic results!' Jamie said.

Potter seemed in inner debate. 'Where is your son?'

'In a private sanitarium about sixty miles from here—where he's under constant guard.' Ward paused, forced himself to continue. 'I never expected anything so horrendous to happen. I was tired of all the fighting. Tired of others telling me how to run my business.'

Jamie stared at him in barely contained rage. 'Because of a careless remark, my mother is dead!'

'I'm sorry. I never meant for it to happen. I'll have to live with this for the rest of my life.' Ward rose to his feet, turned to Potter. 'I'll bring Evan to your office at 10 A.M. tomorrow. But I must have your word there'll be no reporters, no photographers present. Evan would be terrified.'

'No reporters, no photographers,' Potter agreed. 'But you must expect this to be headlined in the local newspapers once your son is in our custody.'

Ward flinched. 'His mother and I have tried through the years to protect him, but I failed him. I realize Evan will

72

have to pay the consequences. I realize now he's a danger to the world—through no fault of his own. I'll bring him in at ten tomorrow morning.'

He left the office. The other three sat in silence—caught up in the drama of the situation. Thank God, Sandy told herself, Adrienne's killer would go to trial. Yet she was assaulted by fresh pain that her death had been caused by a remark spoken in rage. A teenager, a boy with the mind of a nine-year-old, had sought to please his father, with no concept of what he was doing.

'That's one murder solved.' Potter punctured the silence. 'The boy will be tried and found guilty by reason of his mental condition. He'll be institutionalized, no further danger to the community.' He stared into space. 'I doubt that the Lieberman case will be solved this quickly.'

'Have you ruled out the possibility that what we were just told is a diabolical scheme? Noel Ward using his son to commit murder?' Sandy felt compelled to pursue this issue.

'That will come up at trial. My instincts tell me this was a tragic accident. I suspect a jury will be convinced that Evan acted on his own. But one thing is clear—we don't have a serial killer here. Evan Ward was eighty miles away last night, under tight security, when Dottie Lieberman was murdered.'

'This town is running scared.' Jamie gestured concern. 'And there's much hostility towards Noel Ward at the prospect of almost a thousand unemployed if he goes ahead with his outsourcing. A jury might let this color its verdict on Evan Ward.'

In her mind—despite her supposition that the father and not the son might be guilty—Sandy was conscious of Noel Ward's pain. His life and his wife's life would never be the same again. A horrible quirk of fate, and Adrienne was dead and a teenager would spend the rest of his life in a mental institution.

Seated again in her car, Sandy and Jamie dissected what had taken place in Potter's office, both knowing they'd be haunted for a long time by the knowledge that Adrienne's death never should have happened. A crazy quirk of fate— and she'd paid with her life.

'Okay, let's head back for the paper.' Jamie reached for the ignition key. 'I've got a while before my appointment with Nora.'

'This is unreal.' Sandy shook her head, as though to thrust aside disturbing visions. 'Who killed Dottie Lieberman? Why?' *And why do I have this terrifying conviction that there will be more murders?*

Ten

Jamie sat in the dining area of Nora's attractive contemporary. While she brought a carafe of coffee to the table and poured for them, pulled a tray of blueberry muffins from the oven and transferred them to a plate, he told her what had transpired in Potter's office. He understood—she forced herself to be active because this was how she held herself together.

'How do we know that Evan Ward didn't manage to escape and come into town for—for as long as it took to kill Mom?' Nora challenged.

'The police will check it out,' Jamie told her, 'though it's unlikely.' He hesitated, knowing the anguish she was feeling at this moment. Matching his own anguish. 'You're familiar with your mother's cases,' he began. 'Do you—'

'Mom and I worked together on several cases.' Nora picked up. 'I'm familiar with her other cases. The detectives asked for records—where there was hostility towards Mom. I went through her files, pulled these out. Mom wasn't murdered by someone involved in a case,' she said with sudden intensity.

'You suspect someone?'

'I'm wrong. I know I'm wrong!'

'Why don't we talk about it?' Jamie said gently.

'How can I suspect my own father of killing my mother?'

Jamie struggled to conceal his shock. 'Did this come up with the detectives?'

'They know Mom was divorced—years ago. The question

of their relationship now came up for a moment.' Nora paused, seeming in some inner battle. 'I harbor no love for my father—' Her voice deepened in bitterness. 'But how can I tell the police I suspect he might be Mom's killer? I know in their eyes I'm concealing evidence. I have no love for my father,' she reiterated, 'but I can't turn him in unless I'm convinced he's guilty.'

'That'll be hard to know.' Jamie's mind was racing. *How do I handle this?*

Nora's voice dropped to a tortured whisper. 'I remember the very early years when he was a warm, devoted father— and then he changed. People do, you know.' Her tone was defensive now.

'It happens . . .'

'He developed a vile temper, fought with Mom constantly. He was verbally abusive. She was building a career, earning respect. Everything he touched turned to dust.' She closed her eyes for a moment. 'Then one night he hit her— that was the end of the marriage. Jamie, I can't tell the police that he was badgering Mom for the past two weeks, right up to last evening.'

'What did he want?'

'In the divorce settlement Mom got the house—with its huge mortgage. Mom saw me through high school, college and law school—never missing a mortgage payment. Now the house is almost paid off. Dad was screaming at Mom to take out a larger loan on the house so he could buy some franchise, set himself up in business. Mom wanted no part of it.'

'That's understandable.' Jamie searched his mind for knowledge of Craig Lieberman. He had only vague recall. 'He doesn't live here in Westwood now, does he?'

'No, he left town right after the divorce. But he's living just fifty miles away.' Nora was struggling to continue. 'He didn't fight the divorce—and four months later he married a waitress in a cafe where he used to have breakfast. They'd known each other six weeks. He'd pop into the house at intervals—every six or eight months—to see me. Then that stopped. We had nothing to talk about. And just a few weeks ago he started phoning Mom. Sometimes twice a day. At first he was looking for free legal advice—he was starting up a business, wanted to know about S corporations— things like that. And then a couple of weeks ago the calls got nasty—'

'The police didn't push you for information about him?' That would seem a lead to follow. Even years after a divorce, an irate ex-husband had been known to kill his wife.

'No.' Nora's mouth tightened. 'He's been out of our lives—for the most part—for over a dozen years. Once he hit Mom she knew she had to divorce him. Before that she'd tried to hold the marriage together. For my sake.'

'He may be questioned,' Jamie warned. *But without Nora's testimony they'll have nothing.*

'Jamie—as much as I resent him—he's still my father. How can I turn him in when I don't know that he was involved?'

'Hold your own investigation,' Jamie began. 'Know in your own mind if he's innocent or guilty. Then act accordingly. You can't just ignore this, Nora.'

'Will you help me?' Nora leaned across the table. 'By now he must know that Mom was murdered.' She paused in anxiety, brushed with contempt. 'He hasn't even bothered to call.'

'Call him,' Jamie said. 'Sit down and talk with him. Don't be afraid to ask questions. Let him know your feelings.'

'He may refuse to come—even for Mom's funeral.'

'Insist you must talk with him. Tell him the police are asking questions about his relationship with your mother. That'll put fear in him.'

'Will you face him with me?'

'Of course I will.' His voice was reassuring.

'I'll threaten to tell the police about the bad relationship between him and Mom. Right up to the day she died.' Nora was resolute now. 'He'll come. If he can prove he's not involved, I'll say nothing to the police. But if he can't prove that he wasn't in Westwood the night Mom was murdered, I won't hesitate to turn him in.'

Jamie drove back to the paper, his mind on a roller coaster. They must deal with Dottie Lieberman's murder in tomorrow morning's edition. That was on the mind of every man, woman, and child living Westwood. Everybody was terrified that a killer walked free in their town, fearful that he—or she—might strike again. There was no way that Dottie Lieberman was killed by Evan Ward.

No word about Ward's meeting with the D.A. could be published in tomorrow's *Sentinel,* he cautioned himself. That must wait until Ward delivered his son to the District Attorney. And doubts tugged at him. *Did Ward push his son to murder? Was this all a devious cover-up?*

Jamie parked, charged into the building. Walking through the editorial floor, he heard Andrew's voice in agitated conversation. He paused at the door of his former office, stared inside.

Andrew stood by the window, phone in a tight grip. 'Now listen to me!' he interrupted the person at the other end. 'There's no way I can fly back to Iraq tomorrow morning—no matter how hard you've worked to arrange it. I have to remain here for a while—' He paused for an instant, broke in. 'Don't you understand? We buried my mother yesterday. So I'll handle the situation a few days later. They're spinning a pack of lies . . . I'll be in touch in about forty-eight hours—we can work from there.'

Jamie strode past to his mother's office—now his own. He was anxious. Was Andrew in some kind of trouble about his stories from Iraq? He remembered the correspondent he'd met in Iraq who had been so disparaging about his articles from Afghanistan and Iraq. A jealous creep, he thought again, and settled at his desk to focus on the work ahead. There had been times he and Andrew could read each other's mind. Each a half of a whole, he'd told himself so many times.

'How did you make out with Nora?' Sandy hovered in the doorway of Jamie's office.

'Come sit down—let's talk.' He hesitated. 'Nora will understand my confiding in you—that we're a team.'

'This sounds serious.' Sandy sat across him.

'Nora doesn't want to jump to conclusions about her mother's killer—but there's a lead that must be followed.'

Sandy listened while Jamie reported on what Nora had told him.

'How awful if it should be Nora's father.' She felt a surge of compassion for Nora.

'We don't know yet if her father was involved,' Jamie cautioned.

He's right—I have this awful habit of jumping to conclusions. 'I've been thinking about Noel Ward and the outsourcing situation at Westwood Manufacturing,' Sandy began.

'You expect this business with his son to change things?'

'I think we should try for an interview. Explain that if he drops the outsourcing deal, people in town will be grateful. It might affect the jury pool.'

'His son killed. A jury can't ignore that.'

'Ward's decision could temper their feelings. Talk to him,' Sandy urged. 'If we can persuade him to forget outsourcing—keep Westwood Manufacturing here in Westwood—it would be like a memorial to Adrienne. It meant so much to her.'

'To the whole town.' But Jamie was ambivalent.

'Maybe I'm reaching, but could the town make offers that will turn his thinking around? Talk to the Town Council. Ask—'

'You mean, property tax abatement promises?' Jamie broke in. 'Other tax breaks?'

79

Sandy nodded. 'Perhaps talk to the union about some temporary concessions.'

'All right,' he capitulated. 'But I'm not the one to go for the interview. It would be a better move if you approached him. Make him understand that the *Sentinel* will give him approval of the article. He'll see it before it's published.'

'I'll try to get through to him today.'

'Explain that we want to air—fairly—his reasons for considering outsourcing.' Jamie flinched. 'Of course, this whole business might push him into outsourcing if it isn't already a done decision.'

'Chuck has been talking to people. He says it's almost a sure thing. But if it'll help his son,' Sandy clung to this, 'Ward may change his mind.'

'Okay.' Jamie straightened up in his chair. A gesture Sandy recognized. He was determined to go through with this. 'I want you to try for the interview. He would see me as hostile. He doesn't know how close you are to me—and how close you were to Mom.'

'He may refuse to talk to me,' Sandy conceded. 'Somehow, I have to make him understand it'll be helpful for Evan's case.'

'Follow through. And sometime in the next twenty-four hours,' Jamie plotted, 'I'll sit down with Nora and her father. She's determined to face him. And I suspect he'll come when she threatens to tell the police he had a hostile relationship with her mother up to the day her mother was murdered.'

Eleven

For the dozenth time Sandy tried to get through to Noel Ward. Each time she called, she was told he was in conference. She left her name and phone number—but there was no return call.

All right. Try once more. Words forming in her mind that might get past that 'in conference' excuse.

She tried again. A recorded voice came to her. *'Westwood Manufacturing is closed for the day. The office will be open at 8:30 tomorrow morning.'*

Damn! She reached for the local phone book. Try to reach him at home. Adrienne would want them to try to stop Ward from outsourcing. The night before she died, she'd talked about going to the Town Council. That would be a move for Jamie. *But first, talk with Noel Ward.*

She found the Wards' residential phone number, punched in keys.

'The Ward residence,' a calm feminine voice replied.

'May I speak with Mrs Ward,' Sandy said on impulse. 'This is Sandra Taylor of the *Sentinel*. It's important that we talk. It's about Evan.'

'Oh—' The woman at the other end seemed suddenly distraught. 'Please hold.'

Sandy waited, heard a jumble of voices at the other end.

'This is Noel Ward.' His voice—guarded, suspicious—came to her. 'Why do you want to talk to my wife?'

'I wasn't able to get through to you at your office—and it's important that we talk. It's to your advantage,' she pressed. *He knows a newspaper article might work either way. If he refuses to cooperate, the paper might be harsh on Evan.*

'Come to the house at 9 P.M.,' he said after a moment. 'But no photographers. You'll come alone.'

'I'll come alone,' she confirmed. 'At 9 P.M. sharp.'

Off the phone Sandy leaned back in relief. This was a start. They were following in Adrienne's footsteps.

But can I convince Ward to keep Westwood Manufacturing here in town? It depends on what kind of a deal the Town Council will offer—and the union. It'll be Jamie's job to negotiate.

All at once she was conscious that Jamie and Andrew were arguing in the hall. So weird, she thought—the voice of each identical to the other.

'What do you mean? You had circulars run off and delivered all over town! Who told you do that?' *Why is Jamie so angry—or is it Andrew?*

'What the hell's the matter with you, Jamie? We talked about reaching everybody in town with the reward offer!'

'The whole situation has changed.' Jamie was exasperated. 'Why didn't you discuss it with me first?'

'Because I thought you were up to your eyebrows in work—and I could do this. Cool it, Jamie.'

'I can't explain now. You'll know tomorrow morning. After 10 A.M.'

'Oh wow,' Andrew mocked. 'Now you're part of the CIA?'

Sandy heard the sound of footsteps striding down the hall. Andrew, she guessed. Then Jamie appeared at her doorway.

'Did you hear the famous war correspondent?' Jamie jibed. 'The whole floor must have heard him.'

'Minutes after Evan is brought in tomorrow morning, the radio and TV news people will be on the story. It'll be all over town.' For a few moments—when Noel Ward had admitted his son was guilty—she was enraged at Evan. She'd wanted to see him suffer for what he'd done. He'd committed a terrible act—but he'd had no understanding of it. Now her inner rage was directed towards his father.

'How are you making out with the Ward interview? You're getting the run-around,' Jamie surmised. But his eyes were sympathetic.

'It took a while,' she admitted. 'But I'm seeing him this evening at 9 P.M. He's thinking the *Evening News* will run a bizarre story. Maybe—just maybe the *Sentinel* will not try for the sensational approach.'

Jamie came into the room, dropped into a chair—stifling a yawn. 'I had a strange call a few minutes ago. I was heading here to tell you.'

'What kind of a call?' Sandy was instantly alert.

'The committee that was backing Mom for the Town Council seat.' He took a deep breath. 'They're asking me to run in her place.'

'Jamie, that would be great! Adrienne would be so pleased.' Her mind charged ahead. 'And that means a voice on the Council that would fight to keep Westwood Manufacturing here in town.'

'Elections are weeks away. It'll have no—' He stopped short at a sharp ring. 'That's my phone.'

Sandy reached for one of the lines on her desk. 'I'll have Gloria switch the call.' She waited a moment, responded. 'Hello?'

'May I speak to Jamie Moss, please?'

'One moment.' Sandy handed the phone to Jamie. 'I think it's Nora—she sounds upset.'

Sandy sat on the edge of her seat, strained to hear the exchange between Jamie and Nora.

'I talked to my father.' Nora's voice was shrill. 'He's outraged, claims he didn't know about Mom. And he's furious at me.'

'It was in the *Evening News* yesterday. Every morning paper in the county carried the story today,' Jamie scoffed. 'It's been on local radio and TV news as well.'

'I suspect he was upset at my threat to talk to the police about his harassing Mom.' Contempt sneaked into her voice. 'But he'll be here tomorrow afternoon, he said—between 5 P.M. and 6 P.M. You can make it then?' She was anxious now.

'I'll be there at 5 P.M.—stay until he arrives and we've talked.'

'Have you heard any word from the police?' she asked. 'A newspaper gets word fast, I gather.'

'Nothing so far. They haven't had much time,' he pointed out. 'And if there was word, you would have been contacted. They'd probably have questions.'

'They've had time to go through Mom's files on her cases. But then any divorce lawyer runs into hostile defendants. I gave them names, what addresses were available.' Nora sighed. 'I realize it takes time to check them out.'

'Nora, I know what you're going through,' Jamie said gently.

'Craig wanted to be here with me, too—but he and Dad have never even met. I didn't think that would be helpful.'

'No,' Jamie agreed and hesitated a moment. 'Does he know I'll be with you?'

'No. I was afraid he'd balk. I don't know if he's guilty and scared out of his mind—or just nervous about being involved. He knows if I talk to the police, they'll want to question him. But when he comes, I'll insist you be with me—that we've both gone through the same horror and I need you.'

'Make him understand I'm not there to represent the *Sentinel*,' Jamie stressed. 'I'm there as a close family friend—who's going through what you're going through.'

'I'm not letting him off the hook,' Nora insisted. 'I have to know. Did he kill Mom—or is he innocent?'

At a few minutes past 8 P.M. Jamie walked into Sandy's office with a large brown bag, juggling two mugs of coffee. 'Martha called. She's making noises about our not coming home to dinner, but she sent over sandwiches and fruit salad with Andrew.' He chuckled. 'Only Martha could utilize Andrew as a delivery man.'

'He's in her good graces,' Sandy guessed, 'because he's making a big fuss over Claire. And that's good,' she added conscientiously.

'Let's have dinner.' Jamie reached to clear off a corner of Sandy's desk. 'Martha's note said there's more dinner for us in the crockpot on the kitchen range "at whatever insane hour you come home," ' he mimicked affectionately, removing the contents of the brown bag.

'Only Martha would think to send over a paper table-cloth and napkins.'

Only now did Sandy realize she was hungry. The hours had sped past with no thought of a dinner break. So much that the *Sentinel* must cover. The town was besieged: The two murders—one unsolved, which meant a killer was on the loose; the threat of the loss of a thousand jobs. Townspeople frightened that the killer might strike again—and fearful that Westwood was about to become a distressed town.

'If I know Martha,' Jamie began in an effort to lighten the atmosphere, 'the fruit salad will be laced with some fancy liqueur. Oh, and she's added brownies.' He unwrapped them, sniffed. 'Rum-soaked, of course.'

'She's spoiling us,' Sandy said tenderly.

'Drop me off at the police station when you head for the appointment with Ward,' Jamie told her. 'I can walk back from there.'

'Go home from there,' Sandy ordered. 'Don't come back to the paper—everything's under control. You can go to sleep at a reasonable hour.'

'Before my Guard unit went on alert, I thought we'd be

married by now.' His eyes made ardent love to her. 'I wish we'd been married before I went away.'

'Our time will come,' she whispered. So strange, to be living in Jamie's house but not sharing his bed. 'Jamie, we can handle this.'

'Mom so looked forward to being at our wedding.' His eyes darkened in grief. 'But we know we have her blessing.'

They ate with a knowledge of Sandy's imminent interview with Noel Ward. Jamie drained his mug of coffee, rose to his feet.

'More coffee?' he asked Sandy. 'Gloria keeps it going.'

'No more for me,' she said, and Jamie left to replenish his mug.

She cleared her desk, made a phone call to the Composing Room. She smiled at sounds in the hall. Jamie was teasing their part-time Gardening Editor, trying to lighten the dark mood that gripped every member of the staff.

'Hi,' Jamie looked in from the doorway, 'how're you doing?' *It isn't Jamie—it's Andrew! When will I learn not to fall apart when I mistake one for the other? It's Jamie I love.*

'Hi—' Sandy managed a smile.

'Where's the ogre?' he asked, gazing at her with unnerving intensity. 'My other half,' he elaborated. 'I thought he might want a ride home since you're keeping such long hours.' *Andrew knows we drive in together.* 'I'm still hanging on to my rental car.'

'I'll be dropping him off on my way to an appointment.' Not at home—at the police station. But Jamie could walk from there to the house.

'He's pissed at my boy-scout efforts—you know, to plaster every house in town with our reward circular. I rustled up a crowd of kids to do the job. They felt important—and richer,' he added, grinning. 'I took good care of them. It seemed like a great idea. I know how rushed you all are, and I had the time on my hands.'

'Jamie's uptight,' she apologized for him. Why were the two of them so hostile? No, she corrected herself, Jamie was hostile towards Andrew.

'I'd better get moving. I promised Grandma I'd be back to spend some time with her before she hits the sack.'

'She'll like that.' Jamie was close with Claire, but she doted on Andrew.

At 8:50 Sandy and Jamie were in the car. Five minutes later she dropped him off at the police station and headed for the Ward house. Exactly at 9 P.M. she turned into the circular driveway, lined with red and yellow rose bushes in glorious bloom. Towering oaks rose beside the white, multi-columned Greek Revival.

Sandy gazed at the elegant mansion that was the town's showplace. But Noel Ward would give this up in a moment without a regret, she thought—her rage at him replaced for an instant by compassion—if Evan could become a healthy human being.

All right, talk to Ward. Try to convince him it was to his advantage to abandon plans for outsourcing. The jury pool would be more compassionate in their judging of Evan. But her heart was pounding as she left the car and walked up to the house.

Am I out of my mind to think that I can change Ward's mind about so important a move? But I must fight to keep Westwood Manufacturing in town. A thousand jobs are at stake!

Twelve

Sandy reached to touch the bell, heard the echo of chimes within the foyer. A maid in a black uniform and white apron opened the over-sized mahogany entrance door.

'I'm Sandra Taylor. Mr Ward is expecting me.' She strived for poise.

'Yes, miss,' the woman said and gestured her to enter the elegant foyer. 'Please follow me.'

Sandy followed her down the wide hall, its walls hung with paintings. The maid paused before a closed door, reached to open it. 'Mr Ward will see you here shortly.'

Tense with anticipation, Sandy walked into the spacious, high-ceilinged room. All at once self-conscious as she glanced about at the fine antiques, the tall glass-enclosed bookcases that flanked two walls. Moments later she glanced up to see Noel Ward striding into the room.

'Please sit down.' He gestured towards a pair of chairs at one side of the room. 'I'm seeing you against my better judgment,' he told her brusquely, taking the chair opposite her. 'My attorney advised against it. What can you and the *Sentinel* do to help my son? Why would you do it?' He exuded skepticism. Sandy guessed he'd agreed to see her out of desperation.

'We're asking something in return.' Sandy sensed a wall shoot up between them. *He must know how I feel towards him, towards his son. Together they're responsible for Adrienne's death.* 'We're trying to keep this town from becoming a depressed area.'

'I'm not responsible for the future of this town!' He rose to his feet as though in a move to dismiss her.

'Mr Ward, Westwood doesn't deserve to become a ghost town.' *Be cool, don't let emotions get in the way.* 'We'll present the true facts in your son's case.' She forced herself to focus on Evan's situation. 'Evan killed—but we understand he didn't realize that this was a horrible, senseless act. We know his mental condition. We'll present the murder as a tragic error. We'll bring in a pair of psychiatrists to explain how this—this awful situation happened. Our readers—the jury pool,' she emphasized, 'will realize he isn't a monster but suffering from a terrible illness.' *How can I rationalize this way when part of me wants to tear Ward and his son apart?*

'And what's your price?' he demanded. His eyes narrowed, as though anticipating an ugly blow.

'We want you to drop all thoughts of outsourcing. We'll—'

'Do you realize what you're asking of me?' he broke in. His face flushed, his eyes blazing.

'You're wrecking the future of a thousand families in this town—plus all the others who'll lose their jobs as a result. And already some huge firms that have outsourced realize now it was a mistake. They're returning jobs to this country.'

'Do you think I want to move my operations outside this country? I'm being pushed. I have no recourse except to move out to cheap labor—so I can meet the prices of my competitors. If I don't, I'm out of business. I've had to cut out two shifts for the lack of business. I'm losing money every day that I keep Ward in operation in this town.'

'Suppose we find ways to cut your overhead.' Sandy remembered research she'd done for the article in work. Other towns, too, had fought for their survival. 'We'll go to the Town Council, fight with them to provide you with a dollar-a-year property tax for the next five years. We'll talk to the union about wage concessions for the next five years. The union is anxious to keep jobs here—they'll work with you. The Town Council will find other ways to help you be competitive. Perhaps a special tax to provide funds. Work with us, Mr Ward—and we'll work for you.'

'How do I know this will happen?'

'Jamie will approach the Town Council. He'll set up a meeting with you. He'll approach the union, set up a meeting with them. This will provide an atmosphere in Westwood that will be helpful to Evan. The *Sentinel*—the Moss family—will be supportive.' *Adrienne would approve of this—it'll save Westwood.*

'I need time,' Ward hedged. 'Twenty-four hours—then you'll have my answer. I spent a lifetime building up my company. I don't want to lose it.'

Sandy returned to the paper with mixed emotions. Part of her was convinced Noel Ward would cooperate, part was fearful that in the course of the night he'd take his son and flee the country. *Will the two of them be in Potter's office tomorrow morning?* Walking into the *Sentinel* building she was conscious that this appeared a normal evening, where work was in full swing to bring out tomorrow morning's edition of the *Sentinel*. But so much more was on the line.

Approaching Jamie's office, she heard him in impassioned conversation with Chuck. Both men stopped dead as she joined them.

'Did you sell Ward?' Jamie's eyes clung to her.

'He'll have an answer for me in twenty-four hours.' She dropped into a chair with an air of exhaustion. 'I gave him a strong pitch,' she said defensively. 'What happened at the police station? Any leads on Dottie Lieberman's killer?'

'Nothing substantial,' Jamie reported. 'They're digging into her divorce cases—three husbands who wrote her nasty letters.'

90

'You're seeing Nora again tomorrow afternoon?'

'Right.'

'What's with Nora Lieberman?' Chuck glanced from Jamie to Sandy. 'She's got a lead?'

The phone rang, clearing Jamie of a need to reply. Sandy was uncomfortable—they couldn't discuss Nora's suspicions even with Chuck at this point.

'Jamie Moss—Yeah, Nora.' All at once he exuded excitement. 'Yeah, I understand. I'll give Potter a ring first thing tomorrow morning, see what I can dig up . . . Sure, I'll be there a few minutes before 5 P.M.—and I'll talk with Potter earlier. Goodnight, Nora.'

'What's with Nora Lieberman?' Chuck demanded.

'She just received a call from the detectives on her mother's case. They wanted more information on a character named Carl Reynolds. He wrote nasty letters after Dottie Lieberman won a decent settlement for his wife in their divorce case. That was four years ago. For the last three and a half years he's been in prison for armed robbery. Three weeks ago he was released. And he's been seen in Westwood.'

Chuck whistled. 'If he's in town, he'll be picked up. That'll be the next big story in the Lieberman case.' He pulled himself to his feet. 'You two go home—you've had a long day. I'll carry on from here.'

For a few minutes Sandy and Jamie sat in the darkened car in a warm embrace.

'We'd better head for home.' Sandy pulled away in candid reluctance. 'Our time will come, Jamie.'

At the house they paused at the entrance to the living room. To Sandy's astonishment she saw Claire and Andrew sitting hand-in-hand on the sofa. Claire had not left her room in the past five days—except to attend Adrienne's funeral. They were watching a comedy show on television, with Andrew making quirky comments.

'Would you like some tea?' Sandy asked Claire.

'I have a pot right here.' Claire pointed to the tray on the coffee table. 'Andrew made Martha go off to bed, then brought me tea and cookies.'

'We're famished.' Jamie seemed annoyed. *Because Andrew is playing up to Claire? What is it with Jamie?* 'Martha said she left food in a crockpot on the range for us.'

'Not until you mentioned it did I realize I was hungry,' Sandy confessed as they headed down the hall to the kitchen.

'Sit and be served,' Jamie ordered her and headed towards the range.

He heaped a savory chicken stew onto a pair of plates, brought them to the table. Sandy provided silverware, napkins, mugs for the inevitable coffee.

'We'll have to put up fresh coffee,' Jamie decreed. 'Martha probably made that hours ago.'

'Jamie, this Carl Reynolds that Nora told you about,' Sandy began as they sat down to eat, 'could he be Dottie Lieberman's killer?' Her eyes searched his. 'He was in town, he had a motive,' she conceded, 'but my instinct tells me that's too convenient.'

Jamie chuckled. 'Not every murder case takes weeks on end to solve. This could be one of the quick ones. At any rate, Nora still wants to tackle her father. In her mind he isn't in the clear as yet.'

'You said Carl Reynolds has been in prison for armed robbery.' Sandy squinted in thought. 'That doesn't sound like a man who'd smother a woman to death.'

Jamie stared at her with raised eyebrows. 'Right away you're clearing him?'

'No,' she back-tracked, 'but he sounds like a violent man. Not a man to take a pillow and suffocate a woman. I know,' she derided herself, 'I'm depending again on a "woman's intuition," but I just don't believe Reynolds killed Dottie Lieberman.'

'You'd rather it was Nora's father?'

'No,' Sandy retracted. 'I just feel that we're not on track yet. I have this weird feeling that we could be facing more murders.'

Thirteen

Sandy awoke on Tuesday morning with the instant real-ization that within another fifteen hours Noel Ward had agreed to give her his decision about aborting or proceed-ing with the outsourcing for Westwood Manufacturing. And this morning, or so he said, he would surrender his son to the District Attorney. Did he mean that—or was he already in another country with Evan? A country without an extra-dition agreement?

No, it was ridiculous to consider such an action. But Westwood Manufacturing did own a private jet capable of whisking them to freedom. Needing to discuss this with Jamie, she rushed to dress and join him at the breakfast table.

Walking down the stairs she was conscious of the quiet-ness that permeated the house, as though—briefly—life was standing still.

Arriving in the foyer she sniffed the comforting aroma of coffee brewing in the kitchen, fresh bread baking in the oven. Only Jamie and Martha would be awake at this hour; Andrew slept late and Claire would spend most of the day in her room. It was sweet, she thought gratefully, the way Andrew was devoting so much of his time to comforting Claire.

Now she heard Jamie and Martha in conversation. This was a time of day she found reassuring. Martha fussing over Jamie and her, ordering them to eat. Somehow, at this hour, Sandy thought, she felt a closeness to Adrienne.

Jamie and Martha greeted her with warmth—almost as though it was just another routine day, she thought in a corner of her mind. But how could it be just another day when they would go into the office and Adrienne wouldn't be there—and they didn't know who killed Dottie Lieberman, or if the town would be saved from outsourcing?

'You eat your breakfast,' Martha ordered Sandy from her place at the range. 'Coming up in a minute.'

'Or maybe two,' Jamie added with an effort at lightness.

'What do you think?' Sandy asked Jamie. 'Will Ward be there at 10 A.M.?' No need to say where.

'I plan on being close enough to his house to know,' Jamie admitted. 'I'll take Mom's car.'

'You'll be seeing Nora at five this afternoon?' *Did Nora's father kill her mother?*

Jamie nodded. His eyes somber. 'Nora's sure she's frightened him into showing—I'm not sure. And we may have an answer there—but I'm not banking on it.'

Martha brought poached eggs and toast to the table for Sandy, detoured to the radio, switched it on. The voice of a local newscaster filtered into the room.

'The police offer no word yet on suspects in the murders of Adrienne Moss and Dottie Lieberman.' *The word hasn't leaked out yet about Evan Ward. Will his father deliver?* 'District Attorney Potter advises that the entire Police Department is focused on apprehending the killer . . . ' Assuming a serial killer was at large.

Jamie rose to his feet, switched off the radio. 'It's too early in the morning to listen to that,' he told Martha with an apologetic smile.

'There's more coffee in the carafe,' Martha said. 'I'm taking tea up to Miss Claire. But you two finish your breakfast. That's ammunition to keep you going.'

Minutes before 7 A.M., Sandy and Jamie left the house, walked to the garage.

'A week ago nobody thought of locking their garages,' Jamie said in painful recall while Sandy unlocked the door.

'Everybody's frightened. Even the children feel it.'

Jamie walked to his mother's car, reached for the door on the driver's side. 'I can almost feel Mom's presence here,' he whispered.

'She'll always be with us—' Tears blurred Sandy's vision. 'She'd be so pleased to know you'll take her place on the Town Council.'

'Hey, I haven't even been announced yet,' he scolded her. 'I could lose.'

'No chance!'

'Okay, let's head for work. And pray that Noel Ward delivers Evan, and he calls you to say the outsourcing project is off.'

In her office—sitting at the edge of her chair as in all traumatic moments—Sandy clung to the phone. Jamie was parked a hundred yards from the Ward house, cell phone in hand.

'Nothing's happened so far,' he said in exasperation. 'A maid came out about forty minutes ago to bring in the morning newspaper. The *Sentinel,*' he added. 'Since then, nothing.'

'He's not due at Potter's office for another eleven minutes. It's a five-minute drive.'

'I see no other signs of life. Damn, the three of them could have skipped town. I should have checked on the company plane!'

'A hundred to one Potter has the plane under surveillance. If there was any action, detectives would have moved into place.'

'They're coming out!' Jamie's voice was electric. 'The three of them. Evan, his father, and his mother!'

'I'll call Frank—he'll be at the police station when Evan's brought in.' She hesitated. 'No photos,' she decided. 'We have plenty on file.' It was difficult to feel compassion for the two responsible for Adrienne's murder—yet she knew the anguish Ward and his wife were feeling.

'No photos,' he acknowledged. 'And let's pray Ward has the good sense to realize it's to his son's advantage not to go ahead with the outsourcing.'

'He'll want some real assurance that the town will come through for him,' Sandy warned, 'if he agrees to keep the company intact here in Westwood.'

'I'll talk to each member of the Town Council separately, then try to set up an emergency meeting this evening. And I'll insist on talking with the union people some time today.' Jamie took a deep breath. 'Don't expect me back at the paper until after my meeting with Nora and her father. This is going to be a long, hectic day.'

'It's going to work,' Sandy vowed. 'The Town Council— and the union—must understand what's at stake.'

'I'll be in touch at intervals with anything worth reporting.'

'Jamie, remember Dottie Lieberman's funeral.' At Nora's insistence her mother's body had been released. In the Jewish tradition she was to be buried within forty-eight hours of death. 'Be at the synagogue at 10 A.M. sharp.'

'I'll be there,' Jamie promised. 'In the Muslim faith, too,' he recalled, 'early burial is traditional.'

Sandy sat motionless for several moments, her mind charging ahead.

Now she crossed to the small TV that sat on a file cabinet in her office, switched it on, hit the mute button on the remote. The television crew from the local channel would be at the police station minutes after the Wards arrived, she suspected. The TV channel would flash 'BREAKING NEWS.' She'd leave for the synagogue in twenty minutes.

She arrived early, but already the parking area was packed, cars lined up on adjoining streets. Walking up to the synagogue, people talked in whispers—grieving, frightened. Some stores were closed for the hour of the funeral services.

Dottie Lieberman and her daughter were highly respected, known for their pro-bono work in Westwood.

Sandy waited on the stairs for Jamie and Chuck to arrive. Together they represented the paper. Only forty-eight hours ago they attended Adrienne's funeral. After the services they would go to the cemetery for the burial. Dottie Lieberman had been one of Adrienne's three dearest friends.

Returning to her office from the poignant service at the cemetery, Sandy realized she'd left her TV on. She saw 'BREAKING NEWS' flashing across the TV screen, rushed for the remote. The impassioned voice of the newscaster burst into the room.

'Only minutes ago the police announced that the murder of Dottie Lieberman has been solved—'

Jamie sat in the office of attorney Ted Newman and argued with him about the possibility of calling an emergency meeting of the Town Council.

'Jamie, get real. How the hell can we call an emergency meeting for 8 P.M. tonight?'

'By doing that we may save a thousand jobs in this town!' A vein pounded his temple. 'I'm going from here to an emergency meeting with the local union chief. I have to be able to present definite promises to Noel Ward if we're to keep him from outsourcing all those jobs at Westwood Manufacturing to cheap labor in China.'

'What makes you so sure we can switch Ward's thinking?' Ted was skeptical. 'With his son up on murder charges, he'll probably want to get out of this town as fast as he can.'

'Because he's anxious to create some good feelings in Westwood for his son. Damn it, Ted, this is our one chance to save those jobs.' He felt a surge of exhilaration. *Ted's about to capitulate.* 'Would 7:30 be a better time?'

'No,' Newman brushed this aside. 'Let them at least have time for a leisurely dinner. We'll try for 8 P.M. in the Town

Hall conference room. We'll sit down and discuss the situation. With luck we can reach a decision. But I'm making no promises, Jamie.'

Jamie rushed from his meeting with Ted Newman—the most dedicated member of the Town Council—to his appointment with Bill Thompson, the union chief who had organized Westwood Manufacturing after a long battle. He chafed at being kept waiting almost forty minutes.

'Sorry, Jamie,' Bill apologized, 'but we've been having some problems with illegal aliens at a construction site. You know, contractors looking to cut back on costs—and those guys will work for coolie wages. I know they're trying hard to scrape together a living, but our own people need those jobs.'

'I explained the situation when we talked on the phone,' Jamie began.

'Jamie, I know where you're coming from—but I can't ask my people to take cuts in salary and in benefits. We broke our backs to get them a break.'

'Either we find a way for Ward to operate with a profit, or . . .'

'Jamie, this guy is no philanthropist. He won't hang around for peanuts.'

'A fair profit,' Jamie insisted. 'We might be able to convince Ward he can survive in this town if we help him cut back his overhead. Face facts, Ted. The man can't meet competition without cutting overhead.'

'You expect our people to drop down to minimum wages in the possible hope that Ward might hang around for another year?' Bill scoffed. 'They can't survive on that.'

'I'm not talking about minimum wages—that figure is a disgrace to this nation. I'm talking with the Town Council about a tax-free package for a period of five years. But that won't be enough. We may even have to add a local tax to see him through—but first we have to offer him a break in labor costs. Everything out in the open. He shows you his books—you work out an agreement whereby he can stay in business with a fair profit.'

Bill grunted, stared into space. 'I'll talk to my committee. You come up with your end, then there's a fair chance I can do the same. No guarantees,' he cautioned. 'First let's see what you can do.'

Fourteen

Sliding behind the wheel of the car, Jamie glanced at his watch. It was 4:48 P.M. He'd promised Nora he'd be at her house before 5 o'clock, when her father was due to arrive. Between 5 and 6 P.M., he corrected himself. But get moving—she must be nervous now.

Not everybody was buying the police's assumption that Carl Reynolds had murdered Dottie Lieberman. Nora was doubtful. But the police were holding him for arraignment.

Jamie frowned as his cell phone rang, reached to respond. He was running short on time. 'Yes?'

'Jamie, are you getting through to people?' Sandy sounded anxious. *Damn, I should have called in earlier.*

'It's looking good. I'm running late—I'm rushing now to Nora's house. I'll get back to you as soon as that session's over.'

Driving faster than normal, conscious of the passage of time, Jamie turned into Nora's street a few minutes before 5 P.M. He tensed. A car was parked in the driveway. Nora's car, he recognized in relief. Craig Lieberman hadn't arrived yet.

He parked on the street, two houses past Nora's, lest Craig be frightened away. Nora opened the front door with an air of relief. She'd been watching for his approach.

'I'm sorry—I meant to be earlier,' he apologized, following Nora into her comfortable living room. *Thank God for air-conditioning.*

'He's not here yet.' Now Nora seemed apprehensive. 'Maybe he's on the run—'

'He said he'd be here between 5 and 6 P.M. I think you scared him. He'll be here.' Jamie managed to sound reassuring.

'I have to know if he—if he killed Mom.'

'Nora, there's a good chance he's innocent.'

'If it wasn't Dad, and it wasn't Evan Ward, then who killed her?'

'The case against Carl Reynolds has no legs—'

'We both know that.' Nora was struggling to hold herself together. 'I have a call in for a private detective I've used in divorce cases. I can't sit back and wait for the police to come up with Mom's killer.'

Both Jamie and Nora started at the sound of a car pulling to a stop before the house.

'He's here.' Nora hurried to the foyer.

Jamie sat in a club chair with a direct view of the entrance to the living room. He heard the strained—argumentative—conversation between Nora and her father. *He's scared—but that's no indication that he's guilty.*

Nora and her father walked into the living room. Craig Lieberman stopped dead at the sight of Jamie.

'What the hell is he doing here? And who is he?' Lieberman's face was contorted in rage.

'This is Jamie Moss. He's here at my request. You must remember his mother, Adrienne Moss. She was murdered just a few days before Mom, and—'

'What the hell is this crap about me being a suspect in your mother's murder?' he broke in. 'And why do you want him here?' He glared at Jamie.

'Jamie is a longtime family friend—he's going through what I'm going through.' She paused, took a deep breath. 'He knows who killed his mother. I want to know who killed Mom.'

'Mr Lieberman, where were you between 11 P.M. Sunday and 4 A.M. yesterday morning?' Jamie pressed.

'Why should I tell you?' Lieberman challenged. Eyes defiant.

'Because—you may recall—the Moss family publishes the Westwood *Sentinel,*' Nora shot back. 'And if you can't convince us you didn't kill Mom, your face will be on the front page of tomorrow morning's *Sentinel.*'

'I was home,' Lieberman yelled. 'Where else would I be in the middle of the night!'

'You received or made a phone call?' Jamie probed. That could be checked out.

'I was in bed asleep,' Lieberman began.

'In bed with whom?' Nora's eyes were contemptuous.

'By myself!' He radiated hostility. 'Yeah, I forgot—I did make a phone call. Just before midnight. I ordered a pizza from Joe's Pizza on Broad Street.' Now he was triumphant. 'Call Joe's Pizza—they'll tell you. I'm a regular customer.'

Jamie and Nora exchanged a fast glance. 'We'll check it out,' he told Lieberman. 'If the pizza store confirms it, you're in the clear.'

'This is no way to treat your father!' Lieberman lashed at Nora.

'You knew Mom had been killed—and you didn't even bother to call.' Nora was pale, trembling now. 'You didn't care about me. You never did.'

Without a reply Lieberman strode from the living room and out of the house. Moments later Jamie and Nora heard the car pull away from the curb.

'My private detective will check with Joe's Pizza first thing in the morning,' Nora said unsteadily. 'In an odd way I'm relieved that my father probably didn't kill Mom. But I have to know who did.'

In a matter of minutes Jamie was behind the wheel of his car again. He suspected Craig Lieberman's alibi would hold up. Now he called Sandy's private line on his cell phone. Guilty that he'd been so short with her earlier.

'Hello—' Sandy was anxious.

'Everything under control there?'

'Yes—but what's been happening with you? I have to leave soon to meet with Ward. What will I be able to tell him?'

'I spent hours talking to Town Council members—they're calling an emergency meeting for 8 P.M. this evening to discuss how to bail out Ward and keep Westwood Manufacturing in town. I spent time with Bill Thompson and he'll talk with his union committee tonight. There's a good chance they'll sit down with Ward and work out a deal. Nothing promised—but every side understands the situation.'

'Then I must stall Ward until we have a definite package to offer,' Sandy summed up.

'I kept my appointment with Nora,' Jamie told her. 'A hundred to one her father's in the clear.'

'Discounting him and Reynolds, we still have a killer on the loose.'

'For the moment,' Jamie hedged.

'I can't shake off this instinct that says in some weird way Adrienne's murder and Dottie Lieberman's are linked.'

'We know Evan Ward couldn't have killed Dottie,' Jamie reproached her gently.

'I know that!' Sandy's voice deepened in frustration. 'But I'm convinced there's a link that we're missing. In some fashion we don't understand, Adrienne's murder and Dottie's murder are linked. One triggered the other.'

'I'll drop by the house just for a few minutes—to see Grandma, then return to the paper. Martha says she's terribly upset about Dottie Lieberman's murder. First Mom, now one of Mom's closest friends. Andrew said he tried to keep the news from Claire—but the word came through.'

'We've had dozens of calls about Evan Ward,' Sandy told him. 'People with stories about small incidents.' She sounded troubled, Jamie thought.

'You mean stories that make him seem a monster.'

'In truth, he's a sick little boy in a man's body. I know he should be punished—'

'Noel Ward is a powerful man,' Jamie reminded her. 'A wealthy man—'

'He'll do everything to make things easier for Evan,' Sandy acknowledged. 'But he and his wife will forever suffer for what he caused. They'll pay.'

'Until this business of outsourcing threatened Westwood, Ward was considered a good employer. For years his employees resisted unionizing. Let's pray he sees a way to salvage Westwood Manufacturing without destroying a thousand families.'

Sandy returned to her office after a consultation with the Composing Room. Space must be held open on the front page for whatever developed with Noel Ward. As usual these past few days the television set was on but muted. Sandy glanced at her desk clock as she sat down. It was close to 7 P.M. Two hours before Ward's deadline for his decision.

She tensed at the ring of her private line, reached to pick up.

'Sandra Moss.'

'Miss Moss, this is Noel Ward.' His voice was non-committal. 'Please be at my house by 8 P.M. We'll talk then.'

'I'll be there—' She heard the phone disconnect without any further exchange.

Where is Jamie? I need to talk with him. He said he'd just drop by the house for a few minutes. He should be here by now. Is Ward ready to abandon the outsourcing? Or is he—in grief—planning to close up shop, period?

The Town Council was holding an emergency meeting.

The union was willing to talk about a break for Westwood Manufacturing. For a moment she pushed down panic. But how much could she offer Ward with certainty?

Her face brightened. She heard Jamie and Chuck in conversation in the hall outside her office. But now doubt invaded her. *Is it Jamie or Andrew? Why do I feel such fear when I'm not sure? It's natural—identical twins have identical voices. Jamie's the twin I love. The twin I'm going to marry. What does it matter that their voices, their appearances, are identical? It's who Jamie is that makes me love him.*

The two men walked into Sandy's office. Yes, it was Jamie, she told herself in relief—yet she was unnerved that she knew it only because of what he was wearing.

'I brought dinner,' Jamie said with a show of calm, holding up a brown-paper bag. 'I was home and Martha threw together chicken-cutlet sandwiches and a big salad. You know Martha—there's enough here for six.'

'Gloria's sending in coffee.' Chuck settled himself in one of the pair of chairs before Sandy's desk while Jamie distributed paper plates, napkins, and food.

'I'm seeing Ward at 8 P.M. He gave no indication of how he was thinking,' Sandy warned and gazed from one to the other. 'I'm not sure what I can offer with conviction—'

'Tell him the Town Council is sitting down to an emergency meeting even while you're talking with him,' Jamie instructed. 'They're there to work out a tax package that will help him stay in Westwood. The union is discussing a drop in wages for a five-year period. Possibly a short-term cut in benefits. We'll have the complete package set within the next forty-eight hours.' His face tightened. 'Provided that neither the Town Council nor the union people run into opposition—'

'It sounds good,' Chuck conceded, 'but we still have a killer floating around this town. All those people who're chewing their fingernails down to the cuticles about their jobs will feel better if the deal with Ward comes through. But everybody in town—including Ward's employees—is terrified that they'll be the next victim of that murdering creep.'

Fifteen

Sandy rang the doorbell at the Ward house, waited for a response. Her heart hammering though she managed to appear composed. So much depended upon what Ward had decided. And—still—it was difficult for her to face the catalyst to Adrienne's murder.

The door opened. The maid who had admitted her the previous evening beckoned her inside. Wordless, she followed her into the library. Noel Ward sat behind his desk, his face inscrutable.

'Please sit down, Miss Taylor.' He gestured to a comfortable armchair that faced him.

'Thank you.' *Shall I barge right in and explain to him what's been worked out? Or wait for him to tell me his decision?*

'You talked yesterday about plans to make it possible for Westwood Manufacturing to remain in this town.' His eyes searched hers. 'What can you offer me?'

'Even as we're talking,' she quoted Jamie, 'the Town Council is sitting down to work out a package of tax relief and possible financial aid. The union committee is meeting right now to discuss the five-year contract with lowered wages and—possibly—smaller benefits. Jamie Moss will have their decision late this evening.'

Ward paused, as though still deliberating. 'I'll give them five days to offer me a package that I can live with.' He clasped one hand within the other as he forced himself to continue. 'If I'm guaranteed a deal that will allow Westwood

Manufacturing to operate without losing money, I'll keep the company intact in Westwood. My books will be open— my own salary will be modest. But if at the end of five days, you have nothing concrete, nothing signed and deliverable, then I'll move all jobs except for a small office staff to China. Because if I don't, Westwood Manufacturing will be bankrupt within a year.'

'I'm confident we can meet your terms, Mr Ward. Jamie Moss will bring you together with the Town Council and the union officers within five days.' *Am I grandstanding? We hope—we don't know this. Will Council members disagree? Will the union membership go along?*

'My plans will be on hold for five days.' Ward was terse. 'The ball is in the town's court.'

Returning to the paper, Sandy discovered Chuck and Jamie in mercurial conversation in Jamie's office.

'You can't guarantee anything at this point,' Chuck warned him. 'Everybody—including the Town Council and the union membership—is unnerved at what's happening. Not just the outsourcing—they're running scared with a killer on the loose.'

Suddenly—as the two men became aware of Sandy's presence—the atmosphere in Jamie's office was electric.

'What happened with Ward?' Chuck demanded.

'If we can deliver,' Sandy told them, 'he'll play ball. We've got five days to sit down with him to sign agreements.'

'I wanted to be present at the Council meeting,' Jamie said. 'They wouldn't buy that. But the moment the meeting's over, Ted Newman will buzz me. Ditto Bill Thompson from the union meeting.'

'What about the membership?' Chuck probed. 'Won't they be called on to vote?'

'I understand that in emergency situations—and this is an emergency—the committee can act on the membership's behalf,' Jamie reported. 'Bill Thompson will call me. Both will call my cell phone,' he added. 'Which stays on for the night.'

Chuck fought a series of yawns. 'Hell, I'm calling it a night. Ring me when you know the score.' He pushed back his chair, rose to his feet. 'Let me call Bernice to pick me up. My car's in the shop—the transmission's shot.'

'Take my car.' Jamie reached into his pocket for keys, tossed them to Chuck. 'I'll ride home with Sandy.'

Twenty minutes later, after Jamie had checked with the Composing Room staff, he and Sandy headed for her car.

'You drive,' she told him, handing over the keys. 'I'm punchy.'

'Hey, you're doing great.' Jamie pulled the car door open for her, then reached to pull her close on the near-empty parking area, swathed now in shadows. 'Mom would be proud of you.'

'She wanted so much to be at our wedding . . .' Sandy clung to him. *But what did Adrienne mean when she told me to be careful?*

'She'll be there in spirit,' Jamie said.

Sandy forced herself to pull away. This was not their time. 'Let's go home and wait for Ted Newman and Bill Thompson to call.'

The house was night-dark as Jamie turned into their driveway. A low light glowed in the foyer. Claire was sleeping, Sandy thought in relief—and worried, yet again, that she was upset that 'the boys' did not inherit Adrienne's estate. But, in truth, Jamie was inheriting—through her.

Jamie pushed the button that opened the garage door. The garage was empty now except for an unfamiliar car.

'Where's Andrew's Jag?' Jamie stared at the Prius that sat in the Jaguar's normal space. 'It was a rental,' he recalled. 'Andrew must have turned it in—and bought the Prius?'

'That's a plus for the environment,' Sandy said. *Why does Jamie so often seem hostile towards Andrew?*

'Why would he buy a car when he plans to go back to Iraq?'

'Perhaps he's had enough of putting his life in constant danger.' She shuddered, remembering how many foreign correspondents had died in the course of the fighting in Iraq. 'It's a miracle he was able to find a Prius,' she added in obvious admiration.

'Leave it to Andrew to find someone desperately short of cash and willing to sell.' Jamie reached for his cell phone, left the car.

At the door Sandy searched for her house key. Still strange the way everybody locked doors these past few days.

'This key's a joke,' Jamie said, reaching to take it from her. 'Anybody with a credit card could break into the house.'

Walking into the foyer, they heard sounds from the living room.

'Andrew watching television,' Jamie guessed. 'In the dark.'

Sandy and Jamie walked into the darkened living room. Jamie flipped on a lamp.

'Hi—' Andrew glanced up with a casual smile. 'I'm waiting for the 10 P.M. news. Meanwhile, there's the usual re-run of *Law & Order.* Nothing new about the Lieberman murder—but then if there was, you'd know about it at the paper.' He reached for the remote, muted the sound.

'You dumped the Jag,' Jamie noted, sitting on the sofa beside Sandy.

'Yeah, the rental was steep. And with the $25,000 CD Mom left for me, I could swing the Prius.' Andrew grinned. 'The only one in town.' Now he focused on Sandy. 'You're looking beautiful tonight. But then you always look beautiful.'

'Thank you—' All at once Sandy felt uncomfortable. Jamie bristled, reached for her hand. *Does Jamie think Andrew's making a play for me? That's ridiculous.*

'I was talking with Grandma earlier.' Andrew's voice was

gentle. Amused. 'She's worried I'm getting bored here—but she wants me to hang around a while.' He focused on Sandy. 'If that's all right with you?'

'Of course it's all right,' Sandy stammered. *He's thinking about the will. But I've told him—he's always welcome here. It's the family home.*

'Grandma thought I should do an article for the *Sentinel*—about my travels in Iraq.' Andrew's voice was indulgent. 'I think she's worried about my being embedded again with a fighting company near Baghdad.'

'I don't think that's a good idea.' Jamie was flagrantly hostile. 'The *Sentinel* is a local paper. We don't run international news.' *Not true. Doesn't he realize Andrew's teasing him? Why is he reacting that way?*

Andrew shrugged. 'I thought it would please Grandma.'

'Anybody feel like coffee?' Sandy asked, impatient to puncture the leaden atmosphere. 'You know Martha—there'll be coffee brewing in the kitchen.'

'Before she went to bed, about ten minutes ago,' Andrew said, 'she told me she'd just put up coffee. Shall I bring in coffee for three?' he asked lightly, about to rise to his feet.

'I'll get it,' Jamie told him. Exuding annoyance. *What is it with him? Andrew's trying to be nice.*

'It's almost time for the 10 P.M. news.' Andrew reached for the remote, switched on the sound.

In companionable silence Sandy and Andrew listened to the round-up of local news.

'And now to the fighting in Iraq,' the newscaster began, and Andrew hit the 'Power' button.

'Tonight I don't want to hear that.' He grimaced in distaste, rechannelled the conversation. 'The police don't seem to be getting anywhere in the Lieberman case, do they? Probably some transient who's two hundred miles away by now.'

'I don't think so,' Sandy rejected.

'Why not? Your reporter's nose seeing something the rest of us are missing?'

'I have this uncanny conviction that somehow Dottie Lieberman's murder is tied in with—with your mother's murder.'

'Because they were close friends?' Andrew contemplated this for a moment. 'I can see how you feel that way. Thank God, Mom's killer was caught.' His face tightened. 'He won't kill again.'

The phone rang. Sandy leapt to answer.

'Hello?' A tinge of excitement in her voice.

'I'd like to talk to Jamie Moss. It's important.'

'Just a moment, please.' *Ted Newman or Bill Thompson, the union head? But Jamie said he gave them his cell phone number.* 'Jamie,' she called and an instant later he appeared in the door, tray in hand. 'It's a call for you.' She took the tray from him.

'Hello. Jamie Moss,' he said briskly. The voice at the other end was too muted for Sandy and Andrew to hear. 'Sure. I'll set it up first thing in the morning. No problem. Thanks for calling so quickly.' Jamie put down the phone with an air of exhilaration. 'That was Ted Newman. He said he misplaced my cell phone number, tried the house, figured I'd be here. The Town Council has worked out a package. They want to sit down and talk with Ward.'

Andrew was curious. 'What goes?'

In succinct terms Jamie explained the situation. 'The union big wheels are meeting tonight. They must decide whether they have the right to offer a deal without a vote by the membership.'

'With a thousand jobs on the line, who'll reject it?' Andrew countered.

'We'll know when we hear from Bill Thompson.' Jamie was brusque.

'That'll knock the Lieberman murder off the front pages,' Andrew predicted.

'No, we'll have no real peace in this town until the killer has been apprehended. People are scared there'll be another murder as long as he—or she—is on the loose.'

'Dottie Lieberman, like your mother, was very well liked in this town. Who wanted her dead?'

'Wasn't she a lawyer?' Andrew asked. 'Weren't we at school with Nora Lieberman?'

'She was a lawyer,' Jamie confirmed, 'and we went through school with her daughter Nora.'

'Search Lieberman's clients,' Andrew pursued. 'A hundred to one she made a mortal enemy of a husband— or wife—she fought in divorce court.'

'The police are doing that.' Jamie dismissed this with irritation. He swigged down his coffee. 'I was hoping we'd hear from Thompson tonight—' The phone rang again. Jamie lunged for it. 'Hello?'

Sandy leaned forward, trying to read his face as he talked.

'Right,' Jamie agreed. 'I'll set it up first thing in the morning. Thanks for getting back so fast.'

'The union's going along?' Sandy's eyes clung to Jamie.

'They're willing to sit down to talk with Ward.' He glowed with anticipation. 'Tomorrow will be a busy day.'

But we don't know that the pieces will fit together to save all those jobs. Please God, let it work out well.

Sixteen

Sandy and Jamie drove to the office in his car, leaving Sandy's for Martha to use for her morning trip to the supermarket.

'I'll call Ward a little past eight,' Jamie decided as he pulled into the parking area.

'So early?' Sandy was doubtful

'We're not the only ones who keep early hours. I understand Ward is always at his office by 8 A.M.'

'All right,' Sandy approved.

A moment later she dropped her head on Jamie's shoulder—in a sudden need to reassure him. She couldn't erase from her memory the unnerving moments the previous evening when Andrew seemed to be making a light play for her, and Jamie reacted with such anger.

Doesn't Jamie understand that I love him? It means nothing to me that he and Andrew are physically identical. They're two different people. It's Jamie I love.

In the reception area Gloria was just settling at her desk.

'You're late,' she jibed, handing a slip of paper to Jamie. 'Nora Lieberman called ten minutes ago. She said to call her as soon as you came in.'

Jamie and Sandy hurried to his office. He reached for his personal line, punched in Nora's number, hit speakerphone so Sandy could hear.

'Hello—' Nora's voice, pitched high in excitement.

'You have news,' Jamie guessed

'Three things,' Nora said. 'I called my P.I. after you left

115

yesterday. He figured he'd check on it last night—when the delivery man on the night shift would be available. Dad was right.' Her voice echoed relief. 'He was home when Mom was murdered.'

'You were hoping for that,' Jamie reminded.

'Twenty minutes ago Detective Bronson buzzed me. First thing: Carl Reynolds' alibi showed up. She's married—her husband was out of town. She stalled on coming forward. Second, they received an anonymous phone call. A local building contractor made remarks in a tavern last night that seems to implicate him in Mom's murder. They asked if I knew him. I explained that he's a roofer who tried to bilk Mom on a roofing job on her house. She took him to court, won. He was livid. They're picking him up this morning for questioning.'

'What's his name?' Sandy jumped in.

'His name?' Jamie asked.

'Bert O'Reilly,' Nora said. 'He runs a roofing company out on Emerson Street. He inherited the business when his father died a few years ago. When the old man was alive, they had a fine reputation—but something happened . . .'

'Let's see if the police hold him for arraignment,' Jamie hedged. 'He could have been talking after too many beers.'

'Oh, and there's something else.' There was contempt in Nora's voice now. 'He's the son-in-law of the Publisher of the *Evening News*. Jamie, I want the *Sentinel* to stay on this. Maybe readers will come up with more evidence if they know O'Reilly's a suspect. Your mother would do that—you know how close she was to Mom.'

'We'll follow closely,' Jamie promised.

Off the phone, Jamie and Sandy discussed this new lead.

'You can be damn sure there'll be no word in the *Evening News* about Bert O'Reilly being questioned,' he pointed out.

'It's news. Shouldn't we send Frank over to follow up?'

'Run with it. But make Frank understand he must wait

for arraignment before we go into action,' Jamie stipulated. 'O'Reilly could be the killer—but let's sit back and see how this develops.'

'I'll bring in Frank and—' Sandy stopped short. 'Jamie, it's 8:11—you can phone Ward now.'

'Right.' He tried for a reassuring smile as he reached for the phone. 'What's the number at Westwood Manufacturing?'

Sandy supplied it, sat on the edge of her chair as Jamie put through the call. *Ward won't back out now, will he? He must be terribly shaken with his son in custody. But this will set a compassionate tone in the jury pool.*

'Good morning, Mr Ward, this is Jamie Moss.' He paused as Ward responded. 'Yes, we're making progress. The Town Council and the union chief—Bill Thompson—are both prepared to sit down with you and work out a way to handle the situation. I can set up an appointment for you to meet with Ted Newman and Bill Thompson at whatever time you choose.' Jamie seemed to relax a bit. 'Yes, that'll be fine. I'll confirm with them and get back to you.'

Jamie put down the phone, took a deep breath. 'I have to call Newman and Thompson. Ward wants to sit down with them, hear what they have to offer. He said he never wanted to outsource—but he saw his company going belly-up if he didn't. Now let's just hope the three of them can come up with a deal that works.'

Close to 1 P.M. Frank charged into Jamie's office.

'O'Reilly's scheduled to be arraigned Friday evening,' he announced. 'I took Jim along with me—he has photos. Won't this throw the noses of those creeps over at the *Evening News* out of joint!'

'They won't be happy,' Jamie acknowledged. 'All right, go all out now. Dig into O'Reilly's background. Talk to waiters at McFeeters—the tavern where O'Reilly opened his mouth. Find out now much he was drinking.'

'Folks in town will sleep a little better when the word gets out about his arraignment. Not that they'll read about it in the *Evening News.*'

'We can't do anything until tomorrow morning's edition comes out, but we'll be hearing it from the radio and TV newscasters in a matter of hours,' Jamie surmised.

'Yeah.' Frank nodded. 'I saw the local TV crew driving up just as I left the police station.'

'It'll be front page tomorrow morning,' Jamie summed up. 'Work with Sandy on the article. Remember our dead-line.'

Andrew sat with Claire over lunch, served at her request in the library.

'I always have my lunch on a tray in the library while I watch CNN,' she told him. 'That is, I have in the past —' Her face etched in fresh pain. Of late her lunch had been served in her room. Her sanctuary from the world.

'As long as I'm in town, I'll have lunch with you here,' Andrew promised. 'But no television,' he said with mock sternness. 'I demand all your attention.'

Martha came into the room with a tea tray. 'I made blueberry muffins,' she told Claire. 'They're just out of the oven.' *She's pleased that I persuaded Grandma to come downstairs for lunch today. First time since Mom died.*

'The muffins look great,' Andrew said, his smile charismatic. 'Chow here sure beats what I was getting in Iraq.'

'I worked out my own recipe. Dr Maxwell says we all need to cut down on fat. I use less oil and replace it with applesauce,' Martha told him with an air of secrecy.

'Grandma's slim as a showroom model.' Andrew chuckled. 'I don't think she needs to worry about fat.'

Martha clucked in reproach. 'Fat does bad things to the arteries. Miss Claire don't need that kind of trouble.'

Most of the time, he knew, Martha favored Jamie over

him—though she would never admit that. There was always that division since they were kids; Mom and Martha thought Jamie could do no wrong, Grandma was on his side. Grandma loved the letters he sent her from Afghanistan and Iraq. Mom said she bragged about them to everybody.

Grandma made a point of avoiding talk about Mom's will, but he sensed she was upset that he and Jamie were practically disinherited. *But wait a minute! Is Jamie out of the picture? He's sending signals that he's got something special going with Sandy. Mom left almost everything to Sandy because she figured Sandy would be marrying Jamie. I'm the one that's disinherited.*

'Andrew—' Pouring tea for them, Claire punctured his introspection. 'I wish you'd forget this mad need to chase around the world.' She flinched in recall. 'With all the killing in Iraq, I worry so when you're there. Your mother worried—though she'd never admit it. I wish you'd settle down here in Westwood.'

'Grandma, stop worrying,' he scolded her. He remembered—again—the encounter with Jamie, when he'd offered to write an article for the *Sentinel*. The arrogant bastard! The *Sentinel* couldn't afford him. 'What could I do in Westwood? I offered to write an article about my experiences in Iraq, but Jamie turned me down flat. I guess that shows where I stand with the *Sentinel*.'

Claire froze in disbelief. 'Your own brother and he turned you down? You're famous—he should be proud to have you write for the paper.'

'I wouldn't say famous.' Andrew's smile was diffident.

'You write for a national magazine. Your mother, too, was so proud of you. I don't know where her head was when she made out her will!'

'Grandma, it's okay,' he soothed.

'It's not okay that Jamie won't let you write for what should be your own newspaper,' Claire blazed. 'I'm having a talk with that young man. I may not own the *Sentinel*, but I should have a say.' She paused in thought. 'I'll talk to Sandy. She's the official publisher now.'

Seventeen

Earlier than normal, Jamie walked into Sandy's office and suggested they head for home.

'Everything's under control. I like the article you and Frank wrote about Bert O'Reilly—you hit the right tone. The man's being arraigned, sure, but he's swearing he was drunk and talking out of turn.'

'You think he may be dismissed at the arraignment?' Sandy was ambivalent. He'd bragged about 'getting rid of that rotten lawyer who took me to the cleaners.'

'It's a possibility. Unless the police come up with substantial evidence.'

'Any word yet on the Ward situation?' Sandy reached into a desk drawer for her purse.

'No more than I told you earlier. He's meeting with the Town Council at 7:30 this evening, then goes to talk with Bill Thompson and his committee at 9 P.M. With luck we'll have some word before bedtime.'

'I'll call Martha and tell her we'll be home for dinner in twenty minutes,' Sandy decided, reaching for the phone. 'She'll be pleased.'

'No crockpot on the range tonight? No casserole waiting to be heated in the oven?' His smile was tender. 'Martha's put up with a lot from this family.'

Driving up to the house, they saw Andrew's Prius in the garage.

'What does Andrew do all day?' Jamie raised his eyebrows in mock dismay. 'Sleep?'

'He probably needs it,' Sandy began and paused. 'You need it, after the insanity in Iraq.' *In her mind she heard Karen Mitchell talking about the problems that faced identical twins. 'You wouldn't believe the competitiveness they often face. It's as though each is determined to prove his independence—that he's a person in his own right.'* Did that explain Jamie's hostility towards Andrew? He was afraid he wasn't living up to his brother?

'I used to dream about sleeping for twelve hours straight—in a normal bed,' Jamie mused. He frowned, all at once seemed miles away. 'I still feel guilty that I accepted a discharge. I'm always fighting this feeling that I should be in Iraq with my company.' He parked, sat staring into space.

'Jamie, you were wounded three times.'

'More than one soldier goes back after three injuries. But then I was hit with—with Mom's death, and I wasn't thinking straight.'

'I'm glad you're home.' Sandy was defiant.

'Oh God, I missed you,' Jamie whispered, reaching to pull her close.

'I missed you too . . .'

'We'd better get into the house,' Sandy said after a few minutes. 'Martha will have our heads if she's putting dinner on the table and we're not there.'

Walking into the house, they were aware of tantalizing aromas drifting from the kitchen. They heard talk in the dining room.

'Grandma came downstairs for dinner.' Jamie was surprised. 'That's good.' He reached for Sandy's hand, strolled with her into the formal dining room.

The table was set for dinner—with Claire's Lenox china, Sandy noted, and her best crystal. Martha's decision or Claire's? Was this meant to indicate a return to normalcy—to the days when Claire insisted on waiting as late as 10 P.M. for dinner with Adrienne and herself? *'It's fashionable to have dinner at 10 in Europe. But that's my deadline.'*

Claire sat at the head of the damask-covered dining table, with Andrew at her right.

'Sandy, sit next to me,' she ordered with a distant smile for Jamie.

Startled by Claire's imperious instruction, Jamie took his place at the foot of the table. For an instant his eyes met Sandy's. Neither understood Claire's sudden coldness. It was as though Jamie was being assigned to purgatory, Sandy thought. *What's bothering Claire?*

Martha came into the dining room, served steaming bowls of carrot soup. She'd heard the car drive up, Sandy assumed.

'You don't add salt,' she admonished Andrew. 'It's seasoned right.'

'Yes, ma'am.' There was a glint of amusement in his eyes. Sandy suspected this was a running reproach from Martha.

Aware of unspoken tension in the room, Andrew launched into a series of amusing stories about escapades in Afghanistan and Iraq.

'Hey, what about you?' He challenged Jamie. 'You must have had some wild old times in the last seven months.'

'I wouldn't call them wild.' Jamie was somber. 'Not in the war we were fighting.'

Sandy yearned for dinner to be over. And she was disturbed by the knowledge that if she closed her eyes, she wouldn't know if it was Jamie or Andrew speaking. Jamie and Andrew were so close when they were small, Adrienne had told her, they were unhappy at any separation. Until they were ten years old, she said, they fought against having separate bedrooms. According to Karen, that was a familiar pattern. When Jamie and Andrew were to start nursery school, Adrienne deliberately enrolled them in classes in different schools, but they were miserable, cried to be together. Now, Sandy realized, she recoiled from the hostility she felt between them. Perhaps Andrew was just more adept than Jamie at hiding his own feelings.

Martha removed the soup bowls, returned with a platter of grilled chicken laden with mushrooms plus a huge salad bowl.

'No beef in this house,' Martha reminded Andrew with mock sternness. 'Don't expect steak or roast beef.'

'Only because I love you will I accept such a decree,' he drawled. 'If I get desperate, I'll run out for a Big Mac and a double order of French fries.'

'Bite your tongue,' Martha scolded, but she enjoyed these light exchanges with him.

Andrew was the major contributor to dinner-time conversation—avoiding uncomfortable swathes of silence from the others. He had an endless store of amusing anecdotes about his recent weeks in Iraq. Still, Sandy was disturbed that Claire seemed annoyed with Jamie. What had he done to upset her?

After what seemed to Sandy an interminable time, Martha cleared the table and returned with dessert.

'No dessert or coffee for me,' Claire told her. 'I'll have tea—in my room.' Now she turned to Sandy. 'I'd like to talk with you. In my room,' she emphasized. 'Come up when you've finished dinner. Now if you'll all excuse me . . .'

Alone at the dining table with Jamie and Andrew, Sandy made small talk about Martha's superb chocolate mousse.

'Your mother said you two were real chocoholics as kids,' Sandy recalled.

'Right,' Andrew recalled, reaching for his coffee. 'When we were kids, if there was no chocolate dessert on Saturday nights, we knew Martha was punishing us. We were in the doghouse.'

Sandy was startled by the passionate intensity of Andrew's eyes as they met hers. Jamie hadn't noticed, she realized with relief. He was focused on scooping up the final spoonful of his mousse. By now Andrew must realize that she and Jamie were more than friends. What was he trying to do?

'I'd better go up to Claire's room.' Sandy took a final swig of coffee, pushed back her chair. 'She has something she wants to discuss with me.' *They know that—they heard Claire. Why do I feel something ominous is about to hit me?*

Sandy hurried from the dining room, into the foyer and up the stairs. Andrew and Jamie were in the living room now—she could hear a television newscaster reporting on the latest fighting in Iraq. Jamie wouldn't try to find a way to rejoin his company, would he? He harbored such guilt that he was home and out of the fighting.

She paused before Claire's door. Only silence inside. None of the classical music Claire loved emerged from her stereo. That meant she was uptight about something. What had Jamie done to upset her?

She hesitated a moment, knocked lightly.

'Come in.' Not Claire's usual gentle voice.

'I should have brought you a fresh pot of tea,' Sandy apologized as Claire lifted the pot to pour and nothing emerged.

'Martha will bring another pot shortly,' Claire said. 'I'm upset with Jamie—'

'Why?' Sandy strived for a casual tone.

'The way he's behaving towards Andrew. He's refused Andrew's offer to write an article for the *Sentinel* about his experiences in Iraq. Nothing political,' she insisted, 'just an article that would give readers some insight about a foreign correspondent's life in Iraq.' Her face softened. 'You know, a local boy who's made it big in his field.'

'I haven't heard anything about this.' Sandy forced herself to lie. 'I'm sure Jamie has some logical reason.'

'You're the Publisher,' Claire pointed out. Sandy tensed. 'I'd like you to talk with Jamie. I understand his contribution to our country, but he has to understand that Andrew, too, has put his life at risk. Andrew's making a name for himself as a journalist. Perhaps Jamie feels he's in his shadow—'

'I'll talk with Jamie,' Sandy promised.

'Adrienne always fought to treat them evenly—she worked so hard at raising them well. She was always reading some book or article that dealt with it. If Andrew got something, then she made sure Jamie got something of equal value.' Claire paused. 'And she was aware that they were fiercely competitive. But this is wrong,' she insisted. 'For Jamie to tell Andrew he won't accept an article from him for the *Sentinel*. You're the Publisher, Sandy.' *Technically, yes—but once we're married, Jamie will be co-publisher.* 'Make Jamie understand he mustn't treat his brother so shabbily.'

Eighteen

Her mind in chaos, Sandy walked slowly down the stairs. She recognized Jamie's hostility towards Andrew. But why this refusal to run Andrew's article? In truth, it would be a plum for the *Sentinel*. They ran a small-town newspaper; Andrew was published in a national magazine. Readers would be enthralled. Claire was pushing her to confront Jamie—to her it was a question of sibling rivalry. *But Jamie runs the paper—no matter that Adrienne left it to me. I shouldn't be put in this position.*

Arriving at the foot of the stairs, she could hear the TV news report spilling out into the foyer. She couldn't talk with Jamie here. *Make an excuse to go back to the office. He'll pick up I need to talk with him.*

She hurried into the living room. Andrew was sprawled across the sofa, seeming totally relaxed. Jamie sat at the edge of a lounge chair, absorbing the newscaster's report, tense, uptight.

'Jamie, I just remembered something that should go into Frank's article about Bert O'Reilly.' She strived to sound casual. 'I'll run back to the office and make the addition before it goes to the Composing Room.'

Jamie rose from his chair. 'I'll go with you. If some word comes through tonight about the outsourcing deal, I'd like to get it into tomorrow morning's edition. Everybody concerned knows to call me on my cell phone.'

They were silent until they were in the car and headed back for the paper.

'I don't know why, but Grandma is furious at me.' Jamie spoke with a deliberate slowness that told Sandy he was disturbed about it. 'Then she summons you to a grilling in her bedroom. What gives?'

'It's so silly . . .' Sandy sought for the right words. 'Andrew told her you'd refused to have him write an article for the paper. Something just in general, about his experience in Iraq. She—she thought readers would love it.'

'They would,' Jamie agreed, his eyes on the road ahead. 'But I didn't feel it was a good move.'

'Jamie, why?' Sandy was bewildered.

He hesitated. 'It's a—a feeling I have.'

'Why?' she persisted. Most of the time she trusted Jamie's instincts.

'It could be I'm leaning over backwards,' he admitted. 'Back in Iraq I met a correspondent who'd had a run-in with Andrew over there. He could have been talking out of jealously—at the time I convinced myself he was.' Jamie's hands tightened on the wheel. 'He said that Andrew had laughed at him for chasing into the heart of the fighting for stories. Andrew said that Hemingway—back in the '30s in the fight against Fascism—had boasted about doing his best reporting "from the lobby of my hotel in Madrid".'

'You don't know that it's true,' Sandy reproached him after a moment.

'No.' Jamie's face tightened. 'But I can't expose the *Sentinel* to that kind of reporting. You can be sure the *Evening News* would be on the watch for something like that. It could destroy our believability.'

'Could you talk to Andrew about it?' Sandy was troubled.

'No.' Jamie was brusque. 'Tell Grandma you discussed it with me, and I refused to budge.' He took one hand from the wheel to clasp Sandy's for an instant. 'Tell her I felt an article by Andrew didn't fit the *Sentinel's* image.'

Sandy sighed. 'She won't be happy.'

'You're the Publisher.' Jamie shrugged. 'It's up to you to make the final decision.'

'Jamie, stop that!' *Adrienne didn't mean for her will to come between me and Jamie. I won't let that happen.* 'What do you feel is best for the paper?'

'We don't run Jamie's article.'

'Then we don't run it,' she said, an air of defiance behind her words.

'Andrew will be taking off soon,' Jamie soothed, 'Grandma will forget this.' He seemed to be in inner debate for a moment. 'I overheard Andrew on the phone with his magazine. He was arguing about something being a pack of lies. Sandy, we can't take a chance of publishing mis-information.'

But how am I to tell Claire that Jamie's decision is final? I can't say we suspect Andrew of fabricating stories. It may not be true.

The morning was gray, unseasonably cool. Standing under the comfort of a hot shower, Sandy considered how she was to explain Jamie's decision about Andrew's article to Claire. Thank God, Claire never came downstairs for breakfast. She wouldn't have to face the situation until tonight.

After a quick breakfast Sandy and Jamie headed for the paper. She sensed that Jamie, too, was concerned about an impasse with Claire. But she must be firm, Sandy ordered herself. The correspondent that Jamie quoted could be all wrong—but they couldn't take a chance on publishing false-hoods. Even the almighty *New York Times* was suffering from that.

She and Jamie had agreed to drive together to the office each day. With the soaring price of gasoline—and the short-age that the world faced—Jamie considered this the right thing to do.

'I thought I might hear from Ward last night.' Jamie seemed anxious. 'Or from Newman or Thompson.'

'They won't settle that quickly,' Sandy said. 'There's so much to be worked out.'

'You're right, of course. And all sides know that Ward is holding up any move for five days. Five days from yesterday.'

Chuck was emerging from his car as they swung into the parking area. He seemed depressed, Sandy thought.

'I did something I never do,' he grumbled as Sandy and Jamie joined him. 'I took Lester Owens and his wife out for dinner last night.' He grinned. 'Expense account—it was one of those places. I knew it was their thirty-first wedding anniversary. I was at their wedding.'

'You wanted to talk advertising,' Jamie surmised.

'Right. Lester has been one of our biggest advertisers for years. The store runs full-page ads on the slightest provocation, especially with the economy so bad. He was blunt. He said folks in this town were more concerned with their safety—when a killer was on the loose—than chasing down sales. He won't advertise until the climate changes.'

'We can sit out the situation, even with more advertisers pulling out,' Jamie decided. 'We're not retrenching in any way.'

'What's with Ward?' Chuck asked. 'That's most important. If this town is to survive, we need those jobs to remain here.'

'I haven't heard a word from any side,' Jamie admitted. 'But this isn't something to be solved at one meeting.' He tried for an air of optimism. 'They have a lot of angles to consider.'

'Your mother was working so hard to stop the outsourcing,' Chuck remembered. 'Bring this off, and the town will be forever grateful.'

The three of them headed for their individual offices, settled down to preparing another edition of the *Sentinel*. Each was hopeful that word would come through about progress between Ward and Newman and Ward and Thompson.

Shortly past 9 A.M., when Sandy and Jamie were huddled in her office, Andrew sauntered into view.

'I don't believe it,' Jamie jeered. 'What got you up at the break of dawn?'

'I'm without a computer at the house.' Andrew smiled wryly. 'I feel lost. I'll pick up a laptop in the next day or so—but in the meantime I'd like to monopolize the computer in your old office.'

'Sure—' Jamie shrugged. But he seemed wary, Sandy noted. 'But you'll need a laptop to take back to Iraq.'

'Iraq's on hold. In a way,' Andrew amplified. 'I was on the phone with my agent in New York. He suggests I submit a book proposal. He feels I should get it down while it's hot in my memory.'

'Everybody's writing books about Iraq.' Jamie appeared annoyed. *Jamie wants Andrew out of our lives. He keeps dropping hints. Does Jamie think that Andrew could come between us?*

'Okay,' Andrew said briskly, 'let me get back to my personal salt mine.'

At about 10:30 A.M.—after a brief session with the paper's accountant—Jamie charged into Sandy's office.

'I just had a call from Newman.'

'Good news?' Sandy was anxious.

'Nothing's settled yet, but Ward is meeting again this evening with a committee from the Town Council and a group from the union. Ward feels he needs more help than they've offered so far if he's to keep his head above water without outsourcing. But they're still talking,' he emphasized.

'We knew they'd have to have a few meetings to reach a conclusion. Everybody has to bend a little.'

'They managed to do it in that town we talked about,'

Jamie began, stopped dead as Gloria—pale, distraught—burst into the office.

'Bad news!' Gloria paused, struggled to speak. 'Beth McDonald didn't show up at her school this morning. She's teaching in the summer session. She hadn't called in sick. The principal got worried. You know—with all that's been happening in this town—'

'What about Beth McDonald?' Sandy felt her throat tighten in alarm.

'The principal—Leonard Davis—sent a woman from the school cafeteria over to Mrs McDonald's house to check her out. She didn't answer the doorbell. Her car was in the garage. The woman from the cafeteria was worried. She thought Mrs McDonald might have had a stroke or a heart attack. She went to the side of the house . . .' Gloria paused, struggled to continue.

'Gloria, what did she see?' Jamie demanded.

'The drapes in a bedroom weren't tightly drawn. Through a chink she saw Mrs McDonald lying in bed—a pillow over her head. A lollipop lying beside her—'

'Not again!' Sandy gasped.

Gloria nodded. 'Beth McDonald has been murdered! The same way Dottie Lieberman was!'

Nineteen

Shocked silence inundated the room. The three in Sandy's office were a frozen tableau as they struggled to comprehend what Gloria had reported.

'Mrs McDonald was my English teacher in junior high.' Jamie punctured the leaden silence. He'd seen men die in Iraq, both Americans and Iraqis, and it had been agonizing. But this was shattering—an invasion of home. 'Everybody liked Mrs McDonald. She was a favorite teacher! Who could have done this?'

Sandy's face was devoid of color. 'Jamie, don't you see what's happening? What we've suspected. First your mother, then Dottie Lieberman, now Beth McDonald. There must be a link!'

Jamie sought to clear his head. 'We know who killed Mom. And we know that Bert O'Reilly couldn't have killed Beth McDonald—he was in custody. You're right—there's some weird link between these murders that we haven't been able to pin down. The police must see that by now.'

Sandy spread her hands in a gesture of futility. 'They're questioning all the obvious suspects—'

'And coming up with nothing,' Jamie flared.

'The phones are going wild.' Gloria fled to her reception desk.

'Cool it, Jamie,' Sandy coaxed. 'The police haven't had much time. Three murders in the past eight days.'

'When the word circulates about Beth McDonald, this town will explode with fear.' Jamie was apprehensive.

'That must be happening right now.' Sandy's eyes searched Jamie's. 'What can the paper do to make them feel less threatened?'

'That was Mom's first objective when anything bad happened in Westwood.' He sought his mind for answers. 'We need to campaign for heavy police patrolling of this area. Maybe organize volunteer teams. But enough of that for now—we have a murder to cover.'

How can I pretend to be cool in a situation like this? I could be cool in Iraq. Cool when I was wounded. But where will this killer strike next? Sara Adams? She's the fourth in Mom's tight little circle.

'Frank's clear. I'll rush him over to the McDonald house.' Sandy reached for a phone. 'Jim's off today. Who's available for photo duty?'

Again, Sandy kept the TV in her office switched on but muted. Waiting for 'BREAKING NEWS' to hit the screen. Waiting for further word from Frank—stationed along with a crew from the *Evening News* and crews from neighboring communities—along with TV and radio reporters. She'd dug from their files every item about Beth McDonald.

Jamie had been at the high school for almost two hours. He'd called in to report that the school had closed for the day. Counselors were scheduled to appear in classroom tomorrow. Beth McDonald's son—an accountant living with his wife and two small daughters in Philadelphia—had been contacted.

At a TV 'newsbreak', Sandy reached for the remote. Sound filtered into the silence.

'. . . detectives are questioning members of the faculty in an effort to arrive at a motive for the murder of one of our high school's most popular teachers. Beth McDonald was two years from retirement . . .'

Sandy turned to the door as Jamie charged into the office, at the same time muting the TV again.

'Any leads?' She reached for the mug of coffee Jamie extended.

'The police chief held a brief press conference.' He sank into a chair with an air of frustration. 'So far they've come up with nothing. Sure, McDonald had disciplined three or four students in the past year—but that amounted to nothing. Oh, the latest is they're questioning a custodian who left the school under a cloud. It seems he blamed McDonald for his dismissal.'

'Wait a minute!' Sandy's mind was in high gear. She'd come up with nothing in the *Sentinel* files—but what about that craziness several months ago?

Jamie tensed. 'What are we missing?'

'Do you remember that fifteen-year-old accused of rape at the high school last March? No,' she answered before Jamie could reply, 'you had left for Iraq already. But I remember that the principal—what's his name?' She searched her memory.

'Leonard Davis.'

'Mr Davis moved fast to squelch it,' she recalled. 'It didn't even hit the papers—he fought to keep it out.' *He carried on about our ruining two lives if we ran one word about it.* 'He didn't want a scandal in his school. The pretty little fifteen-year-old was portrayed as being hysterical, misinterpreting a shy pitch. The boy's family spirited him off to a fancy boarding school in another state. Mrs McDonald and your mother were outraged. The girl was afraid to go back to her school—even with that young fiend gone. Her parents worked at menial jobs—they couldn't afford to send her to the local private school. Your mother and Mrs McDonald formed a committee to raise funds to send her. The boy's father was outraged.'

Jamie grunted in distaste. 'The young monster ought to be serving time in a juvenile detention center—but I can't see the police bringing in either.'

'Claire's going to be in shock when she hears that Mrs McDonald has been murdered.'

'Andrew will hold Grandma's hand, and she'll feel better,' Jamie said dryly. 'And what's this sudden book proposal he's thrown into the ring?'

'He said he's anxious to write about his experiences while they're still fresh in his mind.'

'He'll camp out here while he writes his book,' Jamie scoffed. 'A damn parasite.'

'All household expenses are paid by your grandmother— out of the check she receives each month from the *Sentinel*,' Sandy reminded him. 'I doubt that she'll complain about Andrew staying on.' *She'll be delighted to have him around.* But the prospect of his long-term presence in the house was disconcerting.

'Why isn't he going back to Iraq?'

'About the rape incident at the high school,' Sandy shifted the subject, 'should we bring it to the attention of the police?'

'They're probably aware of it.' Jamie shrugged dismissively.

Sandy pondered. 'I'm not sure. The school swept it under the rug so fast, the police were not brought in. Nothing appeared in the local papers. We knew about it because Frank's daughter was in the high school—and shocked and scared.'

'Why don't we try to interview some of McDonald's current students? Maybe line up two or three past students as well. This must be traumatic for them. It is for me.' He rose to his feet. 'We'll be here late tonight.'

'Jamie, what about Sara Adams?' Sandy asked.

'What about her?' Then comprehension sunk in. 'If we're right, she'll be the killer's next intended victim!'

'The police should provide her with protection. Now.' Sandy churned with frustration. *What's holding it up?*

'They police don't buy our "three friends of Mom's" theory—they're sure it's just a coincidence. They don't see Sara Adams in danger. Bronson told me they're sure to arraign the school custodian. He made wild threats when he was fired. Bronson said he claims to have been out of town the night McDonald was murdered—but he has no witnesses.'

'Whoever killed her killed Dottie Lieberman, too—and Sara Adams is next on the list.' *How can I talk so calmly about this?*

'I'll phone her.' Jamie was grim. 'Plead with her to leave town until the police have this creep in custody. She has two grown kids—her son Elliot was one year ahead of Andrew and me in school. Her daughter Jennifer is a year behind us. She'll be a hell of a lot safer with one of them.'

Sandy spread out sandwiches on her desk for Jamie and herself. Gloria had provided coffee. Jamie had been trying to reach Sara Adams by phone for the last two hours, was impatient at not being able to get through to her. At the phone again, his face brightened. He was getting through at last. With a sigh of relief he hit the speakerphone button, signaled Sandy to listen in.

'It was my morning to serve at the church thrift shop,' Sara explained. 'I know these are terrible times—I can't stop grieving for your mother and Dottie and now Beth. But I try to keep busy with my volunteer work.' *Mom always said she did more volunteer work than any two women in this town.* 'But we're all so shaken again—we just heard about Beth an hour ago—' Her voice broke. 'Everybody loved her. I can't believe this craziness. Beth taught at the high school for twenty-eight years. Everybody's grieving—and terrified.' *She realizes that her small clique is being assassinated—and she's the last of the four. Okay, go for it now.*

'I think it would be advisable for you to leave town for a bit.' Jamie's voice was deceptively casual. 'Stay with Elliot for a few days.' *Probably longer.* 'Or perhaps with Jennifer.' But Jennifer was way out in California. Elliot was less than two hours away. 'Just until this creep is in custody.' *When will he—or she—be in custody?*

'I was thinking about that,' Sara confessed. 'I mean, my three dearest friends—' Again her voice broke.

'Please, make arrangements to leave Westwood,' Jamie coaxed.

'I'll call Elliot tonight,' she promised, 'when he's home from the office. I feel so awful for Beth's children. She didn't know they were planning a big surprise party for her birthday next week. Both her kids and their families were coming here to celebrate her birthday. Now they'll be coming for her funeral. Jamie, has anybody notified her kids? It would be awful for them just to hear about it on the TV news—' Because three murders in eight days in the same small town would make the national news.

'I'm sure the police are making every effort to notify them. They've probably done so already,' Jamie soothed. 'But focus now on calling Elliot. Make arrangements to stay with him.'

'I know.' Sara took a deep breath. 'I could be next.'

Twenty

The atmosphere at the *Sentinel* was tense. Three members of the staff in addition to Jamie had attended Beth McDonald's English classes through the years, and two others had children in the school at present.

The town was in an uproar at the unexpected closing of the school before the lunch periods. Students and teachers alike were told only that school was closing for the day. No explanation was offered. They were instructed to return as normal tomorrow. But word circulated fast.

Sandy, accompanied by a staff photographer, talked with clusters of students reluctant to leave the school grounds as word filtered through to them. They clung to one another in shock. Sandy returned to the paper to write her article. *I'm not wrong—there's a link between these murders.*

Close to 10 P.M. Chuck strode into Sandy's office, where she and Jamie were preparing Frank's front-page story for the Composing Room. 'So what's holding up the works?' Chuck grumbled. 'We've got a paper to put to bed.'

'We're finishing up here,' Jamie said. 'Copy-editing done. Everything ready for the Composing Room.'

'So you two get out of here. I won't be far behind you.' Chuck hesitated. 'You said you talked to Sara Adams. She's leaving town?'

'She was calling her son early this evening. I gather she's expecting him to drive up for her.' Jamie glanced at his watch. 'It's late for me to be calling, but—'

'Call her,' Sandy ordered. 'I'll sleep better if I know she's

139

out of town.' *It's too late to line up an overnight security guard.*

Jamie reached for a phone, punched in Sara Adams' number, and waited.

'Speakerphone,' Sandy said quickly, and Jamie hit the button.

'Hello?' Sara Adams, sounding wary. *She's scared after all that's happened. Every call laden with threats.*

'This is Jamie,' he said. 'I just wanted to reassure myself that you've reached your son and—'

'Oh, I was so rattled I wasn't thinking straight,' she broke in. Apologetic. 'Elliot and Mary and the baby left this afternoon for a long weekend with friends who have a house in East Hampton. They'll be back Sunday afternoon—they're coming in early to beat the traffic. I'll call Elliot then.'

Jamie exchanged an anxious glance with Sandy. 'I'll ask the police chief to see that a police car drives around your area at regular intervals tonight.'

'Tell her to leave her porch light on,' Sandy said. 'An intruder would figure she was expecting someone—possibly any moment.'

'Mrs Adams, leave your porch light on,' Jamie told her. 'And a light in your living room. I'll brief the police.'

'I'll be all right.' An edge of defiance in her voice. *But she's terrified—she has every reason to be.*

'Ask her if she has a phone number for the house at East Hampton,' Chuck instructed.

'Do you have a phone number for that house in East Hampton?' Jamie asked. 'Or the name of Elliot's friends?'

'Jamie, I can't ask them to give up their weekend. This is the first chance Elliot's had to get away this summer. He's been swamped with work. I'll be fine,' she insisted.

Sandy reached into a desk drawer for her purse. Jamie pulled the car keys from a pocket. Chuck scowled, stared into space.

'Okay, what's bugging you?' Jamie asked.

'Maybe we're being shortsighted.' Chuck was blunt. 'Maybe it's not just your mother's friends on that list. It could be you—or Andrew—or Sandy.' *We talked about this days ago—even Chuck could be a victim. Everybody knew how close he was to Adrienne.* 'I hear this little voice inside me that says all these killings are a kind of revenge against your mother.'

'Ever since six years ago, when some nutcase threatened to kill Mom, the house has been burglar-proofed,' Jamie reminded. 'If anybody tries to get in, the alarms go off.' And the nutcase was in a mental institution.

At prodding from Chuck again, Sandy and Jamie headed for the parking area.

'You're worried about Sara Adams,' Sandy said while they settled themselves in the car.

'I'd feel a hell of a lot better if there was a security guard on duty overnight,' he admitted.

Walking into the house, they were aware that Andrew was watching a re-run of a Vietnam movie on TV.

Jamie grunted in distaste. 'The last thing I want to see these days,' he told Sandy while they headed for the kitchen to forage for their late dinner.

To their astonishment Martha was there.

'I'm baking,' she told them. 'I always bake when I'm upset. Your grandmother's in such a state,' she told Jamie. 'She barely pecked at her dinner, even with Andrew coaxing her to eat.'

'No note for us tonight.' Jamie tried for a lighter note. 'Does that mean no dinner?'

'Sit yourselves down—I'll bring out the casserole. I've been keeping it warm in the other oven.'

Sandy and Jamie ate with a gusto that brought a faint smile from Martha.

'Clean your plates up, and you can have a slice of hot apple pie,' she promised.

Jamie grinned. 'With vanilla ice-cream?'

'He's been saying that since he was five,' Martha told Sandy. 'All right, hot apple pie and a scoop of vanilla ice-cream. When the boys were little, I kept the ice-cream in a freezer in the pantry—and locked.'

'Do I smell something in the oven?' Andrew strolled into the room. 'Martha, you're baking.'

'Apple pie with a scoop of vanilla ice-cream coming up for three,' Martha said with a mock air of martyrdom.

'There was a "news break" a while ago,' Andrew reported. 'About the new murder. They've brought in a former school custodian for questioning. But you probably know.' He squinted in thought for a moment. 'Didn't we have McDonald in high school?'

'We had her for two years. She was great.'

Andrew nodded in recall. 'She was the one who made the two of us wear name tags in her class. You were the good kid—I was the troublemaker. She didn't have much of a sense of humor.'

'What's with Mrs Adams?' Martha asked, striving to mask her apprehension. She knew their theory about the murders.

'Mrs Adams understands the situation.' Jamie was somber. The mood in the kitchen was heavy with anxiety. 'She'd agreed to call her son this evening, have him take her to his house for a few days. But she'd forgot—he left the office early today for a long weekend in the Hamptons. He won't be home until Sunday afternoon.'

'She should have floodlights set up around the house,' Sandy began. 'I know it can't be done tonight, but in an emergency perhaps tomorrow she—'

'Bad scene,' Andrew interrupted. 'It'll just frighten her to death—she won't be able to sleep. And a devious killer would manage to kill the power—she'd be a sitting duck.'

Jamie shook his head in frustration. 'At this hour there's no way to bring in a security guard.'

'Hey, why don't you and I take on guard duty for tonight?' Andrew challenged.

Suddenly Sandy was ice-cold. 'That could be dangerous!'

Andrew's smile was wry. 'Being in Iraq was dangerous. We can deal with this.'

'Sure. We can do that,' Jamie agreed.

'We'll each take a shift—11 P.M. to 2 A.M., 2 A.M. to 5 P.M. Three hours each between now and daylight.' Andrew smiled up at Martha, approaching with apple pie. 'You take the first shift, Jamie. I've got a date with apple pie and ice-cream.'

Sandy was unnerved. 'But you should be armed.' She gazed from Jamie to Andrew.

'We'll be armed,' Andrew reassured her. 'I have a 9-millimeter automatic that I brought back with me from Iraq.' He turned to Jamie. 'Go up to my room—you'll find it in the top left dresser drawer.'

'How did you get it through,' Jamie asked, rising to his feet, 'with all the security today?'

'It was a snap,' Andrew drawled. 'I hopped a ride from Baghdad with a general who likes my writing style. It fit into my knapsack.'

'Call Mrs Adams and tell her what's happening,' Martha ordered. 'Don't scare the daylights out of her by parading around her grounds. But she'll feel better knowing somebody's out there watching over her.'

Sandy had known she'd find it difficult to sleep tonight when Jamie was out there in the night, watching for a killer. A few minutes past 1 A.M. she abandoned the effort. She crossed to a window, gazed out into the darkness. Clouds hung heavy in the sky. No moonlight, no stars. An unseasonable chill in the air.

In a burst of restlessness she changed into slacks and a cotton turtleneck. As though to be prepared for an emergency, she scoffed at herself. All right, go downstairs, put up coffee. Jamie would like that when he came home. With catlike steps she left her room, headed downstairs. An ominous stillness throughout the house. Approaching the kitchen, she was startled to realize someone had preceded her. The kitchen was brightly lit.

'Hi.' Andrew glanced up from the book he was reading.

'You didn't bother trying to sleep.' Her tone sympathetic. *It was so sweet—so thoughtful—of Andrew to have enrolled Jamie and himself in guard duty.*

'Three hours pass fast.' Andrew shrugged. 'At 1:45 A.M. I walk over to the Adams house to relieve Jamie. It's a short walk—better not to disturb the night with the sounds of a car.'

'Jamie said Mrs Adams was so appreciative when he called to let her know what was happening.'

'Grandma will be pleased.' Andrew rose from his captain's chair at the table, crossed to join Sandy at the counter where she was putting up coffee. 'You should always wear that shade of blue. It does marvelous things for your eyes.'

'You'll want coffee before you go to relieve Jamie, won't you?' Sandy was conscious of a sudden pounding of her heart. *This is Andrew—not Jamie. Why do I feel this way?*

'I'd love coffee.' His eyes were carrying on a different conversation with hers. 'I'm jealous. Jamie found the grown-up Sandy before I did.'

He reached to draw her close. *This is insane. What are we doing?*

With an effort she pulled away—pretending this was just a casual moment between them. 'There's more apple pie. Shall I warm up a piece for you?'

Twenty-One

Sandy waited for Jamie to return to the house. A piece of apple pie was in the oven, coffee in the coffee-maker. She was still unnerved by the few heated moments alone with Andrew.

She recalled what Karen Mitchell had said about identical twins seeming sometimes to be one whole, each a half of the other, and reluctantly she remembered stories Karen had told her. About a woman who had been engaged to one twin—and ended up marrying the other.

Oh, this is insane! I love Jamie. Andrew's just playing games with me. It's the old competitive bit, where each wants to outdo the other.

She was aware now of muffled footsteps in the hall. Jamie was home.

'I figured you'd be waiting up.' He walked into the kitchen with a gentle smile. 'You shouldn't have—you'll be up again in four hours.'

'Everything's cool,' she gathered. *This is Jamie—whom I love.*

'Not even a tomcat on the prowl,' Jamie said. 'Do I rate a second piece of apple pie?'

'Coming right up. Along with coffee.' She hesitated. 'I should have made decaf—you'll have trouble falling asleep.'

'Not tonight. I'll be out the minute I hit the pillow.' His eyes were making love to her. But they had drawn lines for themselves in Adrienne's house, Sandy reminded herself. And it was rough.

'Sleep late in the morning,' she coaxed. 'The *Sentinel* will survive if you come in three hours later.'

'Can't,' he rejected. 'I have to be on the phone first thing tomorrow morning—or later this morning,' he corrected himself, 'when offices are open for business. I need to line up a security guard to cover Sara Adams' house for the two nights until her son picks her up and takes her to Albany.'

'Whoever's out to kill her, and we figure that's a certainty,' Sandy conceded, 'wouldn't follow her to her son's house. Or would he?'

'I've been considering that,' Jamie admitted. 'I've been thinking that it might be wiser for someone other than a family member to spirit her out of town. Once she knows Elliot is back, I could drive her to Albany—keeping an eye out to see if we're being followed.'

Sandy frowned in impatience. 'We don't know where that creep is, what he knows. Does he have her under surveillance, waiting for the right moment?' She shuddered at their lack of knowledge. 'Why can't the police position a car in front of her house?' *If Adrienne were alive she'd be on their backs for this.*

'I talked to the police chief. I badgered him. But they're short-staffed since the Town Council cut back their budget.'

'Which shouldn't have happened!' That was one reason she was sure Jamie would win a seat on the Council. Voters knew he'd be the voice to bring about local housecleaning. Much-needed clean-up.

'While the whole town is petrified that a killer is running loose, the police department now has additional worries.'

Sandy was startled. 'What worries? You've said nothing about that.'

'I didn't want to heap more on you,' he apologized. 'An angry group has been forming at Westwood Manufacturing. Word's got around about the meetings with Ward and the Town Council and the union leaders. Rumors are circulating about possible physical action if Ward doesn't make a fast decision to work with them.'

'That doesn't sound like Ward employees!' Sandy protested. 'Ward was known for having a good relationship with his people. They were even reluctant to join a union for years.'

'Nobody feels kindly towards Ward since they know his son killed Mom—and he's taking personal blame. And they're uptight at the prospect of losing their jobs. Many of them have been with the company for twenty years or longer. Suddenly they're facing unemployment lines.'

'Could it be out-of-town union organizers using Ward as an example?' *Physical violence at Westwood? Adrienne would have done anything to prevent that.*

'I considered that,' Jamie confessed. 'I'm going to question Bill Thompson about it. I got word just before we left the paper tonight. Detective Bronson tipped me off—'

'He knows how the *Sentinel* has always fought to keep peace in Westwood.'

'He told me he's working around the clock to catch the killer. A nice guy.' Jamie was reflective. 'He told me his wife went through high school with Mom. He said she had great admiration for Mom. For the way she carried on the paper after Dad died, the way she raised Andrew and me on her own—and for all the good she did for this town.'

'But he can't push through police protection for Sara Adams,' Sandy threw back.

'He explained that right now they don't have the manpower to allot a car to sit in front of Sara Adams' house until the killer is caught. They're doing heavy surveillance on that group from Westwood Manufacturing. Just a few guys so far, but they're angry. Talking nasty.'

'Talk to Bill Thompson first thing in the morning,' Sandy urged.

'That's at the top of my list.' Jamie shook his head in rejection. 'Mom would have been out of her mind if something like this happened. I need to talk to Bill—and to pin down Ward. I'll talk to members of the Council. So much is hitting this town at one time.'

'Get to bed,' Sandy ordered. 'Try to get at least three hours' sleep. Tomorrow will be a rocky day.'

Fearful of oversleeping, Sandy had set her alarm clock for 6 A.M. At last deep in slumber, she came awake with a jolt when it sent its shrill message into her bedroom. Without opening her eyes, she reached to silence it. A hot shower would wake her up, she promised herself.

Twenty minutes later she was hurrying downstairs. She heard voices in the kitchen. Martha was up and active, as usual. She was talking with Jamie.

Andrew would sleep till noon. But it had been so right for him to suggest that he and Jamie act as security guards last night. He'd displayed a tenderness she hadn't seen in him before. Whoever gave the story to Jamie about Andrew screwing up on stories he sent in to his magazine must be wrong. Some stupid correspondent eaten up with jealousy.

"I suppose it's safe to say that Mrs Adams came through the night all right?' Martha exuded bravado. 'Thanks to the homegrown vigilantes.' *So Jamie told her about last night.*

'I'm sure she's all right, but I'll give her a buzz at a respectable hour,' Jamie promised.

'You gonna run the story?' Martha jibed. ' "ADRIENNE MOSS'S IRAQI VETERAN SONS GUARD AGAINST MURDER." '

'Only one of us is an Iraqi veteran,' Jamie pointed out.

'The other says he was embedded with the marines,' Martha reminded. 'That should count, shouldn't it?'

'You'd better watch out, Martha,' Jamie joshed. 'If we're short on reporters, you might be drafted.'

'I want this town to get back to normal.' Her voice was harsh now. 'You and Andrew do that for your mother. And you, Sandy, sit down and eat your breakfast. Running off

148

to work before seven in the morning. You needed two college degrees for that?'

Sandy and Jamie pulled into the *Sentinel* parking area as Chuck emerged from his car.

'Bill Thompson phoned minutes after you left last night,' Chuck told Jamie without preliminaries. 'He said not to bother you until you came in this morning, but to call him as soon as you arrive. I don't know if he'll appreciate it at this hour—'

'He'll be up,' Jamie predicted. 'I'll call.'

'Thompson's hit a problem,' Sandy surmised, settling herself in a chair in his office while Jamie reached for the phone. 'We'll need to run a strong article in tomorrow morning's edition, try to cool the situation.' *This town has never experienced violence over labor disputes. But then it's never been threatened with a loss of a thousand jobs.*

'Bill, this is Jamie,' he said briskly, hitting speakerphone. 'What's the problem?'

'That bastard Ward is giving us big-time headaches. He's asking for a larger cut in wages than the leadership can take on its own. We need to hold a referendum. We can't do that by his deadline.'

'How long do you need?'

'With all the paperwork involved, a couple of weeks.' Bill's voice was streaked with rage. 'Not another three days.'

'Cut it to one week,' Jamie began.

'Whose side are you on?' Bill demanded.

'I want to see a thousand jobs saved.' *Jamie's trying so hard to be cool. He knows what those jobs mean to this town. But the union won't go along with starvation wages. Ward's got to bend a little, too.* 'You can hold a referendum in one week if you dig in, Bill. I'll talk to Ward, and then go to the Town Council and—'

'A tax break won't do it,' Bill broke in. 'Hell, taxes aren't that high in this town.'

'I'm discussing a financial-aid package with the Town

Council,' Jamie reminded him. 'I'm waiting for word. It's been arranged in other towns in similar situations. And Ward's not concerned about drawing a fancy salary—'

'He's asking us for a five-year commitment. What about him? Will he allow our accountants to check his books? What will he be taking out of the company for those five years?'

'Something acceptable to the union.' Jamie pantomimed his uncertainty to Sandy.

'You expect him to go along with that? Get real, Jamie—'

'Let's figure he will,' Jamie pursued, waited for Bill's response. Each second seemed an hour.

'Okay. We'll hold a referendum one week from today—assuming he'll wait that long. But we have to guarantee more than starvation wages,' Bill warned. 'Battle with Ward, see what you can come up with.' Unexpectedly he chuckled. 'You pull this off, you've got that Council seat in the bag. Next step the Mayor's office.'

'One thing more, Bill . . .' Jamie hesitated. 'What's this craziness I hear from the detectives? About an ugly group among the workers threatening violence if Ward doesn't drop the outsourcing plans?'

'It's got to me,' Bill admitted uncomfortably. 'We've been looking into it. I suspect outsiders—trying to use Ward as a trial case. The union is not behind it,' he insisted. 'I've made it clear—the union won't support any violence. We'll fight it. But get moving with Ward—then we won't be hearing ugly rumors.'

'Could it be somebody wanting the outsourcing to go through,' Jamie asked after a moment, 'trying to foment trouble that appeared to be union-backed? That could sway Ward to go ahead with outsourcing.'

'Let him know this has no backing from the union.' Bill was terse. 'We want to keep jobs in this country. Not outsource them.'

'Ward's going to be tough to handle,' Sandy warned when Jamie was off the phone.

'He said he wasn't worried about drawing a fancy salary—he doesn't want to see the company he spent close to thirty years building up go down the drain.' Jamie paused. 'This has been rough on him, too. How can he compete with foreign companies that are paying pennies an hour?'

'It's a tough situation.'

Jamie flinched. 'Because of this rotten outsourcing Mom is dead. But how do we tie in the murder of her two closest friends with that?'

Twenty-Two

In Jamie's office Sandy leaned back in her chair and fought yawns while he went for coffee refills. This was going to be a long, painful day, she warned herself again. So much hanging over their heads.

Jamie strode into the office, placed two mugs of steaming black coffee on a corner of his desk. 'Gloria said that yesterday's *Evening News* carried a front-page story about the high-school custodian's arrest. Over-wrought as usual,' he said in distaste.

Sandy lifted her eyebrows. 'We missed something? I don't think so.' She'd had three reporters looking into the case. They'd come up with nothing of substance. At least, they hadn't thought so—

'According to the *Evening News,*' Jamie said derisively, 'the cops have the two murders—Lieberman and McDonald—sewn up. Not only did the guy threaten McDonald for costing him his job, Dottie Lieberman was his wife's divorce lawyer four years ago. He claimed he was taken to the cleaners in the settlement.'

'Can they go to trial with such flimsy evidence?' Sandy was skeptical.

'He's being arraigned this evening. We'll see.'

Sandy glanced at her watch. 'It's past 8 A.M. Sara Adams must be awake by now, if she managed to sleep at all.'

'We covered the house from a few minutes before 11 P.M.—when she was fine—until 5 A.M. and daylight.' He reached for the phone. 'I'll call her.'

Moments later Jamie was on the phone with Sara Adams.

'Oh, I feel so much better this morning. When my cleaning woman came in this morning, she brought a copy of the *Evening News* with her. I know, it's a rag,' she apologized, 'but the police have got that man in custody.'

'Mrs Adams, don't jump to false conclusions—' He reached for the speakerphone button, his eyes telegraphing his alarm to Sandy. 'There's no substantive evidence that the custodian killed Mrs Lieberman and Mrs McDonald.'

'The *Evening News* says the police are sure this is the killer.' There was gentle reproach in her voice.

'He's being arraigned this evening, but that doesn't mean he'll go to trial. The police have little evidence—just suppositions.' Warning signals shot up in his head as he exchanged an anxious glance with Sandy. 'You need overnight security at your house until we know the killer is in custody,' he insisted. *She wants to believe the police are right. Jamie's facing a brick wall.* 'I'll start phoning around town at 8:30 when offices open up and—'

'Jamie, no,' Sara Adams insisted. 'I feel secure now. They've got that awful fiend in custody.'

'To be safe, we should arrange for—'

'No need, Jamie. It's wonderful the way you're concerned for me—but there's no point now. That killer's in jail. You're a dear, sweet man, and I'm so grateful for your concern for me. I'll be fine. Not that it's necessary,' she cajoled, 'but I'll leave the porch light on all night. And the light in the living room.'

'You did your best,' Sandy comforted him when Jamie put down the phone.

'Maybe the custodian is guilty,' Jamie conceded, 'but I'll have to see stronger evidence to believe it.'

'Call Nora,' Sandy said on impulse. 'The police must have checked with her about the divorce case.'

'Right.' Jamie reached again for the phone. 'I don't know if she's at her office yet. Let me try her house.'

Moments later Nora was on the line. 'A detective called to ask about the divorce case,' she confirmed tiredly. 'I worked with Mom on it. He's a real bastard. Abused his wife, verbally and physically. When we threatened criminal charges if he didn't agree to a substantial settlement, he went berserk, made wild threats. I asked for—and got— a restraining order for his wife, Mom, and me. But that was over six years ago. Why would he wait so long to act?'

'As usual, the *Evening News* was determined to be sensational,' Jamie began.

'They're pissed at the *Sentinel* for its rise in circulation. They'll run anything to build up their own sales. And they're fighting like mad against your winning that Town Council seat.' She chuckled. 'Sure, I read the opposition paper. I need to know everything that goes on in this town.' Her voice softened. 'Your mother used to say, "This is a special town—we're one big family." '

'We don't believe this guy, the school custodian, is guilty. Just a reporter's instinct,' Jamie admitted. 'We're still convinced that Mom's murder—in some weird, unfathomable fashion—is linked with your mother's killing and Beth McDonald's. It's exasperating that we can't put a finger on the link!'

'What about Ward?' Sandy asked when Jamie was off the phone. 'He's always the first at his office, he likes to say.'

'He *is* the first.' Jamie was emphatic, but troubled. 'But it's hard for me to be sympathetic towards him in the circumstances—'

'Your mother was so determined to block his outsourcing.' Sandy was somber. For that Adrienne was murdered. 'You're right—we must fight within ourselves to acknowledge that Ward is in a rough situation with Westwood Manufacturing.'

154

'Okay, back to the drawing board. Let's see if Ward will agree to extend his deadline. Then comes the battle about wages and benefits. And what kind of a deal will the Town Council offer financially? Right now,' Jamie acknowledged for the first time, 'the Council is divided right down the middle.'

'You're asking a lot,' Ward hedged as he sat in his large corner office at Westwood Manufacturing and considered what Jamie had laid out for him. 'I've stalled too long already with the people who'll work with me in China.'

'We have to fight together.' Jamie made it an impassioned plea. 'To save this town and to save your business.'

'I can save it by outsourcing,' Ward shot back.

'Maybe,' Jamie acknowledged. 'But we see companies coming back, admitting serious problems.'

Ward deliberated for a few moments. Jamie sat with clenched fists—waiting for his decision.

'I'll give the union the extra days,' he conceded. 'But I can't handle the situation without financial assistance. A temporary tax, whatever—' He gestured his ambivalence. His eyes veiled. 'What about my boy?' he asked. 'What about Evan? My attorneys are trying to work out a deal with Potter. Evan will forego a jury trial, accept incarceration. Potter tells me that a final decision will rest on your family's approval.'

Jamie was conscious of a coldness invading him. He understood the situation, that Evan was severely retarded, with no comprehension of his actions. *But Evan Ward murdered Mom. Should he be allowed some velvet-lined confinement for the rest of his life?*

'Your mother was known as a compassionate woman.' Ward was struggling for calm. Fighting for his son's welfare. 'What would she wish for Evan?'

'The family will go along with whatever the courts work

out,' Jamie agreed after a moment. *That would be Mom's wish.*

Ward closed his eyes for an instant, as though in prayer. 'I don't want to outsource,' he said painfully. 'Show me a way out.'

Sandy glanced up from her cluttered desk at the sound of Jamie's voice in the hall, in conversation with Chuck. Moments later he strode into her office.

'Ward's going along with the time extension. Bill Thompson's calling for a referendum on cuts in wages and benefits as a short-term measure.' He dropped into the chair across from her desk with a sigh of exhaustion. 'But we've still got a long way to go.'

'I rushed Frank and Jim over to the police station,' Sandy told him. 'The lieutenant is holding a press conference right now about Walter Hendricks.'

Jamie lifted his eyebrows in inquiry. 'Who's Walter Hendricks?'

'The ex-school custodian who's being arraigned this evening,' Sandy reminded. 'Did we mess up somewhere? All we could come up with is that Hendricks has a hot temper, battled with Dottie Lieberman over his divorce case, and accused Beth McDonald of costing him his job. He claims he was home with his current wife the night of both murders.'

'No criminal record?' Jamie prodded.

'Not even a parking ticket.'

'The second wife,' Jamie mused. 'She's his alibi. That's not impressive.' He leaned back in his chair. Contemplative. 'But if she's right, Beth McDonald's killer is still out there.' His face tightened in resolve. 'I'm going to talk to Sara Adams again—'

A phone on Sandy's desk rang. A jarring intrusion. She picked up. 'Sandra Taylor.'

'The lieutenant is taking questions,' Frank reported. 'It

156

looks like they've hit pay dirt. Hendricks' wife just recanted—she's saying now that he wasn't with her the night McDonald was murdered. She said he didn't come home until almost 4 A.M.'

Twenty-Three

The staff of the *Sentinel* were caught up in their 'Big News' mode. An air of excitement permeated the atmosphere. Sandy moved into Jamie's office, to work in tandem with him.

'We should call Nora, have her bring in all the facts about the Hendricks's ugly divorce,' Jamie said between phone calls.

'I'll do it,' Sandy said, reaching for her cell phone—to leave the two on Jamie's desk opening for incoming calls.

Moments later she was talking with Nora.

'I'll bring over every item we have on the divorce,' Nora promised. 'If he killed Mom, I want to see him convicted. I'll do anything to help!'

Five minutes later Sandy was on the phone with Frank.

'I can't get through to Hendricks' first wife,' he reported in frustration. 'Maybe she'll talk to a woman.'

'I'll give it a try,' Sandy said. 'See what you can dig up at the high school. Why was Hendricks fired? And why did he blame Beth McDonald?'

'I'm on my way.'

Sandy was conscious of the poignant relief that was spreading through the town. A serial killer had been captured. Their ordeal was over.

Is it over? Why do I have such doubts?

All at once restless—prodding herself to contact Hendricks' first wife for an interview—Sandy went out to the reception area. Gloria would dig up the phone number for her.

Gloria was alternating between two phones. She gestured her frenzy as Sandy approached. Okay, try to contact Hendricks' first wife later, Sandy decided.

Sandy returned to Jamie's office. He glanced up from his computer.

'The *Evening News* will be twelve hours ahead of us in spreading the word,' he said with a sardonic smile. 'But by now every living soul in town knows, via radio or TV, that the police are sure they've nailed Beth McDonald's killer.'

'And they're trying to pin Dottie Lieberman's murder on him,' Sandy added. 'Why do I feel unimpressed?'

'You're clinging to our theory—'

'I feel this is all wrong. Hendricks isn't the killer.'

'We have to accept facts.' Yet Jamie, too, sounded ambivalent. 'The cops feel they have enough to win a conviction.'

'My instincts tell me they've got the wrong man.' Sandy lifted her head in defiance.

'The way we're moving, we'll get out at a respectable time tonight,' Jamie predicted. 'Call Martha to expect us for dinner around 7:30 or 8 P.M.'

'You're tired of casserole dinners.'

'Could be. Plus we need a decent night's sleep.' All at once there was a heated glow in his eyes. 'I want life to be on an even keel. I want to claim my wife.'

'I want that, too,' she whispered. And remembered—with guilt—that brief moment when Andrew had evoked such arousal in her.

'Instead of going home for dinner,' he said with an air of inspiration, 'let's go out somewhere very special. Tell Martha to forget the casserole—tell her we're going out on a business dinner.'

'A lovely idea.' Her smile was luminous. They would have precious minutes alone in the darkness of the car— escaping the world.

Self-conscious at leaving the paper at a normal hour, Sandy and Jamie headed for the parking area before 7 P.M.—unheard of in these tormented days. But everything was under control, Sandy comforted herself.

Earlier Jamie had called the Colonial Inn to make a dinner reservation. The last time they'd dined here, Sandy recalled, was the night before he had to report to his National Guard unit. They'd known he'd be shipping out to Iraq at any moment.

'I don't think the Colonial Inn will have a waiting line for tables,' Jamie surmised while they settled themselves in the car. 'Though people will be less reluctant to go out after dark with the police making such confident announcements.'

'Which are yet to be proved,' Sandy reminded him. 'But we won't think about that for the hour or two,' she vowed while Jamie reached to pull her close in the protective darkness of an overcast night.

They drove away from the *Sentinel* with a guilty sense of stealing time. The night sky was dark, devoid of moon or stars, the weather, again, unseasonably cool. Jamie headed for the secluded area beside the pond where he and Sandy had made love in those nights before his National Guard unit had been shipped out to Iraq.

Jamie parked, turned to Sandy. 'I used to dream about this in those long, ugly nights in Iraq,' he whispered. 'Never knowing if I'd make it home—'

'I was so scared for you,' she whispered, then fell silent as his mouth found hers.

The moon emerged from behind a sea of clouds as they drove away and headed for the Colonial Inn. Sandy sat with her head nestled against Jamie's shoulder. For the next hour or so, she vowed, they'd forget the horrors of these last ten days. Forget the fighting in Iraq.

'A few people ahead of us,' Jamie noted as he pulled into the parking area before the restaurant, once an elegant colonial-era residence.

'They've heard the news about Hendricks.' *But we don't know for sure that he's the serial killer.*

'We won't think about that—it's off limits here. Banished,' he said with a lordly gesture.

The hostess led them to a private table, as though knowing this was a special night for them, Sandy told herself. Their waiter arrived, offered menus. They focused on the menu, striving for a convivial mood. The waiter's smile was indulgent, Sandy thought—he knows we're in love.

In a corner of her mind, she remembered the heated moment with Andrew. *Am I in love with two men? Each one half of the other?*

'Guess who just came in,' Jamie whispered.

Sandy's gaze swung to the entrance where a party of four was being greeted by the hostess. Eric Potter, another man, and two women. Two couples, she assumed.

As though feeling the weight of their gaze, Eric Potter swung his gaze in their direction, waved a hand in greeting. He excused himself to his companions, headed towards their table.

'I'm sure you've heard the word. We've got the character who killed Lieberman and McDonald,' he told them. 'He thought he had an alibi—the old "I was with my wife all evening, all night." But the wife—the second wife,' he pointed out, 'had a change of heart. She said he didn't come home until 4 A.M. the night McDonald was hit. The coroner said McDonald was killed between midnight and 2 A.M.' Potter glowed with satisfaction. 'Hendricks' wife found out he's playing house with another woman.'

'That seems to settle the McDonald case. What about Lieberman?' Jamie was casual.

'We'll pin it on him.' Potter was confident. 'His current wife is out for blood. She's not sure where he was the night Lieberman was killed.'

'What's the motive?' Sandy prodded.

Potter shrugged. 'We'll nail it. In time.'

He returned to his table. Jamie turned to Sandy. 'And why were we honored with his presence?'

'He knows you're headed for a seat on the Town Council,' Sandy interpreted. 'You're becoming a big wheel in this town.'

'They don't have a strong motive. Hendricks will be held for a grand-jury hearing,' Jamie predicted, 'but that's a long way from a guilty verdict.'

With candid reluctance Sandy and Jamie left the Colonial Inn an hour later. They drove home with Sandy's head on his shoulder and his thigh pressed against hers. Turning into the driveway, they noted the living room and entrance foyer were brightly lighted. Involuntarily Sandy's eyes swept to Claire's bedroom. It was dark.

'Claire must be downstairs,' she told Jamie.

'I'm in the doghouse,' he said edgily.

'I'm there with you,' Sandy reminded him. *Why can't Jamie run Andrew's article? He shouldn't believe an ugly rumor.*

Reaching in his pocket for the key, Jamie froze as he gazed through the glassed area of the front door.

'Grandma heard the car come up—she's going up to her room—'

'Maybe she'd just decided she was tired.' *She's going up to her room because Jamie and I are coming home.*

'All of a sudden I feel like an intruder in her house. Maybe I should try to find an apartment.'

'Jamie, it isn't her house,' Sandy protested. 'It's your mother's house.' *According to Adrienne's will it's my house. When we're married, it'll be his, too.*

'I don't feel comfortable here,' Jamie said in an agonized whisper. 'I grew up in this house—it's the only house I've ever known. But now I feel like an intruder.'

Andrew was sprawled on the sofa. The TV—in soft tones in deference to Claire's presence, Sandy surmised—was providing national news.

'Hi,' Andrew greeted them with a casual smile. 'I guess we won't be battling rain tonight, the way the weathercaster warned.'

'They're wrong as often as they're right,' Sandy shrugged. *Will I ever become accustomed to being in a room with both Jamie and Andrew? It's as though I'm being pulled in two directions.*

Martha appeared with a tea tray. 'Where's Miss Claire?'

'She was tired—she went up to her room,' Andrew said.

'I'll take her tea up to her.' Martha seemed uneasy. 'You'll all want coffee, I suppose?'

'Not us.' Jamie answered for Sandy and himself. 'Thanks, Martha.'

'I'll put up coffee,' Andrew told Martha. 'Go,' he said teasingly and turned to Jamie. 'What shift do you want to take tonight?'

Jamie was startled for an instant. 'Oh, you mean at Sara Adams' house. Not necessary. The cops are sure they've got the guy.'

'You don't sound convinced.'

'I'm not,' Jamie admitted.

'Then maybe we ought to play security guards again,' Andrew said

'I offered—Mrs Adams said no deal. She's convinced she's safe—nobody's going to attack her when this Hendricks character is in custody.'

'We could sort of—take it upon ourselves.' Andrew was thoughtful. 'If you think she's still in danger.'

'No deal,' Jamie rejected. 'She'd be furious. And if she spied us—no matter how careful we were—she wouldn't know it was one of us. She'd be terrified.'

Andrew rose from the sofa, stretched. 'Just as well. I should take myself back to the salt mines. Oh, I bought a laptop today—I can work here at the house. I should be putting more time on the book proposal.' He squinted in thought. 'If I work all night, I won't be disturbing anybody, will I? I mean, the computer keys are not noisy—and the walls in this old house are thick.'

'Type all night if you like.'

Sandy was startled by the sharpness in Jamie's voice. *What has got into him, to be so nasty? Andrew's trying so hard to be helpful.*

She remembered now something else Karen Mitchell had said about identical twins: *'One is usually the leader, the other the follower.'* *Does Jamie resent Andrew for having initiated the security guard situation for Mrs Adams? For being the leader?*

'Oh, I heard something disturbing on the local news,' Andrew added. 'A nasty rumor about a handful of workers threatening violence if Westwood Manufacturing tries to outsource.' He glanced from Jamie to Sandy, back to Jamie. 'Any truth in that?'

'Nothing's secret for more than five minutes in this town.' Jamie grunted in disgust. 'Yes, it's true.'

'Wow, this town is destined to hit the national headlines big time!' Andrew speculated. 'Three murders, a threat of outsourcing, now violence in the air . . .'

Jamie's eyes clashed with Andrew's. *Karen said that identical twins often read each other's minds.*

'Don't think about selling the story to some rotten tabloid,' Jamie warned. 'Westwood doesn't deserve that.'

'Okay.' Andrew shrugged. *It's like Karen said. They each know exactly what the other is thinking. At least, some of the time.* 'I'll go up to my room and get moving on my book proposal. My agent's real hot on it.'

Andrew isn't disturbed about not inheriting the bulk of Adrienne's estate, Sandy thought with relief. *He figures he'll do great all on his own, maybe with a huge sale of his book.*

At regular intervals she was plagued by guilt that she had been favored above Jamie and Andrew. Adrienne knew how Andrew would respond—he had huge confidence in himself and his future. She knew that Jamie would share in the inheritance through marriage to her.

But what had Adrienne meant? *'Sandy, be careful. Be careful . . .'*

Twenty-Four

Sandy and Jamie arrived at the paper later than normal. They'd agreed to allow themselves an extra hour of sleep on Saturday morning.

Chuck charged from his office to greet them. 'Would you believe it?' he chortled. 'With Hendricks headed for trial, I see a sign of a change in business already. I ran into Jake Block when I stopped to pick up a pack of cigarettes, and—' He stopped at Jamie's grunt of disapproval. 'I know—I quit smoking for almost three years. But this craziness—' He winced in recall. 'Anyhow, Jake said he'd be talking to me early next week about a full-page ad in next Sunday's paper.'

Jake Block ran the Emporium, a specialty shop catering to those with expensive tastes.

'He figures Hendricks is as good as convicted,' Sandy said—but without conviction. 'The police have tied him in to Beth McDonald's murder, but how are they doing in connecting him to Dottie Lieberman's?'

'Hendricks hated Lieberman for his divorce settlement,' Jamie reminded them. He reflected a moment. 'That's flimsy evidence. He's not the only husband who hated Lieberman— and Nora—for winning hefty settlements for the wife in question.'

'You're saying Nora could have been on the killer's list?' Chuck paused at the door to his office. 'I know her husband got himself a gun license quick. That's the trouble with serial killers—unless you know the motive, nobody knows who will be next.'

166

This morning Sandy settled herself in her own office while Jamie headed for his Saturday morning meeting with several of the associate editors—most of them part-timers. As usual she found a copy of the morning's edition on her desk.

She sat down to scan the pages, but her mind refused to focus on them. *Do the police have the killer in custody? Why do doubts keep plaguing me?*

Deep in thought, she was startled when her phone rang, invading the morning quiet. 'Sandra Taylor, good morning.'

'Sandy, this is Leona Rogers.' Their longtime next-door neighbor. 'I know it's early, but I just had to call to talk to you. A few of us—members of the Westwood High PTA—got together last night and talked about a memorial to Beth McDonald. We want to start a college-scholarship fund in her name. Can we can count on the *Sentinel* to work with us?'

'Absolutely,' Sandy said. 'I suggest we hold up running the story in the *Sentinel* until after her funeral, though.'

'That'll be fine. I talked with her son and daughter—they're too upset to sit down and work out details with us just yet.'

'It's been an awful shock for them,' Sandy commiserated. She remembered the death of her mother, her feeling that her whole world had collapsed.

'Beth would like having a scholarship in her name—she was always pushing her students to go on to college. Of course, it'll be rough for some of our kids to make it to college if Westwood Manufacturing closes down. One scholarship won't make a dent . . .' Her voice drifted away.

'Jamie and the paper are working hard to keep Westwood Manufacturing in town,' Sandy told her. 'It's too early to know how this will work out.'

'I heard rumors about the union running a referendum.' Leona sounded doubtful. 'Is that true?'

'It's true.' One bright spot in their dark world. 'Of course, we don't know how the workers will respond.' *Be truthful—don't give her false hopes.* 'And Jamie is working to bring the Town Council and Noel Ward together.'

'We saw nothing about this in the *Sentinel!*'

'We considered it premature—we didn't want to raise false hopes.' *I shouldn't have told her. Jamie said we should keep what was going down under wraps until we had an answer.*

'Most people put the outsourcing craziness in the back of their minds when all this horror hit us. I still can't believe we've lost three of our most prominent—much-loved— women in such a short time. But thank God, the police have got that fiend behind bars. I'm not one for the death penalty—but for this killer I could accept it.'

Off the phone, Sandy tried to concentrate on what must be completed in the course of the day. Every time she called Hendricks' first wife, she got an answering machine. She'd tried half a dozen times to get through to his current wife, but each time there was a busy signal. The phone was probably off the hook.

Her thoughts kept detouring to Hendricks' coming grand-jury hearing. She searched among the clutter on her desk for the folder that contained what they'd been able to learn about him. She read, absorbing each word as though it might be a clue to the truth. After being fired as custodian at the high school, he'd held a variety of jobs. A security guard at a local bank, a waiter at a low-scale tavern, most recently a supermarket worker. Each was a little lower on the pay scale.

She paused to digest a morsel of information about his second marriage. His second wife had been a cashier at the supermarket where he'd been employed. They were married five months after his divorce. She quit her job to be a home-maker, but neighbors said they fought constantly. Once the woman next door, fearful that he'd kill his wife in a screaming match, called the police. Though she greeted them with a blackening eye and bruises, she refused to file charges against him.

Originally Hendricks' second wife had said he was with her on the night that Beth McDonald was killed. With her the whole night. Then she retracted, said he hadn't come until 4 A.M. Why? Was it because she discovered he was seeing another woman that night? Or was she lying—as he insisted?

'The little bitch is pissed at me—she wants to see me in trouble. She knows I was there in the house with her the whole bloody night. She's lying!'

Suppose she is lying? Then the killer is still out there somewhere. A killer activated in some weird fashion by Adrienne's death. Somebody close enough to know Adrienne's three best friends. But many people in town knew about their friendship.

Sandy was conscious of a sudden chill. *His next victim— if my instincts are right—will be Sara Adams.*

She left her office, hurried into Jamie's. He was on the phone—hammering with one fist on his desk. It was a sign Sandy recognized as exasperation.

'Sure, it's going to have a political cost—but we have no other choice. We're not the first town to do this.' He paused as someone argued on the other end, then gestured his frustration. 'Yes, I'll be there,' he promised. 'I'll explain what we must do to keep Ward here in town.' He hung up, turned to Sandy. 'Newman,' he explained. 'He's calling a special meeting of the Town Council tonight. He's been having individual meetings with the members. There's some resistance to the new tax to back up Ward. Damn! The Council has to realize what's at stake.'

'I'm worried about Sara Adams.' Sandy sat down.

'You're not buying Hendricks as the murderer?' His eyes held hers. 'You think the police are way off-base?'

'Jamie, you know what I think.' Her own eyes were

reproachful. 'I'm convinced whoever killed Lieberman killed McDonald—and I don't see this Hendricks creep pulling that off. He's not bright—he'd have left some clues. These two murders were planned well. No fingerprints anywhere. No sign of a break-in. And that ridiculous trademark, the single lollipop beside each pillow! That's a sick, diabolical mind. I'll call her,' Sandy decided. Mom—and Adrienne—used to tease her about making impulsive decisions, but Sara Adams' life could be on the line. 'I know, she's convinced the killer's in custody—'

'At the moment the police believe Hendricks is guilty,' Jamie reminded her. 'But he has to go through a grand-jury hearing and a trial, and we don't know what'll come up.'

Sandy squinted in thought. 'I'll tell her the *Sentinel* is planning a tribute to Beth McDonald and I need to talk to her about their longtime friendship.'

Jamie pushed a phone closer to her. 'Call,' he said tenderly. 'You won't rest until you know she's all right.'

Sandy allowed the phone to ring a dozen times. 'She's not home. Early in the day for her to be running around.' Alarm spiraled in her, tightened her throat. 'Jamie, where is she?'

'She does a lot of volunteer work. Didn't you tell me she started the summer-breakfast program at the elementary school?'

'Right. The school's running summer classes for students who need extra help to enter the next grade and to learn English as a second language.' Few people realized that immigrant students had become a problem in small towns as well as in the major cities. Already, property taxes had gone up in order to hire more teachers to cope with this problem.

'Honey, don't jump to dark conclusions.'

Sandy forced a smile. 'I'll try her again in an hour.' *Jamie thinks I'm becoming paranoid.*

'A good thought,' Jamie approved, returned to business. 'Who've you got following up on Hendricks?'

'I gave it to Frank—he's chasing down his first wife for an interview. Frank's wife knows her, which might help. With luck we can use it for tomorrow's edition. I'd better get back to my office. I have a chunk of "Letters to the Editor" to deal with—everybody knows about the labor-union referendum and it's seeping through about fundraising via taxes to help keep Westwood Manufacturing here.' Sandy frowned. 'People are divided on that, Jamie.'

'We must keep Westwood Manufacturing in town. Even if it means a local sales tax to help it stay here.' His smile was wry. 'And, of course, the major objections to that come from the high-livers.'

Sandy rose to her feet. 'Back to the grind. I'll call Sara Adams in a bit.'

By 10:30 A.M. Sandy had made three attempts to get through to Sara Adams. Now she called the elementary school to ask if she had been there this morning.

'No, she hasn't,' the office secretary reported. 'She's here most mornings, though.'

At 11 A.M.—warning herself she was becoming paranoid—Sandy left the paper to drive to Sara Adams' house. Perhaps there was some problem with her phone that she didn't know about. At least, clear your own mind, Sandy told herself.

It was a lovely day, she thought—sunny, hot without being humid. Children played on front lawns, rode bikes. Laughter in the air. Sandy waved to a pair of women in lively conversation on a porch. The town seemed almost back to normal.

But the *Sentinel* was missing its longtime Publisher. A lawyer noted for her pro-bono work was gone. A teacher at Westwood High would have to be replaced next month. It would be a long while before the town fully recovered.

Sandy pulled into the driveway of Sara Adams' charming white colonial, set on a spacious, beautifully landscaped half-acre. Rose bushes in glorious bloom lined the long path to the columned porch. Pots of colorful coleus sat on the steps.

There were no sounds from the central air-conditioning unit, no car in the driveway.

I'm over-reacting. She's dashing around on her volunteer work. It's not hot, but Adrienne used to tease her about switching on the air-conditioning before anybody in town.

Still, she was here—try the doorbell. She touched it, heard the chimes sounding inside the foyer. Nobody home. That was normal for Sara, with all her volunteer commitments. She'd been long widowed, her son and daughter out of the house into lives of their own. It was natural she wished to keep busy.

Then at all once Sandy froze. Her eyes fastened on the front door. It wasn't closed. Her heart pounding, she reached to push the door wider. Would Sara have gone away and left the house unlocked? Not these days.

Her heart pounding, she walked into the house, paused in the foyer.

'Mrs Adams?' Only silence greeted her. 'Mrs Adams,' she tried again. Again, no response.

Struggling for calm, she walked through the lower floor. Part of her admired the lovely furnishings—the traditional style that Adrienne, too, had loved. Everything was in perfect order. Yet the silence that seemed to echo through the house was unnerving.

Fearfully, she gazed up the staircase to the second floor. Steeling herself to explore further. Again, she accused herself of being paranoid. Mrs Adams had left the house in a rush. From habit she hadn't bothered to lock the door. Only in the last horrendous two weeks had people locked their front doors during the day.

Feeling an intruder—yet consumed by a need to convince herself that Sara Adams was all right—Sandy walked up the stairs. Later she'd laugh at herself for this morbid fear.

'Mrs Adams,' she tried again as she reached the second

floor. 'Mrs Adams?' But there was no response. *She's just not at home.*

The bedroom at the head of the stairs—its door open—bore the air of a room awaiting guests. The next was decorated for small children. For the grandchildren, Sandy assumed. She opened the door to the large bedroom across the hall, gazed inside, then clutched at the door for support.

The face of the woman lying motionless in the queen-sized bed was covered by a pillow. Her arms were extended, fingers spread as though in fight. And beside her lay a single lollipop.

Twenty-Five

Sandy ran from the bedroom. Her heart pounding. She closed the door, paused—fighting for breath. Her mind in chaos.

It's happened again! A serial killer is running loose in Westwood. Who killed Sara Adams?

Call the police. Then call Jamie. Clutching the banister, she made her way down the stairs. Shaken, cold with shock.

The sun had disappeared behind ominous clouds. The living room was bathed in shadows. A storm seemed imminent. Sandy reached to switch on a lamp beside the phone. No results. The light bulb must be dead, she told herself, and crossed to switch on another lamp. The electric wires had been cut. That was why the central air-conditioning unit had been silent. The phone lines, too, Sandy discovered, had been cut.

She hurried out to her car, pulled the cell phone from the glove compartment, debating again. Call the police first, or Jamie?

Jamie, she decided. Wherever he was, he'd have his cell phone with him. He answered on the first ring, as though anticipating an emergency.

'Jamie Moss.'

'I'm at Sara Adams' house.' Sandy's words tumbled over one another. 'Jamie, she's been murdered!'

'Oh, my God! Are you all right?'

'Yes.' She tried to sound convincing. *How can I be all*

right? I'll never be able to erase those moments from my mind. 'I haven't called the police—I'll do that now—'

'You know not to touch anything.' He was brisk, yet she felt his solicitude.

'Of course. Jamie. There's a red lollipop on the pillow. It's the same fiend again! Debbie Lieberman, Beth McDonald, and now Sara Adams!'

'Call the police. I'll be there in minutes.'

Sandy sat in the car, clutching her cell phone in a trembling hand. She called the police station, explained what had happened.

'Don't touch—'

'I know,' she said, trying not to show impatience. 'I won't touch anything. I'm sitting in my car in the driveway. This follows the pattern. A pillow over her face, a lollipop nearby. Walter Hendricks couldn't have done this!'

'Detectives are leaving now,' the police officer on desk duty told her. 'We'll send over the coroner.' He hesitated. 'You're sure she'd dead? No ambulance needed?'

'She's dead.' Sandy shivered. 'I saw her hands, stretched out as though she'd tried to resist. Rigor mortis had set in. She's dead.'

Off the phone, Sandy sat behind the wheel, shoulders hunched, cold despite the warmth of the afternoon. Dark clouds hung in the sky, seeming to reflect the latest brutal death in Westwood. She felt a surge of relief—Jamie was charging towards the house in Chuck's car—

When will this horror end? Who will be next? So fast! It's happening so fast!

Now she saw a police car swing around the corner, following behind Jamie. He brought the car to a screeching stop, leapt out, sprinted towards Sandy.

'Jamie, it was so awful—to walk in on her like that! The front door was open—I thought perhaps she'd just forgotten to lock it. Then I went upstairs—just to be sure—' Her voice broke.

Jamie pulled her close. 'You shouldn't have gone in alone. You should have called me.'

'Why can't the police nab this monster?' *How many more will be murdered before he's caught? What are we missing about him?*

Two detectives sprang from the police car, strode towards Sandy and Jamie. Again, Bronson and Ryan.

'So we're off to the races again.' Bronson was grim. 'Let's go into the house and get the facts down.'

While they walked into the house, Sandy saw the coroner's van arrive. Several neighbors had emerged from their houses across the road, gathered now in a huddle. The coroner's arrival sent fresh fear through them. The town would be in panic when the news broke. Nobody would feel safe.

Why didn't we listen to Andrew last night? He was sure he and Jamie ought to cover Sara Adams' house last night— even against her will. If they had, she would be alive.

Jamie hovered solicitously over Sandy as they stood beside her car after almost two hours of intensive questioning by Bronson and Ryan. Both detectives were outraged by their lack of success. Now—at last—Bronson had accepted their theory. 'This could be a vendetta against Lieberman, McDonald, and Adams. We've got a lot of digging to do.'

'Sandy, you've had enough for one day.' Jamie's eyes were tender. 'Go home and get some rest.'

Sandy shook her head. 'Jamie, I discovered the murder— this is my story. I want to write it. I'm not assigning it to anyone. The police must come up with answers! How much more can this town take without exploding?'

'There's one tiny piece missing,' Jamie said. 'We know this fiend isn't going to stop. We just don't know who will be the next target.'

'It could be anybody who was close to Adrienne.' *It could be Jamie—Andrew—Claire—me. What's his motive? But why do we all keeping thinking 'he'? It could be a woman.*

A woman who sneaks into the house while her victim sleeps.
'I think it's time we had a more effective security system set up at the house,' Jamie decided. 'I'll make calls as soon as I'm back at the paper.' He paused and groaned. 'Here comes the news brigade—the word got around fast.'

The local TV channel's van was rushing towards the house. Right behind were cars from the *Evening News* and the local radio station. Out-of-town media would follow as the news circulated.

'Okay, let's get back to the paper.' Sandy reached for the door of her car. 'We have a rough day ahead.'

Within another hour the news had spiraled through Westwood. Again, the *Sentinel* phone lines were jammed. The police would say nothing as yet. Residents hoped the *Sentinel* would be more forthcoming. Gloria had been given a statement to read off to all callers.

'*Yes. Sara Adams was murdered in her bed.* Sentinel *staffer Sandra Taylor made the gruesome discovery this morning. The police have no suspects as yet, but it's believed the killer of Dottie Lieberman and Beth McDonald has struck again.*'

Sandy sat at her computer, struggled to write tomorrow morning's lead story. At unwary intervals she was assaulted by recall of the moment she'd walked into Sara Adams' bedroom and found her there. Why did that signature lollipop haunt her? It was the killer taunting them with a clue they couldn't comprehend.

No rush, she admonished herself. Get it right. It would be a report of Sara Adams' killing—and at the same time a memorial to her. No woman in town, other than Adrienne, had worked so assiduously for local causes.

'How're you doing?' Jamie walked into her office with yet another mug of black coffee.

'It's slow,' she admitted, reaching for the coffee as though for a lifeline to reality. This morning seemed an horrific nightmare.

'Let me take it on,' he said gently. 'Or Frank. You're too close. You've been traumatized—'

'No.' Her eyes clashed with his. 'This is my story—I have to write it. I can provide a firsthand report—I was the person who found her.' She closed her eyes for an instant, as though reliving those traumatic moments. 'I'll have the rough ready before you have to leave for the Town Council meeting. You and Frank go over it, tell me what's missing.'

Alone again, she sat immobile, staring into space. Chuck had warned them that the town would be deluged with news people from all over the country now. Westwood would be turned upside down. All of a sudden they'd have traffic problems.

Four murders in ten days. That was fodder for the tabloids. So the first was solved, Sandy conceded. Still, she couldn't erase from her brain the conviction that all four were connected.

Had anyone contacted Mrs Adams' son vacationing in East Hampton, her daughter in California? Jamie knew both—but the police must have taken care of it. With modern technology they could track down almost anyone. She tensed, winced. Almost anyone—except a killer who'd struck three times in Westwood.

Close to 3 P.M. Jamie walked into the office with a brown-paper bag and two mugs of coffee.

'You didn't bother with lunch,' he accused her, then managed a wry smile. 'Neither did I. It's "break" time.'

'I'm hungry,' she admitted in surprise. 'I didn't realize it until I smelled the coffee.'

'I called Collins Security about a fast installation at the house. We aren't the only ones thinking along those lines. They said they'll pencil us in for the Thursday a week after next. Who in this town bothered with a security system up till now? Only businesses.'

Sandy's hand—about to reach for half of her turkey sandwich—froze in midair. 'I just remembered. Beth

McDonald's funeral is being held tomorrow afternoon. The *Sentinel* should send flowers.'

'I'll ask Gloria to take care of it,' Jamie soothed her.

Sandy's throat tightened. 'And now Sara Adams' son and daughter will be making funeral arrangements for their mother. It's unreal.'

Chuck strode into the room with the air of a man barely containing his fury. 'I've heard everything now! I just spoke with Nora Lieberman. Some big-city tabloid contacted her to write about her mother's murder. Offered a bundle. The title they suggested—"The Deadly Secret in Westwood, New York—and Who Will Be The Next Victim?"'

'It would help if we knew the answer.' Jamie pounded on the desk with one fist.

'Oh yes, the tabloids will be pouring into town,' Sandy predicted. 'It's going to be a—'

'They're here already,' Chuck broke in, bristling with contempt. 'At least one. I kid Bernice about reading those creepy supermarket tabloids, but she's addicted. She brought one home yesterday from the IGA, didn't show it to me until this morning. She didn't want to give me an ulcer over dinner, she said.'

Sandy bristled. 'What did it say? All in purple prose?'

'Pretty melodramatic,' Chuck admitted. 'But you know— it's uncanny. They're hinting, too, at a secret link between Adrienne's murder and the three others. Of course, they make it sound as though Adrienne wasn't just a hard-working, dedicated small-town newspaper publisher. She was a modern-day Hearst, and her murder was a cover for dark and dirty secrets—and now these other murders. To keep the secret hidden, they imply.'

Jamie swore under his breath. 'Forget about that now. The Town Council's meeting in a few hours. They're letting me talk.' He took a deep breath. 'They've got to go along with a local sales tax to provide Ward with funds to stay operating here in Westwood.'

179

'A Council meeting on a Saturday night,' Chuck grumbled. 'Not everybody will be happy about that.'

'The meeting is at 7:30,' Jamie told him. 'If we hear good news, it'll make tomorrow morning's paper.' *But the best of news can't wash away the horrors that have engulfed Westwood.*

'Why so early?'

'They figure it'll be a long night,' Jamie said. 'I'll be there,' he reiterated. 'I fought hard for the privilege. Some figured I had no place there.'

'In a few weeks you might be a member of the Town Council.' Sandy defied such thinking. The election was almost forgotten these past ten days.

'A lot can happen between now and election day,' Jamie warned, 'and I was a late-comer.'

'Standing in for your mother,' Chuck pointed out. 'That will count for a lot of votes.'

'You'll be the youngest member of the Town Council. It's time we had a young voice,' Sandy declared.

'Campaigning will take a huge upswing once we're past the current insanity. The *Sentinel* will be a strong voice for you, Jamie. If I were a betting man,' Chuck said, 'I'd lay everything I had on you.'

'I'm sending somebody over to the IGA,' Sandy said in sudden determination. 'I want to see that tabloid rag.'

Twenty-Six

Andrew sprawled in the lounge chair he'd commandeered for his bedroom, his laptop across his knees. He scowled—the book proposal he'd promised to rush to his agent was slow in taking shape. He heard the sharp ring of a phone somewhere in the house.

He aborted his normal reaction to leap to reply. There was no extension in his bedroom, only in Jamie's.

'Andrew!' Martha called from the foot of the stairs. 'Phone call for you.'

'Tell them to hold on,' he yelled back. 'I'll pick it up in Jamie's room.'

He hurried down the hall to Jamie's room, strode inside, picked up. 'Hello.' He noted the framed photo of Sandy on the night table, the photo of Sandy and Jamie on the dresser.

'Andy, why haven't you got back to me?' The querulous voice of Carl Davis, the managing editor of *American Weekly,* assaulted him.

'Hell, man, don't you understand my situation?' He hated having anybody call him Andy—he always made that clear. His name was Andrew—as in Andrew Carnegie. Carl Davis knew that, damn him. 'I've only been home a little over a week—I just buried my mother. Give me a chance to get my act together.'

'We've done everything we can to refute these stories about you fabricating your reports from Iraq. It's becoming a real flap. Give me facts, man!'

'I'm sitting on a hot story right here,' Andrew shot back.

181

So Jamie wouldn't allow him to do an article for the *Sentinel*. He could do a whole series for *American Weekly*. 'Haven't you heard about the serial killer on a rampage here in Westwood?'

'I never heard of Westwood until you came along,' Carl shot back, but Andrew sensed his antenna was shooting high. 'I may have heard a line about it on the TV news,' he conceded. Over-casual. *The old boy's sniffing like a bloodhound after a 'possum.* 'You know, when news is light—and they want to report something beside the war in Iraq—these items pop up.'

'This is big, Carl.' Excitement spiraled in Andrew. 'Three women have been murdered in this town in the past few days, and nobody has a clue to who's guilty—'

'You said your mother had been murdered,' Carl said with an air of sudden recall. 'Any connection?'

'Not that we can see—but three other women have been murdered since,' he reiterated, paused. 'All three longtime friends—and close to my mother. They've discovered who killed my mother. Some teenage retard. But the three other women were murdered by somebody too shrewd to be caught. The police don't have a clue.'

'Move fast,' Carl ordered, 'while the case is hot. What about my shipping up a photographer?'

'No need. I can arrange for a photo spread right here in town.' One of the *Sentinel's* photographers would grab at a side job with big-city pay-off. 'I'll e-mail an opening article late tonight. It's right here for the picking. Scrap something unimportant—run it in the new issue.'

Off the phone Andrew stretched out on Jamie's bed to plot an article. Not the tabloid scene, he cautioned himself—high horror, with class. He was intrigued by the signature bit. The lollipop left on the bed of each murdered woman. This was a master murderer.

His gaze focused on the photograph of Sandy on the night table. He was conscious of arousal. He thought back through the years—the way Jamie came on to great chicks, and how *he* always won them over.

Jamie never learned to turn on the charm full wattage. Jamie left that to him.

He was making inroads with Sandy. She wasn't sure what was happening to her. Outwardly, he and Jamie were carbon copies—inside was a different story. He was adventurous, took chances, was eager to gamble for high stakes. Jamie was so damn serious about everything—no taking chances. Women loved men who took chances. That was when he felt fully alive.

I'm a foreign correspondent, putting my life on the line. Jamie runs a small-town newspaper. He's satisfied with that.

I felt Sandy's reactions when we were alone in the kitchen the night before last. Another couple of minutes and I'd have had her in my arms—and loving it. But then her conscience kicked in. Hell, she's too much of a woman for Jamie.

Jamie checked his watch. The Council meeting would probably start late—it always did. But he meant to be there at 7:30 P.M. sharp. Should he have worn a suit and tie? No, that would say he was nervous about this meeting. Approach it with an optimistic flair.

He left his office, crossed to hover in Sandy's doorway. 'It's a quarter after seven. I'm hitting the road.'

'What about dinner?' Sandy was shoving papers into a briefcase. *Will there ever be a time when we go home without work?*

'I'll eat after the meeting. Tell Martha to leave something for me.' He grinned. 'I'll probably need it by then.'

'Good luck.' Sandy managed a shaky smile, held up crossed fingers.

'I'll need it. Go home,' he scolded her, 'this is Saturday night.' His face softened. 'We should be doing something cool. Not chasing around on business.'

'Our time will come.' Sandy pushed back her chair, rose to her feet.

'I'll walk you out to your car.' *What's that guarded look in her eyes? Is she unsure about our future together?*

'Make the Town Council understand they can't afford to miss out on this deal with Ward,' Sandy said with a surge of urgency. 'So it'll cost us all something—but in the long run it'll be worth it. I shudder at what this town could become if Westwood Manufacturing closes down here, sends all those jobs to China.'

'I'll put up a fight,' Jamie promised, reached for her hand as they headed for the parking area. No need to try to hide their feelings for each other from the staff. Everybody knew by now.

Or is Sandy having second thoughts?

Driving through town, Jamie was conscious of more than normal activity along Main Street. His hands tightened on the wheel as he noted the out-of-town license plates. News crews from New York City, Boston, Philadelphia. He saw TV vans. People in Westwood would wake up to an invaded town in the morning, he warned himself. Nobody would be happy except the hotels and the restaurant owners. But he'd known it was only a matter of time before this invasion mushroomed.

He arrived at the Town Council meeting room at 7:30 P.M. sharp. Only Ted Newman had arrived. He sprawled in a chair at the head of the conference table.

'Hi,' Newman greeted him. *He looks depressed. What's up?* 'We're the only ones who can tell time.'

'Did you get around to more private talks with each member?' Jamie strived to sound casual.

'It's like I told you—they're split right down the middle.' Newman leaned forward, clasping his hands on the table. 'You mention raising taxes and right away you're asking for trouble.'

Jamie sat down. 'If we don't put this through for Ward

a thousand jobs leave town. The union seems set to play ball. I talked with Bill Thompson. He's aware of some grumbling, but he's fairly certain the referendum will give the go-ahead. The union asked for more time—Ward gave it to them.'

Newman gazed at him with curiosity. 'How the hell can you work with Ward when you know his rotten kid killed your mother?'

Jamie took a deep breath. 'It isn't easy. But we have to be realistic. His kid is retarded—he has no concept of what he did, other than his determination to please his father. It was one of those tragic mistakes—and there'll always be anger in my heart that it cost my mother her life. But Mom was devoted to this town. She'd want to save those jobs. That was the major project at the *Sentinel* before—before she died.'

'This is going to be one tough fight,' Newman warned then fell silent because three Council members were walking into the meeting room. Cars could be heard pulling into the parking area.

In ten minutes the meeting was in full swing. Jamie listened to the arguments pro and con, conscious that his presence here was resented. He fought apprehension. Voices grew heated—loud and menacing.

'Why should the whole town pay to keep Noel Ward in business?' Bruce Johnston demanded. 'Why should—'

'Because it'll save this town from becoming another "depressed area," ' Jamie interrupted, ignoring the fact that he was not to speak until the members of the Council all had their say. 'The union members are being asked to take a cut in wages and benefits. From what we hear, that's going to be okayed. If Westwood Manufacturing is outsourced, a lot of people in this town will be out of work. Every business in town—clothing stores, furniture stores, you name it—will suffer. This doesn't just affect the workers and their families. It affects all of us. The *Sentinel* will be in bad shape. Its advertising will fall to nothing. Circulation will drop because people won't spend money on a newspaper. The banks will foreclose on houses when workers won't be able to meet their mortgage payments. We have no choice—we have to keep Westwood Manufacturing in business!'

Jamie leaned back in his chair—exhausted. Total silence in the room for a moment.

'All right,' Ted Newman said. 'Let's have a vote. I'm sorry, Jamie, you'll have to wait outside.'

Twenty-Seven

Jamie paced in the small foyer off the meeting room. The voices inside were loud, bellicose. Only now and then could he make out snatches of what was being argued. No point in kidding himself. If the Town Council didn't go along, then the union membership would vote against wage and benefit cuts. There had to be cooperation across the board.

Jamie paused, strained to hear what was being said in the meeting room. A quietness pervaded now. His heart began to pound.

Newman is calling for a vote of the Council members. Here it comes. Whether a thousand jobs are saved—or Westwood is about to become a distressed area.

A few minutes later the door opened. Newman beckoned to him. Jamie strode into the room. A swift glance about the faces of the Council members told him nothing.

'We've arrived at a conclusion,' Newman said, almost casual—though Jamie knew the battle he'd staged. 'If you can come to us with confirmation that the union membership agrees to cuts and benefits—for a specified period of time—then the Council is prepared to vote for a temporary tax to raise funds to help Westwood Manufacturing to continue operations here in Westwood.'

'The referendum is scheduled for next Tuesday.' Relief surged through Jamie. 'You'll have your answer then.'

Walking into the foyer at close to 9 P.M., Sandy saw Andrew coming down the stairs.

187

'Hi.' He lifted a hand in greeting. 'In time for a fashionably late dinner.'

'I'm famished,' Sandy admitted.

'Dinner in Iraq could be anywhere from 8 P.M. to midnight—and we ate because we were hungry. A hot cheeseburger was considered gourmet food.'

'You haven't had dinner yet?' Only Martha would put up with their insane hours. Or contrive to deal with them.

'I was working, didn't think of it until Martha yelled up to me that it couldn't be held up much more than another five minutes—so "you'd better get your butt to the table." '

'When Martha says that, we obey.' *Why do I feel uncomfortable being alone with Andrew this way? He's going to be my brother-in-law.* 'To the dining room.'

'When Jamie and I were growing up, I remember how Martha always considered Saturday night dinner special.'

'She never stopped believing that.' *Jamie will be tied up at the Town-Council meeting forever. I don't want to have dinner alone with Andrew. Not when he looks at me like that. Jamie and I never told him about our getting married— but he must know by now.*

'Saturday nights—when Jamie and I were kids—Martha broke her rules and came up with some fantastic dessert,' Andrew recalled. 'The rest of the week dessert was some fruit concoction or a low-fat ice-cream or yogurt deal.'

'Is Claire coming down?' Sandy was ambivalent: A third at the dinner table would be fine—but she and Jamie were in the doghouse in Claire's book.

'No deal.' Andrew was somber. 'Another murder was tough for her to handle. I had lunch with her in her room, and then she decided to take a nap. I think Martha slipped something into her tea. She'll probably sleep for hours.' He sighed. 'This craziness . . . '

'Driving home tonight was like driving through a ghost town. Everybody's reeling from shock again. Almost no cars moving. Some shops closed early.' Sandy slid into her regular place at the table—which Martha always set for four, just in case.

Andrew sat opposite her. His eyes were sending disturbing messages. *Why isn't Jamie home by now? What's happening at the Town-Council meeting? I hope he's putting up a fight. Andrew would*, she thought involuntarily, and was brushed with guilt.

'Jamie and I gave you a rough time when you were little,' Andrew reminisced. 'Teased you all the time—but then you were so adorable when you got angry with us.' Under the table his foot reached out to touch hers.

At first she though it was accidental. He was tall and long-legged. But his eyes told her differently. *Was this what Karen had meant when she talked about the fierce competition between identical twins?* She felt a flicker of panic. *Why am I reacting this way to Andrew? It's Jamie I love.*

She shifted her foot away from Andrew's, ignored the gesture. She smiled in relief as Martha came into the room with two plates heaped high.

'This ain't just a plain salad,' Martha told them. 'Just look at all those shrimps—sautéed in white wine. And where is Jamie?' she demanded. 'He loves shrimps.'

'He's at that special meeting at the Town Council,' Sandy told her. Martha must know that. She knew everything that went on in this house.

'Have your salad. Then I'm serving the pork tenderloin if Jamie's home or not.' Martha was grim. 'Some things don't wait. It'll be good later—but it won't be great. The broccoli will be a disaster if he doesn't show up in the next five minutes.' She hurried back to the kitchen.

Now Andrew made a point of being friendly but impersonal. *He's sensitive—he recognizes limits.* He became the charming raconteur, regaled her with amusing stories about his experiences in Iraq.

'Of course, it wasn't all fun.' He gazed into space, as

though recalling painful skirmishes. 'I was embedded with a company—I saw everything they saw.' *Jamie's wrong in believing that correspondent who claimed Andrew did his reporting from safe hotel lobbies and bars.*

Martha came back into the dining room, began to clear the remains of the pork from the table.

'Martha, what about dessert?' Andrew asked in mock impatience.

'It's coming. Be cool.' She grunted in disapproval. 'With all the leftovers in this house we should have a couple of dogs and a cat.' But they could have no pets, Sandy remembered, because Claire was wildly allergic to both dogs and cats. Her face softened in recall. Like her, Jamie adored everything on four feet.

'I picked up this mutt in Mosul,' Andrew said quietly. 'He'd been following me around. He was so skinny—just skin and bones. I kept feeding him. I tried to figure out how I could bring him back home with me.' He sighed. Martha glared at him. *No dogs in this house because of Claire's allergies.* 'Then we were leaving town. He was running about twenty feet ahead of me, chasing after something—I wasn't sure what. There was an explosion. He was gone.'

'Poor little guy,' Sandy commiserated.

'Well, it's about time.' Martha was staring at the entrance to the dining room. Her face reflected deep affection along with reproach. Jamie was home.

'Martha, you've been doing another Saturday special.' Jamie sniffed in appreciation. 'A roast?'

'Pork tenderloin. It would have been better half an hour ago, but you'll have to make do.'

'What's for dessert?' Andrew asked, pantomiming his anticipation.

'It's coming!' Martha was hurrying from the dining room.

Sandy's eyes clung to Jamie. 'What happened at the meeting?' It was all she'd thought about for the past two hours.

'We've got a good chance of seeing the town come through.' He sat beside her. 'The Council will go along if the union accepts wage and benefit cuts—and Bill Thompson is ninety percent sure the membership will agree.'

'What about the gang that was fighting it?' Andrew was curious. 'Are they going to get nasty?'

'Thompson said not to worry—he can deal with them.'

'Any news about the Adams murder?' Andrew asked. 'Any briefing from the police department?'

'Just that one briefing earlier today.' Jamie frowned. 'They concede now that some link exists between the three murders, but they haven't been able to figure out what it could be.' He grunted in exasperation. 'Anymore than we can.'

'Jamie, break down the meeting for us,' Sandy urged. 'Tell us what happened.'

'I was early as usual . . .'

Sandy and Andrew listened while Jamie reported on the meeting, then Martha charged into the room with a laden tray. Salad with shrimps and a huge serving of pork tenderloin for Jamie, and three portions of tiramisu.

'You eat everything else before you hit dessert,' she warned Jamie. Sandy and Andrew were already tackling theirs with relish.

'Yes, ma'am,' he promised and reached for his fork. *This is the way she used to tease him and Andrew when they were little kids. I love the relationship between Jamie and Martha. Sometimes I think she's cold to Andrew—*

Martha was all at once somber. 'I was cooking and I didn't have a chance to watch the evening news. Are the police coming up with any suspects in the Adams case?'

'They're making the usual noises.' Andrew shrugged. 'Who would want to murder her? The way I hear it, she was always fighting for some cause in town.'

'Like Mom.' Jamie's face was etched in fresh grief.

'They were four fine women. We know who killed your

mother,' Sandy's eyes turned from Jamie to Andrew, 'but who harbored some vicious hate for Dottie Lieberman, Beth McDonald, and Sara Adams?' She felt a fresh surge of frustration. 'The same fiend killed them.'

'You're asking who hated those three ladies—and your Mom?' Martha grunted. 'That's easy.' Three pairs of startled eyes zeroed in on her. The atmosphere electric. 'Eugene Matthews.'

Andrew abandoned his tiramisu. Sandy and Jamie seemed frozen in place. 'Who's Eugene Matthews?' Andrew asked.

'He used to run that nice family-style restaurant at the edge of town. Gene's Place. It closed up almost three years ago,' Martha said. 'But until just before it closed, the four ladies used to have dinner there every Friday evening for ages. And then they stopped going.'

'Why?' Jamie probed.

'The food fell off. Folks said Gene was hitting the bottle. After the four ladies stopped going there Gene was sure they talked around town. He finally had to close up, took a job cooking at that diner on Winston Road. He made noisy comments about the "four witches", claimed they'd run him out of business.'

'In a way,' Jamie seemed to be searching for words, 'it could have been a copycat deal. Mom was out of the way so he figured he'd finish the job, take out the other three. Martha, why didn't you bring this up before?'

'I never thought of it until just now,' she said tartly.

'Who's that detective you're always talking to?' Andrew frowned in thought. 'Bronson,' he said before Jamie or Sandy could reply. 'Let's take this to Bronson.'

'Right away!' Sandy prodded. 'We don't want to wake up tomorrow morning to hear about another murder.' She turned to Jamie. 'This can't wait.'

Were three wonderful women murdered because of a psychotic's assumption they'd ruined his business?

Twenty-Eight

'I have Bronson's card somewhere.' Jamie reached into his pocket, came up with the card, dinner forgotten.

'Wouldn't it be more practical to take Martha over to the police station and have her give a statement?' Andrew pushed back his chair. 'I'll go with you, Martha.'

'No!' She was unnerved. 'I ain't going to the police!'

'They'll want a statement. Hey, you'll be a heroine,' he coaxed her.

'I don't want to be a heroine,' Martha tossed back.

'If this Eugene Matthews is a murderer, you want to help catch him,' Sandy intervened softly. 'Before he kills again . . .'

'Can't we do it first thing in the morning?' Martha's eyes exuded alarm.

'The police should be on this lead immediately. Before he strikes again. They'll be grateful for the tip,' Jamie encouraged.

Martha seemed to be reaching for inner strength. 'I'll go now,' she agreed. 'With Sandy. If Miss Claire wakes up and rings her little bell, you go up to her,' she told Andrew. 'Just tell her I fell asleep real early tonight.'

Why did she insist on going with me instead of Andrew or Jamie? But she knew the answer. Martha meant for Andrew to be there in the event Claire summoned her. Martha—who knew everything that happened in the house— was aware that Jamie and she were out of favor with Claire.

On the short drive to the police station, Sandy struggled

to convince her this would not be traumatic. 'Martha, this is important. You're providing the police with a definite lead.'

'Maybe he ain't guilty.' Martha was unsure now. 'Maybe he's just a loudmouth, like that Bert O'Reilly.'

'We don't know that he's guilty,' Sandy conceded. 'Let the police dig for the truth. This town needs answers.'

At the police station they were directed to a conference room where Detective Bronson waited for them.

'Don't be nervous,' Bronson told Martha after introductions, 'just tell us what you know.'

With candid reluctance Martha repeated what she'd told the others earlier. *Why is she so upset about this? She wants the killer caught. Is she afraid he'll get to her before he's in custody?* 'Maybe I'm jumping too fast,' she concluded, anxious now. 'I mean, lots of people say things they don't mean.'

'We're not convicting the guy,' Bronson soothed her. 'We'll check him out. Tonight.' *Before he can kill again— if he's the killer.* 'If he's clean, we drop him from the suspect list. No harm done. But if he killed three women, we want him.'

Sandy and Martha returned to the house. Jamie or Andrew—or both of them—had cleared the dining table, put up coffee. They sat in the living room with coffee mugs within reach and watched CNN.

'Hey, it wasn't so bad, was it?' Andrew joshed as Martha and Sandy walked into the living room.

'I don't like police stations.' Martha was grim. 'Miss Claire still asleep?' Her face softened. 'I figured she might sleep through the night.'

'What did you slip in her tea?' Andrew pretended gruffness.

'What the doctor told me,' Martha snapped, turning to leave the room. 'Wash those mugs before you go to bed. We don't need no roaches in the kitchen.'

'Shouldn't we be heading back to the paper?' Sandy's eyes met Jamie's.

'New headline for tomorrow morning's edition?' Andrew's smile was indulgent.

'We can't make any accusations,' Jamie said, 'but people in this town will be more comfortable to know the police are following up a fresh lead.'

Sandy sat in silence beside Jamie—both in deep thought as they drove through the near-empty streets. Her mind was in turmoil. She was conscious of hostile currents in the house the past few days. Like a cluster of dark clouds threatening to unleash a storm at any moment.

It disturbed her that Claire was furious with Jamie and her. Claire had said nothing more since that brief encounter about Jamie's refusing to run Andrew's article, yet her anger seemed to permeate the household. It was a house divided, Jamie, Martha and herself on one side—Claire and Andrew on the other.

She was also unnerved by the simmering hostility between Jamie and Andrew. Adrienne had talked about how close they'd been during the growing-up years, yet now they were barely civil to each other. No, she corrected herself with painful honesty. Jamie was hostile towards Andrew. Andrew pretended to ignore Jamie.

'I realize we have a rough night ahead of us,' Jamie said, apology seeping into his voice, 'but I'm famished. I didn't get around to eating at the house—not when Martha came up with that pronouncement about Matthews. Let's make a quick stop at that all-night diner on Hamilton Road. Okay?'

'Sure.' They'd been through these quick front-page changes before. 'We can deal.'

The diner was near deserted at this hour. A waitress ambled over to take their orders. Without bothering to consult the menu, Jamie settled for a turkey sandwich and coffee. Feeling compelled to order something in addition to coffee, Sandy asked for fruit salad. Involuntarily her eyes sought the wall clock.

'We won't take long,' Jamie promised. His foot sought hers under the table. She remembered Andrew taking this same approach and felt an odd guilt that she recalled this. 'I was thinking,' he said suddenly. 'I know we have to wait a respectable period before our wedding, but you could wear an engagement ring. Couldn't you?'

She was startled by the wistful glow in his eyes. 'I suppose so.' She hesitated. 'I mean, people won't be surprised.' And it wouldn't be disrespectful to Adrienne's memory.

'Before I left for Iraq, Mom gave me the key to her box at the bank, along with instructions that it should be in joint ownership. The ring that Dad gave her when they became engaged is in the box. Mom wanted you to have it.' His eyes searched hers. 'Will you wear it?'

'Jamie, yes,' she said with sudden intensity. If she wore an engagement ring from Jamie, Andrew would back away. She wouldn't feel these disconcerting thoughts—

'The bank's closed for the weekend, of course—but I'll get there early next week.' He was elated.

They ate quickly, returned to the car. The night was overcast again, unseasonably cool. She hunched her shoulders in reproach.

'You're cold,' Jamie said and reached in the darkness to pull her close.

For a few minutes, she told herself defiantly, they'd forget everything else.

Jamie swung into the parking area at the *Sentinel*.

'We weren't entirely wrong in our conviction the other murders were, somehow, related to Mom's—if this Matthews character is guilty. He saw Mom mowed down that way, and something clicked in his sick brain. He went after Mom's three friends.'

'*If* he's guilty . . .'

Jamie pulled to a stop, hesitated. 'You're not convinced?'

'No. There's no real evidence. It could have happened that way—but I don't know.'

'We'll know fast enough.' He uttered a long, painful sigh. 'Let this insanity be over. Let us get on with our lives.'

'If what we suspect is right, then the—' Sandy hesitated a moment, 'then the killing spree is over.' She reached for the door on the passenger side. 'Let's settle down to business.' But she remained immobile in her seat, her mind charging ahead. 'What can we say in tomorrow morning's edition?' she challenged. The Sunday papers were to hit the newsstands and the delivery circuit in another seven hours. 'What do we know?'

'Readers will feel some relief that the police are questioning a new suspect. No name, though,' Jamie stipulated. 'Not until he's held for arraignment. All we can say is that the police have a new suspect who held a grudge against all three murdered women—and was vocal about it. He has a history of violence.'

'It'll be tight to reset the front page,' Sandy hedged.

'We've done it before. Let's move.' Jamie opened the door on his side. 'We have work to do.'

Walking in the darkness of the parking area to the *Sentinel's* entrance, Jamie reached for Sandy's hand. 'We'll work up a small article,' he emphasized again. 'But front page.'

'I'll check the records—see if we have anything else on Eugene Matthews,' Sandy said.

'Let people go to church tomorrow morning—or whatever they do on Sunday mornings—and feel a little less anxious. With luck, they'll be able to leave their doors unlocked again, go to bed without fear of what they might encounter in the course of the night.'

'It seems so absurd that three women could be dead because of a suspicion they said nasty things about Eugene Matthews.' Sandy recoiled from this possibility.

'You feel let down,' Jamie sympathized. 'You were

focused on the police unmasking some ugly, dark secret.'

'I have these vibes.' She shrugged. 'Maybe just a reporter's overactive imagination.'

The *Sentinel* office floor was late-night quiet, only essential areas lighted.

'I should alert the Composing Room,' Jamie began, then froze for an instant. 'What is Chuck doing here at this hour?'

'What took you so long?' Chuck jeered. 'I was just ready to hit the hay when I got this frantic call from a woman who cleaned our offices for several years. She—'

'Eugene Matthews' wife,' Jamie suddenly realized. 'Rosie Matthews.'

Chuck nodded. 'She was almost hysterical. She said the cops just came into the house with a warrant. They took her husband away. He's a bad scene,' he said in distaste. 'Four years ago, not long after she married the creep and stopped working, she called me. She didn't know what to do. He was beating her every night. I went with her to the cops, got a restraining order. But what do you know? Two weeks later she moved back in with him. But what's this business about his being the latest suspect?'

Jamie reported what Martha had told the family. 'At the time he was losing the restaurant he complained all over town how Mom and her friends had bad-mouthed him, blamed the loss of business on them.' Jamie flinched. 'The whole ugly scene comes back to me now. It was about three years ago. I went to Rosie and told her to warn her husband he'd be sued if he didn't stop making accusations. After that he faded into the background. I thought it was past history.'

'The police will need to come up with some solid evidence to convict him,' Chuck warned. 'I'll take any bet that Rosie will lie for him, insist he was at home with her on each of the three nights. Let's pray the cops find enough to convince a jury.'

'If he's guilty—' Sandy felt uncomfortable. *Are we jumping too fast?* 'Perhaps he's just a stupid loud-mouth—like the O'Reilly character.'

'Let's dig into the files,' Jamie decided. 'Let's see what else comes up on Eugene Matthews.'

'Don't dig too long,' Chuck said. 'We have a Sunday front page to reset.'

Twenty-Nine

S andy came awake slowly. Aware of rain pounding against
the windows. A chill in the air. Her alarm hadn't gone
off, she realized in sudden dismay. She was fully awake
now. Ten minutes past 10 A.M.! Now she remembered. This
was Sunday. She and Jamie had been at the paper until
close to 3 A.M., had agreed to sleep late this morning. No
urgent need for their presence. The *Sentinel* staff could
manage.

Totally awake now, she tossed aside the coverlet, reached
for her cell phone—always on her night table on the chance
there'd be some *Sentinel* emergency. By now Detective
Bronson's cell phone number was engraved on her brain.

She punched it in, waited. *Should I be calling him at this
hour on a Sunday? But like the crew at the paper, he must
be accustomed to calls at odd hours.*

'Bronson here.' He sounded as though the call had awakened him.

'Detective Bronson, I'm sorry to be calling on a Sunday.
We're working on tomorrow morning's edition of the
Sentinel. If Eugene Matthews is being arraigned, we
should—'

'Tomorrow evening,' Bronson broke in. 'He's pleading
not guilty. He's claiming he'd been out drinking with
buddies. That they left him on a bench on the Village Green
when he passed out well after midnight. He says he woke
up around 3 A.M., dragged himself home. We have enough
to hold him for arraignment.'

'Then we can identify him by name?'

'Be our guests. But thus far evidence is weak,' he cautioned. 'Sufficient for an arraignment, but a guilty verdict? We don't know.'

'Thanks so much. We'll check again later, if we may.'

'You won't have anything else until arraignment.' Bronson was brisk. 'We'll talk then.'

Sandy heard a soft click at the other end. The conversation was over. All right, shower, dress, head for the paper. As usual, Frank would be in charge of the Sunday desk. But she ought to dig into the files, try to come up with more background on Matthews.

She pulled a turquoise cardigan from a dresser drawer to wear with her muted green slacks and T-shirt. All at once a wave of self-consciousness swept over her. Andrew said she should always wear turquoise. *'It does marvelous things for your eyes.'*

She left her bedroom, rushed downstairs. Was Jamie awake yet?

Arriving in the foyer she heard voices in the dining room. Jamie was awake, talking with Andrew. She tensed. Encounters between Jamie and Andrew could become contentious. Again she remembered Karen's words: *'Identical twins are so close—yet astonishingly competitive.'*

'Come on, Jamie,' Andrew scoffed, 'these small-town cops are never going to solve these murders. They wouldn't have solved Mom's if Noel Ward hadn't come forward that way.'

'We've got a solid police force,' Jamie shot back. 'I'm not saying they'll bring the right guy to trial in a matter of days or even weeks. This Eugene Matthews may be the killer—we don't know. This has been a brutal period—one murder after another this way. In time Bronson and his crew will have the killer behind bars.'

'Shall we bet?' Andrew derided. 'No,' he drawled. 'Not good old, reliable Jamie. You don't bet.'

Sandy walked into the living room. The contentious moment was dispelled.

'Martha's a little grumpy this morning,' Andrew warned. Cool, laid back. Jamie was uptight. 'I don't think she liked being dragged to the police station last night.'

'How are you doing with your book proposal?' Jamie asked Andrew—making it sound almost a challenge, Sandy thought. 'You'll be chasing down to New York soon to talk it over with your agent.' *Is he trying to tell Andrew to get out of town? Does he think Andrew will come between the two of us? That's crazy!*

'You can have waffles topped with strawberries or strawberry pancakes,' Martha announced from the doorway. 'I ain't runnin' a restaurant this morning.'

'Waffles will be great,' Sandy said. *Martha's still upset about going to the police. Is she afraid Matthews will try to hurt her for this?*

'If you want more coffee, Andrew, have it fast,' Martha ordered. 'Miss Claire will be downstairs in a few minutes. She said you're taking her to church this morning.'

'Right, Martha. And I've had plenty of coffee.'

'You want more coffee, Jamie, come and get it,' Martha told him and hurried from the dining room.

'I went over to talk with Rosie Matthews about an hour ago. I woke early,' he explained to Sandy. 'From habit, I guess. Chuck was concerned that she didn't seem to understand that if her husband goes to trial, the court will appoint an attorney to represent him. They can't afford attorney fees. I figured I should put her mind at ease on that score.'

'And it was a cagey way to interview her,' Andrew interpreted. 'Smart thinking.' He took a final swig from his mug, rose to his feet. 'I'll go wait for Grandma in the foyer.'

'Rosie's upset,' Jamie told Sandy, his expression troubled.

'That's natural, Jamie.'

'She's scared to death at the prospect of appearing in court—'

'She knows she'll be called as a defense witness,' Sandy pointed out. 'She's Matthews' alibi. He'll insist he was home with her when Sara Adams was murdered.'

Jamie took a deep breath, exhaled. 'She admitted to me that Matthews came home after 3 A.M. on Friday—or technically 3 A.M. Saturday morning. She's afraid not to cover for him, but terrified of lying on the witness stand. The police have a motive. If Rosie tells the truth, they'll know he had the opportunity.' Jamie seemed to be in some painful inner debate. 'We'll have to see how it plays out.'

Thirty

Driving away from the house, Sandy and Jamie focused on the referendum, scheduled for Tuesday.

'I can't see how it can go wrong,' Jamie said, but Sandy heard an undertone of wariness in his voice. *He's always so realistic—like Adrienne.* 'Noel Ward agreed not to make any decision about outsourcing until the referendum's over. Thompson is optimistic, but we won't know for sure how the workers feel until the voting's counted. The Town Council has agreed to what they're calling the "Westwood Manufacturing Rescue Tax." Along with the proposed cut in wages and benefits, that should keep the company in town.'

'Your mother would be so happy to know the town was able to stop the outsourcing.' *But because of all her efforts she was murdered.*

'Don't crow until it's definite.' Jamie slowed down. Sunday-morning traffic was heavy, in a town where church-going was a way of life.

Sandy gazed at small groups gathered in conversation along Main Street. 'They're all talking about Eugene Matthews,' she surmised. 'Even before this, he would never win a popularity contest in this town.'

'I worry that people are so anxious to know the killer is not out on the street and preparing to kill again that they might rush to judgment.'

'You think he's innocent?'

'I know how many people on Death Row are proven

innocent years or decades after sentencing,' he hedged. 'I don't want to feel that we're responsible for condemning an innocent man.'

'You want to see something beyond circumstantial evidence.' Sandy was somber. 'And you're right.'

'What do we know that can be proven beyond a reasonable doubt?'

'We know that he lied about being home with his wife,' Sandy began. 'We know he talked around town about his rage against your mother and her three closest friends. We—'

'His lawyer will question his drinking buddies,' Jamie broke in. 'When did they drop him off at the Village Green? Could he have come out of a drunken stupor to go and kill Sara Adams? Did he have the opportunity to kill Dottie Lieberman and Beth McDonald?'

'His court-appointed attorney won't be set until tomorrow morning. In the meantime, let's dig,' Sandy said with resolve. 'Let's see if we can come up with solid facts.'

'We'll do that.' Jamie exuded determination. 'We'll check the taverns where Matthews and his buddies might have been drinking. Discover what time they left, what condition he was in. We're reporters from the *Sentinel*—people will talk to us.'

'You're friendly with people at the coroner's office,' Sandy pursued. 'Find out what time they figure Sara Adams was murdered.'

'The coroner's office isn't giving that information to us. And it's—'

'And it's Sunday,' she anticipated Jamie's reminder, 'but you can make a call to somebody and come up with an answer.' *People trust Jamie—the way they trusted Adrienne. It would be good to know the police have the killer. We could begin to live again.*

'Martha's worried that she pinpointed Matthews, that he's being held for arraignment because of her. She spoke without thinking of possible consequences.'

Julie Ellis

'Jamie, why are you and Martha so insecure in this?' Sandy protested. 'Bronson is convinced Matthews will be held for trial. If he's not guilty, that'll come out.'

'You said Bronson has doubts, too. He told you, "We have enough to hold him for arraignment. I don't know about a conviction." '

'Whatever we dig up, we give to Bronson. You're hoping for conclusive proof that Matthews is a fiendish serial killer. Or proof that he's innocent.' Sandy's mind charged into high gear. 'Let's talk with Frank. He'll know at what sleazy tavern Matthews and his buddies would have been drinking on Friday night.'

Frank sent them off to Pete's Tavern. 'It's that dive on Lombard Street—they'll eat greasy cheeseburgers and guzzle cheap beer.'

When they arrived, Sunday brunch was being served to half-a-dozen seedy patrons. The aroma of sizzling bacon blended with that of cheap beer. Jamie's eyes swept about the room. A short, chubby man in a white apron spied them, moved towards them with an expansive mile.

'That's the owner, Nick Spano,' Jamie told Sandy. 'He'd do anything for Mom. She saved his hide when a dirty politician was out to close him.'

'Hey, Jamie, what brings you into this neck of the woods?' His smile admiring as it rested on Sandy. 'I know it ain't the grub.'

'We need some info, Nick.'

'Sit down, let's have coffee and talk. The coffee ain't bad.'

'This is Sandy Taylor. Sandy, Nick Spano. His father opened this place before any of us was born.'

'Yeah, my old man was Pete.' Nick gestured to a waitress to bring them coffee. 'So, what do you want to know?' he asked Jamie.

'Was Eugene Matthews here on Friday evening?'

'Yeah, Gene and his pals were here Friday. They get

206

noisy after a while—I throw them out. And that Gene, he was drunk as a skunk.'

'What time was this?' Sandy probed.

'Close to 2 A.M.'

'And Matthews was not in best of shape?' Jamie looked up as a waitress long past her prime sauntered towards them with the coffee. 'Hi, Mabel. How's your boy doing?'

'Best thing your mom ever did for me—givin' him a job deliverin' the *Sentinel*. With a few bucks in his pocket, he's a cool kid. No more troubles.'

'He's a good paper boy,' Jamie told her.

Now Jamie made a point of casual conversation while Nick sat with them over coffee.

'Jamie, you think Gene might be the serial killer who's driving people out of their minds?' Nick seemed dubious.

'We don't know,' Jamie said. 'But he's being arraigned tomorrow evening. We'll see what happens then.'

Back in the car Jamie sat immobile, staring into space for a moment.

'Nick said Matthews left the tavern at 2 A.M.,' Sandy broke the silence.

'Let's see if we can find out what time the coroner says Sara Adams was murdered.' Jamie reached for his cell phone. He came up with answers on the third call.

'Don't quote me on this,' the voice at the other end warned. 'The cops don't take to anybody in the coroner's office giving out information before they're ready to disclose it. But they figure Sara Adams was killed between 11:30 P.M. Friday night and 3:30 A.M. Saturday morning.'

'Thanks, Zach—I owe you.' Jamie put down the phone with an air of conviction. 'He could have done it.'

'Drunk as he was?' Now it was Sandy who was unsure.

'Matthews left Pete's Tavern around 2 A.M. and his buddies dumped him on a bench at the Village Green. About a quarter of three we had a brief thundershower. I woke up for a moment, glanced at the clock, and went back to sleep.

He didn't lie on that bench long in a thundershower. It woke him up fast.'

'Now what? Do we take this to Bronson?'

Jamie chuckled. 'What do you want to bet that Bronson and his partner have tracked this down by now? But I feel better for knowing it.' He glanced at his watch. 'That was a good morning's work. Why don't we drop in somewhere for a quick lunch?'

Sunday lunch was a popular diversion in Westwood. The first two diners they checked on had a line waiting for tables.

'Let's live it up, go for lunch at the Colonial Inn,' Jamie decided. 'At their fancy prices there's always an empty table.'

With an air of escaping duty, Jamie and Sandy headed for the Colonial Inn. As Jamie anticipated, they were seated immediately.

'Oh, this is good.' Sandy leaned back in the leather upholstered captain's chair. Enjoying the damask tablecloth, the crystal vase of red roses, the elegant atmosphere. 'I'm tired and hungry.'

The lunchtime waitress was young and bubbly, made wise suggestions about the Sunday specials. They were in the midst of enjoying their green salad generously dotted with shrimps when another diner, a well-groomed man in his fifties, left his party to stride to their table.

'I've been meaning to call you, Jamie,' he said. 'This town lost its shining light when your mother died. We still can't believe she's gone.'

'Sometimes I tell myself I'm having a nightmare.' Jamie's face reflected his grief. 'Judge Watson, do you know our new Publisher of the *Sentinel?* Sandra Taylor, Judge Watson.'

'We've never met,' Judge Watson said, 'but I've read your articles in the *Sentinel,* Miss Taylor. Solid stuff.'

'Thank you, Judge Watson.' *He's shocked to hear me*

introduced as Publisher. Why did Jamie do that? For all his denial, he's still upset that his mother virtually disinherited him.

Judge Watson leaned forward, somber now. His voice low. 'Jamie, when are you going to start serious campaigning for that empty seat on the Town Council? It's barely five weeks until the election.'

'Other things have got in the way.' Jamie's face was eloquent.

'I'm pleased at how you're fighting to stop the outsourcing, but don't lose sight of that seat,' Judge Watson warned. 'Put the *Sentinel* to work for you. It's time!' He hesitated. 'Some insider information drifted my way—as it does from time to time.' His smile was wry. 'The *Evening News* is about to launch a smear campaign against you.' His gaze held Jamie's.

Sandy saw Jamie tense.

'I'll be okay.' But he seemed unnerved. *What are they talking about?*

'Look what it did to John Kerry.' Judge Watson was grim. 'He'd be sitting in the White House today except for the dirty lies circulated endlessly about him.' He turned now to Sandy. 'Pleasure to meet you, Miss Taylor.'

Sandy sat, tense and bewildered. What could anybody say about Jamie that wasn't good?

'Things get misinterpreted, thrown out of context,' he said after a moment.

'What kind of things?' *I thought he was sure to be elected—as Adrienne would have been. What don't I know?*

'Judge Watson was remembering an—an incident that happened ten years ago. When Andrew and I were just past eighteen and all enthralled with having our driving licenses.' Jamie seemed to be searching for words. 'Andrew was celebrating the way he liked best. Drinking too many beers. He drove through a red light at fifty-five miles an hour—in a thirty-mile zone. He knocked down a classmate. The kid died.'

Julie Ellis

'Jamie, how awful!'

'Andrew and I changed places—I took the wheel. We both testified that the classmate had jumped out between cars.' *He lied for Andrew—and has been doing penance ever since.* 'Andrew was legally drunk—he would have gone to jail.'

'Judge Watson's afraid the accident will be dredged up?'

Jamie closed his eyes for a moment. 'Judge Watson was on the case. He let me off with a hundred hours of community service—the kid jumped out from behind a car. It's on my record,' Jamie emphasized. 'Not Andrew's.'

210

Thirty-One

Sandy and Jamie abandoned thought of dessert. They settled for coffee—both anxious to be in the privacy of the car where they could talk without being overheard. Everyone in town was sure Jamie would be elected, Sandy remembered. His opposition appeared to have no chance of being elected. But the *Evening News* was waiting for the propitious moment to launch the smear campaign.

They left the restaurant, hurried to the car. The sultry heat seemed to be intensifying. Dark clouds hovered overhead.

'The election will not be the slam-dunk we expected.' Jamie opened the car door for Sandy, strode to the other side. His face exuding frustration, he sat beside her. 'Leave it to the *Evening News* to dredge up that mess. It shouldn't have happened. I tried to make Andrew let me drive. He refused. He was sailing high. If he'd been driving thirty miles an hour instead of fifty-five, he might have been able to stop.' He switched on the ignition now. 'So I won't be elected to the Town Council. That won't be the end of the world. Right now what concerns us is that the union referendum on Tuesday goes the right way.'

'Yesterday's *Evening News* was nasty.' Sandy grimaced in recall. 'How can they say the new tax is bad for the town? "More taxes may be dumped on innocent residents," ' she mocked. ' "Vote out the Town Council members up for re-election. Stop the union from selling out its membership." '

'The *Sentinel* will keep pushing for union members to vote in favor of a cut in wages.' Jamie moved the car ahead with a sudden rush of speed that brought a murmur of protest from Sandy. 'It's a temporary deal—they know that. And it's better to have a cut in wages than no wages at all.'

'What about this business of Eugene Matthews?' Sandy was uncertain. 'Should we report what we've learned to Detective Bronson?' But she continued before Jamie could reply. 'He's already been through that routine,' she chastised herself. 'He knows that Matthews left Pete's Tavern at 2 A.M. He knows Sara Adams was killed between 11 P.M. Friday night and 3:30 A.M. Saturday morning. Rosie said he arrived home around 3 A.M.'

'That means Matthews had just an hour to sober up, walk over to Sara Adams' house—and kill her,' Jamie estimated. 'And that's a long walk.'

'He was lying on a park bench on the Village Green when that brief thundershower hit town. That was enough to wake him up,' Sandy concluded.

Jamie squinted in thought, reached for the cell phone. 'Let me give Bronson a buzz.'

'He won't like it,' Sandy cautioned. 'He said he'd have nothing new before the arraignment.'

'So I'm a nosey reporter.' Jamie punched in the number of Bronson's cellphone.

'Bronson—' A hit of annoyance in his voice.

'Jamie Moss,' he said. 'You're probably aware of it, but Sandy and I thought—'

'Forget about Eugene Matthews,' Bronson cut him off. 'There'll be no arraignment tomorrow evening. Matthews was released this morning. Sara Adams put up a fight. Bits of skin were found beneath her fingernails. The lab came up with a report. They don't match.'

Rain pummeled the car as Sandy and Jamie headed back for the *Sentinel*. Lightning darted across the sky. Thunder issued ominous warnings.

'It's another of those quick storms,' Jamie said, leaning forward as he drove because visibility was poor. 'In twenty minutes it'll all be over. We're having such weird weather this summer.'

They raced through the rain to the entrance to the paper, huddled beneath the umbrella kept in the car for such emergencies.

Carol, the weekend receptionist and part-time book editor, greeted them sympathetically. 'You're both probably soaked to the skin.'

'In this heat we'll dry out fast,' Sandy predicted.

'Any special calls?' Jamie asked.

'Usual Sunday crap,' Carol shrugged. 'I could deal.'

They stopped at Frank's office for a brief conference, then headed for Jamie's office. Tomorrow morning's front page would carry an unexpected story.

'I'll work up the Matthews story,' Jamie said. 'You focus on the union referendum. Then we'll edit each other.'

'I have this feeling that we ought to be fighting to push the referendum through—not just writing about it. So much depends on the union membership okaying the wage cuts.'

'Honey, it's late to try for a public meeting—' But Jamie, too, seemed troubled.

'I'll call Bill Thompson. Ask if there's anything else we can do.' Suffused with determination, Sandy reached for the phone. *In a crisis like this he'll be at his office.*

Someone picked up on the first ring. 'Westwood Workers' Union.'

'Bill Thompson?'

'Bill speaking.'

'This is Sandy Taylor at the *Sentinel*. Tomorrow morning's paper will carry front-page coverage on the referendum, of course—stressing its importance to this town, but Jamie and I have been searching our brains for something else we might be able to do. Any suggestions, Bill?'

'You bet.' Bill's booming enthusiasm reached Jamie as

well as Sandy. 'It would be a huge help if the *Sentinel* could set up a crew to contact each member of the union, explain the urgency of this move. I know they've been hearing it from our guys and the *Sentinel*—but often the personal approach is more effective.'

'We can do that.' *We must do that!* 'We'll need names.'

'I'll fax you our membership list, with addresses and phone numbers.'

'Fax the list right away,' Sandy said. 'We'll go to work on it. Personal, face-to-face calls,' she decided. 'That's more effective than phone calls. We'll bring in everybody involved with getting out the *Sentinel,* divide up the list.' Counting all the part-time editors that would amount to about twenty-six. A thousand names, divided by twenty-six, she figured mentally. A daunting task—but it must be done.

'Stand by your fax machine.' Bill Thompson was jubilant. 'The list is about to go through.'

Sandy and Jamie enlisted Frank and Chuck to set up crews for the following day's in-person campaign while they themselves worked on the front-page stories. Chuck's wife and Frank's mother joined in, signing up friends and neighbors to participate.

'Folks will be terrified to learn a serial killer is still roaming our streets,' Chuck's wife declared, 'but let them understand we must get out there and save a thousand jobs!'

The day sped past. Minutes before 6 P.M., Chuck strode into Jamie's office.

'Front page set yet?' Chuck was slightly querulous. Meaning, Sandy thought, he was tired and uneasy. 'We've got a paper to get out.'

'All set,' Jamie soothed. 'How're you doing with the crew for tomorrow?'

'Do we have enough people?' Sandy pursued. A thousand to be visited within a dozen hours tomorrow!

'Everything's under control. With volunteers we're up to

214

fifty-one people—counting the three of us. We each have to cover twenty union members. That means—'

'Hold it,' Jamie interrupted. 'When do we talk to them? They'll be at work during the daytime hours.' The evening and midnight shifts had been eliminated over a year ago.

'They're working only one shift,' Chuck acknowledged, 'but the hours are staggered. Some work 8 A.M. to 4 P.M., another group 8:30 A.M. to 4:30 P.M., and the third comes in at 9 A.M., leaves at 5 P.M. It's all broken down on Bill Thompson's list.'

Jamie nodded. 'We'll tackle some as they arrive, some as they come off work, others after hours at home. They'll listen—they know what's at stake.'

'If our list includes members we know personally,' Sandy plotted, 'we might try to take them to lunch.' Her own list, her mind pinpointed, included two women who'd served with her on volunteer committees. Try for a lunch date.

'Names and schedules will be posted all over our premises. Chuck's wife and Frank's sister-in-law are supervising volunteers. We've got a handle on this.'

But a serial killer is still on the loose in Westwood. And nobody knows who will be the next target.

Thirty-Two

Simultaneously exhausted, exhilarated, and fearful about the Tuesday referendum, Sandy and Jamie left for home slightly past 6 P.M.

'No need to phone Martha tonight,' Sandy said with a wry smile. 'She never considers serving dinner before seven o'clock.'

'What's happening?' Martha greeted them in the foyer on their arrival. Fanning herself with a folded newspaper page. 'You two working half a day? And don't complain about the heat in the house—we're stuck with it.'

'What happened to the air-conditioning?' Jamie was instantly solicitous. 'Grandma needs it.'

'It conked out in the middle of the storm. I dug up an old fan from the basement,' Martha told them. 'You know how Miss Claire insists on storing everything. I set it up in her room. But it don't work too well.'

'I'll get on the phone with the repair people,' Sandy began and stopped dead as someone seemed to be struggling with the front door.

'I'll get it.' Jamie moved forward to open the door.

Perspiring and breathing heavily, Andrew came inside, a huge carton in tow. 'I drove over to the mall in the next town,' he explained. 'Grandma is supposed to have air-conditioning when the temperature goes above seventy-five degrees in the house, and it feels like eighty-five, at least.'

'I'll give you a hand.' Jamie moved forward to help.

Grudgingly, Sandy thought in astonishment. It was so thoughtful, so sweet of Andrew.

'As long as you're all home, I suppose you'll be wanting dinner right away. The table's all set—I just have to steam the vegetables and grill the salmon. Eight minutes tops.' Martha made a show of martyrdom, but the others realized it was phony. Every meal was a crisis, a challenge she enjoyed facing. 'By the time you set up the air-conditioner for Miss Claire, I'll have dinner on the table.'

Jamie and Andrew carted the air-conditioner to Claire's room. Sandy joined Martha in the kitchen. Belatedly she realized Martha didn't know yet that Matthews had been cleared.

'Martha, you can stop worrying about Eugene Matthews,' she began. 'He—'

Martha froze, a lid in one hand. 'What about him?'

'He's not our killer. The police have released him.'

'They're sure?' Martha seemed ambivalent.

'They're sure. They found bits of skin under Sara Adams' fingernails, where she'd fought him off. The lab reported they weren't from Matthews.'

'So the killer is still up for grabs.' Martha frowned. 'Anyhow, nobody can say I sent an innocent man to Death Row.' *Yet she seems upset that Matthews had been cleared.*

As Sandy had expected, Claire didn't come downstairs for dinner. *Claire's still furious at Jamie and me. She has lunch every day with Andrew—either in her room or downstairs—but she won't come down for dinner. In her eyes Jamie and I are in purgatory.*

At the dinner table she was unnerved by Jamie's thinly veiled hostility towards Andrew. *They're twin brothers— identical twins. They couldn't be any closer. How can Jamie feel this way towards Andrew?*

Jamie wanted Andrew out of the house, out of Westwood. That came through loud and clear. Andrew was settling in

217

to write his book—which would delight Claire. *Does Jamie feel threatened by Andrew's success?*

After dinner the three settled themselves in the living room with a second round of coffee. Sandy shared the sofa with Jamie. Andrew sprawled in a lounge chair, flipped the TV remote from channel to channel.

Martha appeared in the doorway. 'If anybody wants more coffee, there's a carafe in the kitchen,' she announced. 'I'm taking Miss Claire her tea tray.'

Sandy and Jamie talked in low tones about the next day's campaign. Andrew settled on a news channel, though from time to time he tuned in to the conversation.

'The union bosses must be sweating it out,' Andrew commented in a lapse in the conversation between the other two. 'I saw today's *Evening News.*' He chuckled at Jamie's affronted glare. 'You're supposed to read the competition, know what garbage they're spreading.' Jamie's grunt was eloquent. 'The *News* claims the union bigwigs are selling out the membership. And a segment of workers are agreeing. I hear some nasty incidents have occurred in the last couple of days.'

'A few bad apples.' Jamie shrugged this off. *But we won't know until after the referendum if they've having any effect.* 'It means nothing.'

'Get real, Jamie,' Andrew scoffed. 'What workers are accepting lower wages these days?'

'You watch the TV news,' Jamie snapped back. 'It's happening in major industries across the country! The problem is that CEOs are still clamping on to huge bonuses.'

'The union's trying to save jobs!' Sandy jumped in. 'The *Evening News* is a conservative rag that cares nothing about ordinary people. And it's not just the workers who're taking cuts at Westwood. Noel Ward is committing himself to minor compensation for the next five years. He doesn't want to outsource. He's being pushed. He's trying to save his business in a ghastly price war!'

218

'You're gorgeous when you're on a crusade,' Andrew said, his smile dazzling. *He's baiting Jamie. Living in this house is like living in an armed camp.*

'Tomorrow's going to be a rough day.' Sandy rose to her feet. 'Goodnight, Andrew, Jamie.'

'I'm turning in, too.' Jamie flushed at Andrew's knowing grin. 'I'll walk you to your room, Sandy.' He reached for a magazine that lay on the coffee table. 'I'll read a bit before I go to sleep.'

His eyes dared Andrew to make any insinuating comment.

Sandy knew she would have difficulty sleeping. Too many disturbing undercurrents in this house. After brief periods of troubled slumber, she awoke to a glorious sunrise. By the time she had showered and dressed, she could hear morning sounds downstairs. Jamie was already up and at breakfast. She hurried down, was taken aback by the way Jamie and Martha aborted what seemed an intense conversation as she arrived in the kitchen.

'It's a good day for our campaign.' Jamie attacked a plate of pancakes with a show of enthusiasm. Seeming relieved by Sandy's arrival. 'I'm getting good vibes about it.'

'No vibes about our serial killer?' Martha challenged Jamie. Their eyes were in covert exchange and the atmosphere was suddenly supercharged. 'It's time for this town to live in peace.'

Sandy gaped from Martha to Jamie in shock. Her mind in chaos. *Is Martha accusing Jamie? But that's insane.* Now Adrienne's last words to her zigzagged across her mind. *'Be careful, Sandy. Be careful—'*

No, I can't believe the killer is Jamie. No way!

'Sit down and have your orange juice,' Martha ordered Sandy. 'Whole-wheat pancakes coming up. You'll be racing around all day—won't bother with lunch,' she predicted, bringing a carafe of coffee to the table.

'Oh, I need that, Martha.' Sandy glanced at her watch,

turned to Jamie. 'I suppose it's too early to call the air-conditioning people.'

'Wait until 8 A.M.,' Jamie advised.

They polished off breakfast to Martha's satisfaction, headed for the car. This would be a harried day, Sandy warned herself. They had a paper to get out plus union voters to approach. And always hanging over their heads was the knowledge that the killer of three prominent women remained unapprehended.

'It must be all over town now that Matthews has been released,' Sandy surmised, reaching to switch on the car radio while Jamie backed out onto the road.

A 7 A.M. news report confirmed her suspicions. She remembered Chuck's oft-repeated lament that the radio and TV news had usurped the newspapers' role in alerting the public. Now the brief report on the suspected serial killer was followed by the union referendum.

'CEO Noel Ward announced that all workers at Westwood Manufacturing will be given an hour's paid leave to enable them to vote in today's referendum.'

'Ward accepted your suggestion,' Jamie approved. 'Poor guy, he's in a rough spot. Even if we see this outsourcing stopped, and we pray we do, Ward has to live with the fact that his son will never see freedom again.' *And Jamie and I will never forget that his son murdered Adrienne.*

When they arrived at the *Sentinel,* Gloria was already on duty. Phones were ringing despite the early hour. She glanced up with relief as Sandy and Jamie walked into the reception area.

'Oh, thank God! Ted Newman wants to talk to you right away, Jamie. He says it's urgent. He tried you at home, but you'd left already.'

'I'll get right to him.' Exchanging a loaded glance, he and Sandy rushed to his office. He closed the door behind them.

'The Town Council can't have changed their minds about the new tax?' Sandy was fearful.

'I don't see how that could happen.' Already Jamie was punching in Ted Newman's home number. He hit speakerphone so Sandy, too, could hear.

'Hello—' Newman picked up on the first ring.

'It's Jamie. What's up, Ted?'

'I don't suppose you read last night's *Evening News?*'

'No—'

'We don't read that rag here, either—but I got a call first thing this morning. I was still in bed. It seems the *Evening News* has launched its campaign against your running for Town Council with a wild shot.' Apology in Ted's voice now. 'I don't remember it—but they've got a front-page story about your driving through a red light, running down and killing a teenager. About ten years ago?'

'The *Evening News* wasn't publishing ten years ago. Who dredged up that crazy incident?'

'Jamie, tell me it isn't true.' Ted sounded exhausted. 'We can't afford to have you lose that Council seat. The opposition is a disaster.'

'It happened—' Jamie struggled to continue. 'The kid jumped out from behind a car. I—I didn't see him until it was too late.'

'But you were driving through a red light?'

'I drove through a red light, hit a classmate. It was dark—he jumped out from behind a car,' Jamie repeated.

'We need to talk, Jamie!'

'Not today or tomorrow.' Jamie struggled to clear his head. 'I'll be all tied up with the referendum. Let's talk Wednesday morning.'

Thirty-Three

Sandy sat at her desk—relieved that an air-conditioning firm promised to be at the house early in the afternoon. Martha could deal with it, she reassured herself. In this heat wave, business was booming, she gathered. They were lucky to get service.

Now a dozen questions about tomorrow morning's edition charged across her mind. The referendum was a major story—Jamie had assigned two reporters to that. Driving in, she and Jamie decided she was to follow up on Eugene Matthews' release.

Try for a press briefing by the police, an interview with the D.A. Then call on the Ward union members on her list. She reached for the phone, scheduled a reporter and photographer to stand by for a possible police briefing. Have a reporter and photographer at Town Hall, when District Attorney Potter headed for his office.

Checking her assigned list of union members, she confirmed that she knew two women on the list. The three of them had served together on committees. Call them and invite them out for lunch.

The atmosphere at the *Sentinel* was supercharged this morning. Everyone was conscious of what was at stake tomorrow. Even their own jobs could be on the line in the domino effect that would follow outsourcing.

Some of the staff had been in action before the work day began, Sandy realized. In the course of the day she became aware that she wasn't alone in utilizing the lunch hour.

Preparing to leave at 4 P.M., Sandy reminded herself that Jamie would be without a car. She rushed to the Composing Room, arranged for him to borrow one from an employee who worked from 4 P.M. to midnight, then reported this to him.

'You've covered your list?' she asked in sudden alarm.

'You bet,' he told her and grinned. 'One guy owes me a hundred bucks. I asked him, "How do you expect to pay me back if Westwood Manufacturing goes overseas?" '

Sandy took a deep breath. 'I still have to reach another five. I'm headed there now.'

'It looks good,' Jamie confirmed, 'but we won't be sure until the votes are counted.'

A little before 8 P.M. Sandy arrived home. She opened the front door and flinched. The air in the house was hot, humid. The air-conditioning people hadn't come. They'd sworn they would.

Sounds emerged from the dining room. Martha talking with Andrew.

'I know it's hot,' Martha told Andrew while she placed a huge salad before him, 'that's why you're getting a cold dinner.' She glanced up as Sandy walked in. 'They came,' she said, her tone ominous, 'but they need some piece of equipment. The head guy said they'd phone for it, have it shipped FedEx. They'll have it in the morning.'

'This is cool compared to the days in Iraq.' Andrew grimaced in recall. 'You wouldn't believe the heat over there this time of year.'

'I'll bring your dinner and a pitcher of iced tea,' Martha told Sandy. 'Green tea. That's healthy,' she said with satisfaction.

'Claire's not coming down for dinner?' Sandy asked Martha.

'Not in this heat,' Martha reproached her. 'She's sitting before the unit up in her room.'

But even if the central air-conditioning was working,

Claire would stay there. She's still furious at Jamie and me. Like Jamie, I feel like an intruder in the house—despite Adrienne's will.

'I hear that character Matthews is off the hook,' Andrew commented as Martha left the dining room. 'I read this morning's edition of the *Sentinel.*' A jocular tone in his voice.

He's teasing me. It doesn't bother him that Adrienne didn't leave the paper to him. I guess the Sentinel *is small-time stuff to him. Despite its financial value.*

'You heard it on the late TV news last night,' Sandy said after a moment. 'We're always scooped by TV and radio news.'

'Newspapers are not dead. News magazines are not dead,' he added with relish. 'My magazine sees its circulation soaring.' But all at once his eyes seemed guarded.

Is he running into trouble about his Iraqi reporting—as Jamie suspects? Was he fabricating his stories, the way that other correspondent told Jamie? No, that's absurd. Andrew's too bright for that.

A sound in the foyer told them Jamie had arrived. He headed for the kitchen.

'Our knight in shining armor—well, maybe not shining,' Andrew drawled. 'But if this outsourcing is stopped, he'll be Westwood's big hero.'

'I think he did that in Iraq,' Sandy said softly.

'What about his medals? Three Purple Hearts? I'm impressed.'

Jamie strode into the dining room, a pitcher of iced tea in one hand. 'What's with the air-conditioning? You talked to them this morning, didn't you?' he asked Sandy.

'Martha says they came, but they have to order some part—it'll be here in the morning.'

'We've endured worse heat in Iraq.' Andrew dismissed this with a chuckle. 'Right, Big Brother?'

Jamie shrugged, sat down, poured himself a glass of iced

tea. He sipped in obvious pleasure. But his eyes seemed on a different path, Sandy told herself. *Why is he looking at Andrew that way? Like a prosecuting attorney about to strike a blow.*

'In this heat you're walking around in a long-sleeved shirt?' Jamie whistled in derision.

'Better than a sun block.' Andrew reached for the pitcher, poured into his glass.

'You wrote in one article about running around in Iraq heat in little more than a g-string,' Jamie recalled.

'Ah, you read my Iraqi reports.' Andrew turned to Sandy. 'I didn't realize Big Brother was a fan.'

'Andrew, why are you wearing a long-sleeved shirt in the midst of a heat wave?' Jamie was supernaturally calm.

Sandy's heart began to pound.

'I'm hiding ugly scratches.' Andrew seemed amused by Jamie's interrogation. 'I was coming home from a walk.' He turned to Sandy. 'A long walk clears my head when I hit a block in writing. I ran into two little girls a few houses down the road. They were frantic. Their kitten had climbed up a tree, was afraid to come down. What could I do? I managed to get up there, brought him down. Poor little fellow was scared—he scratched me. I know, of course, about Grandma's allergies. I showered, changed clothes, cleaned up the scratches. I figured it was wise to keep them covered in case I hadn't got out a lingering kitten hair. So I'll sweat a little more—I won't be causing Grandma an allergy attack.'

'That would be the two little Miller girls,' Sandy recalled. 'They're adorable. That was sweet of you, Andrew.'

Why is Jamie scowling that way? What is this horrible resentment he feels towards Andrew?

Thirty-Four

The atmosphere at *Sentinel* this Tuesday morning was ominous, exuding tension, uncertainty. It assailed her as she moved about the building. This was the way it must be before a crucial battle in wartime, Sandy thought, settling herself at her desk. The union voting today would decide if the town's major employer remained in Westwood or outsourced to China—or wherever Noel Ward chose to go. The field was horrifyingly wide.

While the whole town was still unnerved by the series of murders, for a few hours this was superseded by the effort to save a thousand jobs. But the town still grieved for the four women who'd died by foul means, Sandy reminded herself. The streets were still deserted at night. Doors locked, windows locked.

Sandy focused on her next move. Should she call Ward? No chance he'd renege if the union membership accepted wage cuts. But she needed reassurance. She glanced at her watch. It was moments before 8 A.M. But he'd be in his office. At their last encounter he'd given her his private phone line.

'Noel Ward.' His voice was crisp, wary. His son's case was still in serious negotiation, trial by jury dismissed.

'Good morning, this is—'

'Good morning, Sandy. Any new developments?'

He's edgy—not sure about his next move.

'I spoke to Bill Thompson,' she reported. 'He tells me he'll have a crew counting ballots as they come in. By

226

9 P.M.—when the voting stops—he said they should have a final tally within minutes. He says everything looks good.'

'We'll know that when the votes are counted. I don't want to move the manufacturing to China. But without their help—even with the Town Council's new tax deal—I won't be able to carry on here.'

'It'll be a long day for all of us,' she commiserated. 'But our response yesterday was encouraging.'

'From your lips to God's ear, as my mother used to say.' Ward's anxiety crept through. 'We'll know in roughly eleven or twelve hours.'

At intervals through the day Sandy or Jamie checked with Bill Thompson on the vote count. Around 7 P.M.—too uptight to focus on anything else—Sandy went to Jamie's office.

'Time to check with Bill again?' She struggled for poise. 'By now we should know the results—voting's been heavy all day.'

'I'll buzz Bill again.'

Bill was jubilant. 'I don't see how we can't win. It looks like a landslide. Workers need their jobs—they understand the situation.'

An hour later, exhausted from strain, Sandy and Jamie decided to call it a day. A pair of reporters and a photographer were stationed at the union headquarters—awaiting official results. The headline for tomorrow morning's edition of the *Sentinel* was being held up for the confirmation of election results. At Chuck's insistence Jamie had written an upbeat article about the saving of a thousand jobs in Westwood—and how many additional jobs would be saved because of this.

Sandy and Jamie stopped by Chuck's office.

'Here's your front-page story.' Jamie handed Chuck the article.

Chuck grinned. 'You two look like the proverbial Cheshire

cats. Go home, have a good dinner, go to sleep. We've made it.'

At the house Martha greeted them with a triumphant smile. 'I heard a car drive up—I figured it was you two.'

'The air-conditioner people were here,' Sandy said in relief.

'The way I hear it,' Martha pursued, 'everybody in town's saying Westwood Manufacturing won't be going anywhere. You pulled it off!'

'When's dinner?' Jamie asked and grinned. 'We forgot to have lunch.'

'Go into the dining room. You'll be eating in ten minutes. Tell your brother. He's been asking for the last hour.'

Andrew walked into view. 'I have no standing in this house,' he complained with mock ferocity. 'Martha wouldn't give me a crumb to eat until you two came home.'

'We're eating in ten minutes,' Jamie told him. 'What's on the news?'

'Iraq as usual,' Andrew said. 'And the word seems to be that Westwood Manufacturing is staying in town. You're a hero, Big Brother.'

'Sandy had as much to do with this as I did.' Jamie pulled her close for a moment. 'But thank God, we were able to pull it off.'

'You can start with the soup,' Martha called from the kitchen. 'Move your butts to the dining room.'

'Martha, soup in this weather?' Andrew called back in reproach.

'It's cold soup,' she said. 'Gazpacho.'

Jamie chuckled. 'When we were kids, Martha always made gazpacho for our birthday dinner.'

'Your favorite,' Andrew told him. 'I loathed it.'

After dinner Martha joined them at the TV. The local channel was full of the union-voting results. Chuck phoned a few minutes past 9 P.M.

'It's official—though Bill Thompson hasn't announced

it yet. Westwood Manufacturing stays put. It was a tough battle, but we won!'

Twenty minutes later Noel Ward called, asked for Sandy. 'Hello, Mr Ward. We're in business!'

'I wanted to thank you and Jamie for fighting for this. And I want to say again I'll eternally grieve for Mrs Moss's death. My fault—and Evan's paying for it.'

It was past 11 P.M. when the TV was switched off and everyone—stifling yawns—headed for their respective bedrooms.

'You'll have that Town Council seat wrapped up,' Andrew told Jamie as they headed upstairs. 'You'll be the town hero.'

In his night-dark bedroom Jamie tossed from one side of the bed to the other. Futilely seeking a position conducive to sleep. You're too wired, he told himself. So elated by the way the pieces had come together to halt Westwood Manufacturing being outsourced.

What Mom had fought so hard to accomplish was now a reality. He felt a sense of peace—but only for a moment. It was dispelled as his mind taunted him that three murders remained unsolved. And the suspicions he'd struggled to ignore were all at once spotlighted in his mind.

I can't be right. I don't want to be right.

He reached to touch the button that lighted the clock on his night table. Wow, it was almost 2 A.M. Sleep had eluded him for almost three hours. No point in lying here this way. Do something constructive. Work on the editorial for Thursday morning's edition. Follow up with a strong article deploring the trend towards outsourcing.

He'd take it easy—forget the computer at this hour. Dictate instead. He searched in his night-table drawer, came up with the recorder. He adjusted his pillows into a comfortable sitting position, deposited the recorder on the night table. *Not there, it might tumble over. Put it behind the radio.*

Now he settled himself against the pillows, switched on the recorder. His mind was a blank. *I'm too tense. Turn on the radio. Find something relaxing.*

Strains of Schubert's 'Serenade' infiltrated the room. Keep the volume low, he exhorted himself, fiddled with the dials until the music was a soothing whisper. Now, zero in on what was accomplished through the combined efforts of the Town Council, the union, and Noel Ward.

Before he could begin to dictate, he was startled by the sound of his door being stealthily opened. Andrew walked inside, closed the door behind him.

'You're awake—' Andrew moved towards the bed. *What's he carrying in that Barnes & Noble tote? He's brought me a book to read? He's wearing the same pajamas as me. Claire gave them to us when we came home—she suspected we'd been sleeping in our clothes in Iraq. Andrew never wears pajamas—he sleeps in the raw.* 'I thought you'd be asleep by now.'

'Then why come to my room?' Jamie countered.

'Because it's time for a change in my life, Big Brother.'

'You're giving up on the book and going back to Iraq?' *What's he carrying in that tote?*

'I'm not going anywhere.' Andrew moved closer to the bed. 'You are, Big Brother. You knew what Mom was doing to me when she left everything except our piddling bequests to Sandy.' His voice was a monotone with an under layer of menace. 'Grandma told me—you expect to marry Sandy. You'll have everything. The paper, the house, Mom's stock portfolio. She was cutting me out—and that wasn't nice.'

This is the other Andrew, the charismatic charmer in eclipse. This is the one who did those horrible things when we were kids—and I tried to cover for him. But Mom knew. Martha knew.

'You killed Mom's three friends. You're the one.' Jamie kept his voice matter-of-fact. *I've suspected that from the beginning. I forced myself to drive it out of my mind. He*

killed that kitten Mom adored—and my Doberman puppy when I was ten. 'I can't cover for you this time, Andrew.'
'But you will, Big Brother—because I'm going to become you. Who will know the difference?' he mocked. 'You'll be Andrew, who can't bear there being two of us—and one so mistreated by our mother. I'll be Jamie. Who'll know the difference? Sandy? Martha? Grandma?' He shook his head in a gesture of triumph. 'They'll find one of us on the floor—throat slashed. Bad, bad Andrew—who battled with Jamie and lost.'
Andrew's eyes left Jamie for a moment to focus on the contents of his tote. He reached inside. Simultaneously Jamie's hand slid to the floor, groped for the gun that lay there each night since he'd acquired it.
Andrew brought out the Bowie knife that he'd won when he was in a camp contest and kept hanging on a wall in his room. He lunged towards Jamie. Jamie fired. The sound was supernaturally loud in the night silence.
Andrew gasped in disbelief, collapsed on the floor, blood gushing from a wound in his chest.
Jamie leapt from the bed, dropped to his knees, felt for a pulse. Andrew was dead. His brother was dead.
'Jamie!' Sandy's voice—shrill with terror—preceded her. The door swung wide. She hovered there. Frozen by the tableau that met her gaze. Andrew lay on the floor in a pool of blood. Jamie leaned over him.
'He's dead.' Jamie's face was a mask of anguish. 'He meant to slash my throat. He killed Mom's three friends. Because Mom loved them. Sandy, I was to be next—'
'Oh, Jamie!' Her voice was a tortured whisper.
'He didn't realize that what we were saying was being recorded.' Jamie rose to his feet, reached for the recorder, switched it off. 'It's all on here. His confession—his threat to slash my throat.'
Martha rushed into the room. 'Jamie, you're all right?'
'I'm all right,' he said gently.

Martha's eyes darted to Andrew's body. 'He burst into your room. He meant to kill you!'

'Call the police, Martha. Tell them that Andrew murdered Dottie Lieberman, Beth McDonald, and Sara Adams,' Jamie instructed. 'Tell them I have his confession on my recorder.'

Thirty-Five

The police cars had finally pulled away. The coroner's crew had removed Andrew's body. Sandy and Jamie sat with Detective Bronson in the early morning sunlight that suffused the living room while Martha poured a fresh round of coffee for them.

'Claire is still asleep?' Sandy asked her, dreading the moment when Claire discovered Andrew was dead.

'She'll sleep another hour or two,' Martha predicted, lowering herself into a chair with an air of exhaustion. The near-empty carafe on the table beside her. 'I slipped a sleeping pill into her last cup of tea last night. Dr Maxwell ordered it,' she told Detective Bronson defensively.

Bronson stifled a yawn. 'It's not often I appreciate being awakened at 3 A.M.,' he told Sandy, 'but I needed to know this case was solved. We'd never encountered anything like it in this town.'

'We can live in peace again,' Sandy said, and it seemed a benediction.

'No problems for you, Jamie,' Bronson assured him. *But it'll be a long time before Jamie can put this behind him.* 'Come down later this morning and give us a formal statement. But the answer's here.' He indicated the recorder resting in his jacket pocket. He hesitated. 'You were suspicious of your brother all along?'

'I didn't want to believe it.' Jamie's face exuded anguish. 'Andrew was like part of me.'

'I suspected.' Martha was defiant. 'I knew what was

233

happening all those years you were growing up, Jamie. Your mother and I knew you were forever covering for Andrew. It hurt her so much—she tried so hard to get help for him.'

'He refused to be helped.' Jamie closed his eyes for an instant—as though to banish ugly recall. 'Mom sent the two of us to a psychiatrist. After the second session, Andrew refused to go. Mom couldn't bring herself to have him taken there by force.'

'Every day of his life Miss Adrienne lived in fear of some awful tragedy,' Martha said. 'We were scared of what he'd try next.'

'She said to me in her last moments, "Be careful. Sandy, be careful," then added, "Don't." But I couldn't imagine what she was trying to tell me.'

'It's over,' Jamie said with fresh strength. 'The nightmare is over.'

Bronson rose to his feet. 'This town will live in peace again. People won't be afraid to walk the streets at night. And because of you two,' his eyes swept from Jamie to Sandy, 'Westwood won't become a depressed area of boarded-up stores and staggering unemployment. No doubt in anybody's mind that Jamie Moss will be our new Town Council member.'

Detective Bronson took off with the air of a man who'd seen a difficult mission accomplished.

'No need to lock the door.' Martha uttered a huge sigh of satisfaction. 'I'm going out to the kitchen and make us a celebrating breakfast. The works,' she declared. 'Honeydew, waffles, Canadian bacon—low fat,' she pointed out, 'and this morning I'll overlook the nitrites. And if you can still eat, I'll warm up the cheese Danish I baked and threw into the freezer three weeks ago.'

'It's past our usual breakfast time by an hour. We'll eat,' Jamie promised and Martha headed for the kitchen.

'Adrienne would be so grateful that the outsourcing was stopped.' Sandy reached out for Jamie's hand—as though to reassure herself that he'd not been hurt. 'And so proud that you'll win a seat on the Town Council.'

'We weren't wrong in suspecting a link between Mom's death and the death of her three friends,' Jamie reflected. 'Andrew was able to hide his true feelings from others, but I always knew what he was thinking. Almost always. He was furious that Mom left him out of her will—except the $25,000 bequest.'

'But why did he kill her three friends?' Sandy was bewildered.

'He'd always resented them. He demanded all of Mom's attention. In a sick corner of his mind, he was punishing Mom for her friendship with them. With each case some little thing triggered a murder.'

'The lollipop left beside each body—what was he trying to say?'

'He was remembering how after Dad died Mom's three friends came to the house on Friday evenings to play bridge after dinner. Up until we were about ten, one of them would bring lollipops for Andrew and me. They were sweet, warm ladies—but Andrew cursed them for those lollipops. "We're ten years old," he'd rant, "and they treat us like we were in diapers." By then Andrew was stealing cigarettes and smoking them in his room.'

'It's all over, Jamie.' Sandy's face was luminous. 'You're free. A whole person.'